Praise for

"Catherine Mann's mili̶̶̶̶̶̶̶̶̶̶̶ ̶̶̶̶̶ ̶̶̶̶̶ ̶ ̶launch you into a world chock-full of simmering passion and heart-pounding action. Don't miss 'em!"

—*USA Today* bestselling author Merline Lovelace

"Exhilarating romantic suspense."   —*The Best Reviews*

"A great read."   —*Booklist*

"Terrific romantic suspense that never slows down . . . An action-packed story line."   —*Midwest Book Review*

"As gripping in its suspense as it is touching in its emotional pull."   —*Romance Junkies*

DEFENDER

CATHERINE MANN

BERKLEY SENSATION, NEW YORK

THE BERKLEY PUBLISHING GROUP
Published by the Penguin Group
Penguin Group (USA) Inc.
375 Hudson Street, New York, New York 10014, USA
Penguin Group (Canada), 90 Eglinton Avenue East, Suite 700, Toronto, Ontario M4P 2Y3, Canada
(a division of Pearson Penguin Canada Inc.)
Penguin Books Ltd., 80 Strand, London WC2R 0RL, England
Penguin Group Ireland, 25 St. Stephen's Green, Dublin 2, Ireland (a division of Penguin Books Ltd.)
Penguin Group (Australia), 250 Camberwell Road, Camberwell, Victoria 3124, Australia
(a division of Pearson Australia Group Pty. Ltd.)
Penguin Books India Pvt. Ltd., 11 Community Centre, Panchsheel Park, New Delhi—110 017, India
Penguin Group (NZ), 67 Apollo Drive, Rosedale, North Shore 0632, New Zealand
(a division of Pearson New Zealand Ltd.)
Penguin Books (South Africa) (Pty.) Ltd., 24 Sturdee Avenue, Rosebank, Johannesburg 2196, South Africa

Penguin Books Ltd., Registered Offices: 80 Strand, London WC2R 0RL, England

This is a work of fiction. Names, characters, places, and incidents either are the product of the author's imagination or are used fictitiously, and any resemblance to actual persons, living or dead, business establishments, events, or locales is entirely coincidental. The publisher does not have any control over and does not assume any responsibility for author or third-party websites or their content.

DEFENDER

A Berkley Sensation Book / published by arrangement with the author

PRINTING HISTORY
Berkley Sensation mass-market edition / April 2009

Copyright © 2009 by Catherine Mann.
Excerpt from *Hotshot* copyright © 2009 by Catherine Mann.
Cover art by Craig White.
Cover design by Annette Fiore.
Interior text design by Laura K. Corless.

ISBN: 978-0-425-22802-9

BERKLEY® SENSATION
Berkley Sensation Books are published by The Berkley Publishing Group,
a division of Penguin Group (USA) Inc.,
375 Hudson Street, New York, New York 10014.
BERKLEY® SENSATION and the "B" design are trademarks of Penguin Group (USA) Inc.

PRINTED IN THE UNITED STATES OF AMERICA

10 9 8 7 6 5 4 3 2 1

To Morgan Mack Mitchell—a precious blessing to all who knew him. Thanks to the generous gift of organ donation, we were touched by the warmth of Morgan's shining smile for eight and a half years.

And to his grandmother, K. Sue Morgan, an invaluable mentor, talented author, and treasured friend.

ACKNOWLEDGMENTS

To my editor, Wendy McCurdy, and my agent, Barbara Collins Rosenberg, endless thanks for your fabulous feedback and faith in my flyboys. Joanne Rock and Stephanie Newton, what would I do without your brilliant insights, inspired critiques, and excellent taste in chocolate? Suzanne Brockmann, Lori Foster, and Merline Lovelace, your continued encouragement and support mean the world to me. Karen Tucker, R.N., your proofreads and medical fact checking are invaluable. Julia Morrison, I adore you, maestra extraordinaire, *Star Trek* expert, and sister dear. Sergeant "Root"—Air Force Special Ops gunner—you have my deep appreciation for your help with the rescue-scene info and for your twenty years of brave service to our country. My deepest gratitude to USO performers, crews, and staff who so generously give their time and talents to entertain our troops!

And most of all, thank you to my family who somehow believes I can accomplish anything. My children, my miracles—Bricc, Haley, Robbie, and Maggie—I love you all. Rob—my very own flyboy hero—I can't thank you enough for sharing with me your military expertise, unflagging support, and, of course, your love.

PROLOGUE

★ ──────────────────────────────────────

Smoke trailing from the ass of his plane and terra firma approaching at meteoric speed, Captain Jimmy Gage figured he was about fifteen seconds away from being road-kill.

Punching out of a C-12 wasn't an option. No ejection seat. He would have to wrangle this plane to the ground on his own, since the other pilot had slumped, unconscious from inhaling smoke and gas fumes before Jimmy could get his own mask on, then strap on his partner's oxygen.

Major Nathan "Socrates" Breuer was still out cold, even sucking down the pure stuff spewing from the mask.

This troll through the sky should have been a standard medical transport along southern Afghanistan's craggy landscape. They had completed their drop off and were on their way back to base. He even had a seasoned instructor pilot on board.

Who was still stuck in la-la land.

The left engine's slowing groan told him it wasn't reaching max revolutions. His best guess? Sand junking up the fuel tank, which started the whole cluster-fuck effect until an O-ring somewhere in the fuel system failed. Now that engine flamed out of control, the other coughing.

Jimmy fought to level the wings and shoot through a narrow ridge, muscles straining under his sweat-soaked flight suit. He'd dodged ground fire, shoulder-launched missiles, even handled crappy-ass weather, only to be jacked by engine failure. As if it wasn't bad enough that he had to fight human bad guys scurrying around in those tunnels and caves, technology proved to be a lethal enemy as well.

What had his first instructor taught him to do when this sort of thing happened? Oh yeah, say something cool over the radio, then decide whether to go for the scatter or depth record. Hell, that was funny at the time. Not so much now.

The small cargo plane bucked under him. Yoke in hand, he battled for control, constantly adjusting the trim to maintain the best glide angle, defying the shuddering beast to split apart before he could wrestle it to a flat patch in this godforsaken sandpit.

If they survived this crash landing, somebody would need to scoop them up and out ASAP. Time to say something cool. What was the coded Mayday word today? Oh yeah, badger. Who thought this shit up?

He keyed the microphone and transmitted, "Fin six-seven, Fin six-seven, badger, badger, badger. Thirty miles south of bull's-eye. I have an engine fire, and I'm not gonna make it to anything that looks remotely like a runway. How copy?"

A tinny voice came through his headset, "Fin six-seven, Choctaw zero-four, We're passing your info to the operations center and heading your way. How long until you are on the deck?"

Jimmy thanked God and a couple of major saints that there were other friendlies in the area. He glanced out over the nose, searching for a flat spot or road to put down the fast-sinking aircraft. Good instincts and top-dollar training guided his hands as he readjusted his angle to eke a touch more glide from his wounded bird, just missing the mountain range on his left.

He radioed up again. "Roger that, Choctaw, pass to the ops center that I will be requiring rescue forces, and if they wanted to get them moving my way überquick, I would really appreciate it. My engine is barely putting out any power, and I will be . . . well, let's call it *landing* in about two minutes."

He stole a glance at his slouched-over partner. "Socrates, my friend, this is going to hurt me way more than you."

A stretch of desert spread ahead. Jimmy banked the dying craft on approach to the barren patch of salvation ahead.

A very small scrap of sandy salvation.

His thermos clanked his thigh before rolling back along with the rest of his gear ping-ponging around the cockpit. He peeled his helmet off the ceiling after the near vertical dive. "Lucky for you I am a god of aviation and the greatest pilot since . . . well . . . ever."

Jimmy lined up on the bikini-sized area and slowed the C-12 to near stall speed. He pulled up slightly to stay clear of scrub bushes and boulders, just avoiding that stall.

Then he chopped the power.

He yanked the fire handle and cut off fuel to the smoking engine. The plane screeched along the ground in an uncontrolled skid. Scraps of metal peeled off of who the hell knew where. Sparks showered over the windscreen and past the side windows. The left wing struck a small tree, and Jimmy's world started a Tilt-A-Whirl so long he could have sworn the almighty cosmic carnie dude gave him a double ride until . . .

Stillness.

Silence.

And thank you, almighty carnie dude, alive.

Jimmy shook his head to get his bearings. Blood filled his mouth. He'd bitten his tongue and had a new appreciation for the word *whiplash*, but his arms and legs moved in all the right directions.

Still, his first crash sucked as much as he thought it would. And it would suck monkey butt a lot worse if the plane exploded before he hauled himself and Socrates out.

He peeled off his oxygen mask, flung his harness aside, and set to work freeing Socrates. "Come on, old man, let's blow this pop stand."

Jimmy hooked his hands under the guy's pits and lugged him toward the door behind the pilot seat, which, of course, was jammed. The cosmic carnie dude's benevolence had run out, or else he'd picked a mighty inconvenient time for a smoke break.

Damn it. Jimmy kicked at the door, once, again, a third teeth-jarring time before it finally shook loose and jettisoned outward to the ground in a poof of throat-clogging sand.

He grabbed Socrates by the collar and hefted him the rest of the way out of the hatch. The blistering heat swamped Jimmy. No matter how many tours he pulled in this sandbox, he would never get over the sensation of being mummified in an electric blanket cranked on high.

His flight suit sealed to his back with sweat, Jimmy opened an access door in the rear of the aircraft to check the emergency locater transmitter fixed to the floor of the compartment. The blinking red light indicated the radio signal was working, broadcasting on the international distress frequency so that they could be found. He considered turning it off since bad guys could use it to find them just as easily as the good guys.

Weighed the risk.

Decided to leave that red light flashing.

If there were bad guys around, they certainly knew where the smoking plane crashed. And rescue was high on his list. This enemy wasn't known for hospitality.

His neck itched at even the thought.

This might look like the ass end of nowhere, but he expected terrorists would scurry out of their desert holes any minute now. Time to tap into some of that survival training.

Step one: stop, drop, and puke. No, wait, that wasn't right.

Oh yeah, get away from the neon sign that was his smoking airplane. Hoof it a good distance toward a niche in one of those mountains, and dig in until the good guys came winging over the horizon.

Scouting for the nearest outcropping, he patted down his survival vest that contained water and food as well as a bunch of Boy Scout crap. Signal mirrors, matches, fishing lures, and line. Man, he hoped he wouldn't be here long enough to need food. He definitely wasn't hip on eating desert rats.

He skimmed over the rest of his vest to check his gun. Not standard Boy Scout issue, but the 9 mm in his vest and big ass knife in his boot were a part of who he was now.

Outfitted as best he could be, back to step one, which would be a lot easier if he didn't have to carry two hundred pounds of comatose aircraft commander. He patted Socrates' face.

"Come on, dude, you gotta wake up for me. There's some heavy shit going down, and we need to book it out of here."

No go. Nathan Breuer wouldn't come to if a *Sports Illustrated* swimsuit model started washing a Corvette twelve inches from his face.

Gunfire sputtered in the distance. Given the echo off the craggy landscape, he couldn't tell how many or how close. Definitely time to go to ground, set up shop in a thicket, an overhang, something of that order. A cave if he had to, but he didn't cotton to the notion of being cornered with no escape route.

Jimmy ducked his shoulder into Breuer's gut for a fireman's carry. "Okay, old man, up we go." Jimmy grunted. "You're packing on the pounds, Major Ton O'Bricks."

He eyed a jagged outcropping a couple of hundred yards ahead. Not as close as the scraggly bushes, but at least with the rock at his back, he would have one less side to protect.

Jimmy started hoofing it east of the mangled C-12. "After this, we're due a serious bar crawl, and you're buying." He oofed Breuer more securely in place, combat boots pumping pace. "And you're laying off the Krispy Kremes, too."

He half-expected Breuer to roar out in protest over that one, but no luck. The unconscious pilot stayed dead weight over his shoulder. Perspiration popped along Jimmy's gritty skin, crusting the sand before sweat could reach his eyes.

"Not too much longer. We're almost there." He kept talking to distract himself from the shots popping in the distance. He did that a lot. Talked. And Major Breuer always listened, nodding sagely, until he finally offered up something profound that made Jimmy want to etch it on a stone tablet.

Socrates wasn't just his fellow pilot or some drinking pal. This was his mentor. A patient man with vision who'd—God only knew how—found something of value in a short-tempered, foul-mouthed lieutenant when others vowed he was too much of a loose cannon to trust with a multimillion-dollar aircraft.

How fucking ironic *he* hadn't failed. The plane had, and now Nathan Breuer's life depended on him. "It sure would be nice if you'd hook me up with some of that Socrates aviation wisdom right about now. Of course, we aren't really flying anymore, so perhaps that wisdom would be like tits on a porcupine."

Just when he thought his screaming muscles would stage a revolt, Jimmy found a sunken-out wadi running alongside the rock wall. With their backs covered, they could lie belly flat, grafting right into the wadi with some scrub brush on top of them until help hailed over the horizon.

He flipped Socrates off his shoulder and set to work. Five minutes later, his hands so caked with sand he could no longer bend the joints, he'd cleared out enough room for them to take cover. Then the quiet set in, the waiting, the damned helplessness as he gripped his 9 mm and listened to Socrates' shallow breathing.

A rumbling sounded in the distance. Good guys or . . . well, the crappy alternative? The growling engine grew louder as a rusted-out truck rounded a cave outcropping.

His fist tightened around cold metal. He started to squeeze the trigger to plug a bullet in the engine block but didn't want to give away his locale. Three men stood in the back of the barreling truck, AK-47s raised, eyes directly on his hidey spot.

They sprayed the ground in front of him. The pops hit so fast, sand spewed in his face, nose, mouth. He squeezed off shots, trying to down as many of them as he could through the haze of sand. He heard a groan, but he couldn't see.

The truck skidded to a stop with a fresh spray of desert. The driver leapt out, along with the three men in back, one of whom sported a blood-soaked sleeve.

Fuck. Pissed-off bad guys.

A boot came down on his wrist. Double fuck. He bit back a scream at the impact of bones snapping. His gun dangled from his useless hand.

He'd been in some hairy bar fights in his time, outnumbered and outgunned when some bozo pulled a knife, but nothing like this. Four-to-one odds, since Socrates was still down for the count. The numbers part didn't daunt him as much as those AK-47s tipped with bayonets.

The roar of pain in his ears dulled enough that he could hear the men arguing—and helicopter blades chopping the distant air with hope. Now would be a mighty fine time for backup. How about a missile strike straight to that rusted-out truck with an explosion strong enough to stun the quad squad?

Except reason open-fired on hope. Even if the helicopter reached them, the MH-53 couldn't risk shooting for fear of hitting the wrong guy.

Game over. Time to take one for the team. He raised his hands and dropped his weapon.

Silence seemed the best choice while they barked back and forth to each other in Arabic. The apparent leader—a lean man with golden eyes—stepped ahead of the pack.

Adrenaline pumped his senses on overload to the stench of sweat, sting of tight muscles, grainy wind taunting him with the helicopter serenade. *Okay, Afghani Al. What's the verdict?*

"Al" booted Socrates in the side. The sound of cracking ribs snipped the air. Socrates didn't move.

Bile bit the back of Jimmy's throat. *Come on, old man. Wake up, damn it.*

Twice more, Al worked to rouse the unconscious pilot curled on his side. Nathan Breuer wasn't playing possum.

Jimmy fought the urge to beat the shit out of Al and screw the consequences that would inevitably come from the three Al posers who seemed to get off from watching their big kahuna in action.

The leader glanced at the horizon with the helicopter chop, chop, chopping away against the backdrop of a sinking sun, then cranked back to Jimmy. "How sad you not run faster."

Al plugged a bullet into Nathan Breuer's head.

Jimmy didn't think, *couldn't* think. He launched forward. Two of the insurgents grabbed his wrists, legs, whatever they could catch on his flailing body. Dimly he heard his arm pop out of the socket. But he felt nothing except rage and instinct and an animalistic need to kill the bastard who'd blown off the . . . *oh God* . . . the back of . . . *God no* . . . his friend's skull.

He pumped a knee upward. Probably not the wisest move he'd ever made, taking on four armed enemies, but the callous execution still stunned him stupid.

A fist met his face. His vision went red. He stared through the haze of blood at Al holding the AK-47 he'd used to splatter Socrates' blood all over the rock wall.

The bastard kicked the dead man onto his back and smiled. "Now we run very fast."

A gun kissed Jimmy's temple, and some piece of reason stilled him. He absolutely could *not* put his parents through the hell of losing another child. The helicopter crew might not be able to stage a rescue now, but hopefully they could get a bead on wherever these bastards ended up taking him.

The fight flooded out of him, soaked up by the greedy, parched desert. One of the men tied his hands and feet, then dragged him by his bound wrists toward the corroded truck, engine still humming. Apparently *their* technology was holding out fucking fine today.

Al climbed into the cab while the other three tossed Jimmy in the truck bed. His face slid across stones and a ragged shard of rusted wheel well. He heard himself groan at the impact of metal against his shoulder, but he didn't register pain; he barely registered the bearded men guarding him.

The engine revved, jerked, barreled across the desert, tires spewing a cloud of sand behind them. Reality bombarded him as Jimmy stared through the tan-colored haze at his mentor's lifeless body.

He'd committed the unforgivable sin. He'd left his dead comrade behind.

ONE

Sixty seconds ago piloting this flight had been all gum-drops and rainbows. In an exploding flash, Captain Jimmy Gage's day turned to dog shit.

His cutting-edge new CV-22 was still tooling through the late afternoon sky just fine. The folks speedboating along the Mediterranean Sea, however? Not so good.

"What the hell?" He braced his hand against the control panel while aftershocks from the detonation below reverberated upward. This day may have turned to dog shit, but God willing, not nearly as bad as three years ago.

He needed to get his head out of his ass and focus on the radio in his helmet, which squawked to life. A crap ton of voices crowded the airwaves until even his flight-trained ears threatened to go on overload.

He peered through the windscreen, stick shuddering in his grip. Dots still danced in front of his eyes from the blast. Blue water stretched ahead to the distant Turkish coastline. The small boat of USO performers they'd been escorting to a naval aircraft carrier stalled behind, in flames.

Training overrode questions. Time to get his butt in gear.

There were three pilots up front and only one flight engineer in the cargo hold at the moment. Smooth would have his hands full scooping survivors from the sea in back.

Jimmy switched his headset to hot mic so he could hear everything and respond, while keeping his hands free to work. "Vapor, swap seats with me. I'm heading back to help out Smooth."

"Roger that," Vince "Vapor" Deluca jockeyed by and into the copilot's seat beside the aircraft commander. "Holy shit, what a mess down there. Coming left."

Jimmy charged past the bulkhead, already channeled into his new role. He was a test pilot these days, and being able to fly any plane, any crew position, anytime had been a requisite for graduation. Thanks to his new job in a dark ops test squadron, he could do his damned level best to ensure technology became an ally rather than an enemy, as it had three years ago.

This was a personal mission he now lived every minute, in tribute to Socrates. It was a mission that carried extra weight today.

This should have been a shadowy slip across international waters under the guise of escorting a handful of new USO performers to an aircraft carrier off the coast of Turkey. The flight had provided the perfect cover for them to slip into Incirlik Air Base and meet up with CIA and NSA agents already in place, all focused on locating and rescuing Chuck Tanaka, a member of their test squadron who had been kidnapped in the region a week ago by God only knew what kind of monster.

Chuck wasn't the only service member to have gone

missing in the region, but he was the only one with an experimental tracking device embedded under his skin.

No way in hell was Jimmy leaving behind another brother-in-arms.

"Hotwire?" the commander's voice barked. "Smooth? Can either of you give us more on what's happening?"

Jimmy leaned out the open side hatch, wind roaring around him. Acrid gusts from the flames stung his nose, his eyes. He blinked his vision clear. The explosion hadn't taken out the entire speedboat, a good sign.

Except a hole gaped in the bow of the navy boat, sucking in water fast. An accident or deliberate?

He'd faced plenty of hairy situations during combat and test pilot school—not to mention his four-month stint as a POW punching bag—but tossing in the wild card of panicked civilians added an element of unpredictability to any situation that had nothing to do with gauging the odds of technology. Normally he thrived on the charge of an intense assignment, even a good old head-cracking, chair-smacking bar fight to let off steam that had never quite emptied out of him even three years after Socrates' murder.

Jimmy tore his eyes from the mesmerizing flames licking up from the damaged boat hull and studied the survivors bobbing in the waves. "The boat's listing, gonna submerge soon. People are jumping overboard left and right, trying to get to the life raft, Colonel."

Their squadron commander, Lieutenant Colonel Scanlon, had come along due to the sensitivity of their real mission. The delay this explosion caused could very well steal precious minutes that ended up costing Chuck or one of the other missing servicemen his life. From his own captivity, Jimmy knew the inhumane lengths some twisted souls would go to, to extract sensitive information from military targets, and back then he hadn't even been part of the dark ops test squadron, with more explosive information to protect.

But he couldn't think of his friend now or the international ramifications of the top secret data stored in his brain.

"Bringing it around," their colonel drawled over the airwaves. "How many are in the water?"

The CV-22 banked hard and fast, the tilt-rotor tackling the tight turn with ease. Built to replace the MH-53 helicopter, the CV-22 hovered with blades on the wings overhead and could shift the rotors forward to fly like a plane at twice the speed of its predecessor. They needed every ounce of that agility today.

Jimmy gripped the side of the hatch, hooking a gunner's belt around his waist for safety, although his balance was sure after ten years of flying. Smoke from the explosion snaked inside, reminding him of another time, of a crash best scrapped from his mind right now.

Already jam-packed with top secret intelligence gear to trace their lead in Turkey, the cargo hold would be crammed to the gills fast once they pulled everyone from the water.

"I count nine swimming toward the deployed life raft, sir."

Lucky for them they couldn't see the sharks.

Jimmy, however, had a bird's-eye view of the too many black shadows slithering just beneath the surface.

"Nine? Hell, if there are more, we'll be hard-pressed to take them on. Vapor, are there any ships close enough to get over here and help pick these people up?"

"Negative contacts on the radar," Vapor answered. "We'll have to pluck them out ourselves. Shit, is that a shark?"

"Okay, then," the commander drawled through the airwaves. "Let's move out about three hundred yards and get turned around. Hotwire, prepare to work your ass off."

"Roger that, sir." He made tracks around equipment strapped to the deck, his boots clanking metal on his way toward the lowering back ramp.

"Copy all, boss man," Vapor responded. "Sierra Four,

Sierra Four, this is Prey Two-one. We have a boat on fire and sinking fifty-four miles due north of your position. We estimate nine in the water, but there could be more. Can you get a helo heading this way?"

Chatter from the aircraft carrier buzzed in the background while Jimmy worked with Smooth to rig the rescue hoist for deployment. The CV-22 downshifted into a hover over the burning boat.

There had been talk initially of flying the performers. The local coordinator, however, had decided the speedboat had more of a "navy" feel and chose to go with the small boat for a prima donna theatrical effect.

Damned bad-luck choice for the people in the ocean. But worse for Chuck, if these people's need for drama ended up costing him even one extra minute of pain.

Jimmy kept his voice as steady as his hands. "Colonel, waters are beyond choppy. That life raft could capsize at any second."

"All right, boys, let's get some people out of the ocean."

The hovering aircraft descended, closer to the rocking raft, nearer still. Jimmy stared out the cavernous back hatch as the nine people waving wildly became clearer, the sharks tougher to monitor even with Smooth's help.

Smooth swiped spray from his face. "How about you work the winch, and I'll monitor them coming up to the ramp?"

"Got your back." Jimmy deployed the winch outward, a three-person rescue hook like the forest penetrator used in helicopters. "Colonel, ease up on the raft anytime."

"Roger. Don't let me get too close before you lower the sling into the water. We don't need to be shocking these folks with the static electricity in that line."

A burst of wind growled louder than the engines. The tilt-rotor nudged so low, spray speckled his flight suit.

Jimmy played the cable toward the water, the *whump, whump, whump* of the rotors overhead sweeping foamy

ripples. "Line is on the way down. Twenty feet . . . ten."
The hoist slapped the surface by the orange rubber life
raft. "Contact with the water. Ready to move in."

"Roger, Hotwire," the Colonel replied, "easing up.
Keep a good eye on all of them, and make sure the rotor
wash doesn't push anyone under."

"We're watching," Jimmy affirmed. "Keep coming
forward. Forward. Ten feet more. Good, hold it right
there."

A man slid from the raft, the boat captain from the
looks of his navy uniform. He grabbed the rescue hook
and shouted back to the others. A woman in a glittery
costume detached herself from the side. With the help of
the navy dude, she pulled the horse collar over her head
and under one arm like a sash. The guy seemed to have
things in hand below, so Jimmy held his position by the
winch. Two more women joined her, facing each other on
the three-seater apparatus.

So far, so good.

"I have three in place. Bringing them up." Jimmy set
the winching mechanism into humming motion. Easy.
Easy. Eyes glued to the trio to be sure all arms and legs
were clear of the line. The whir of the winding cable
blended with the roar of wind and rotors. "Survivors clear
of the water."

Destroyed boat parts swirled below, with jagged edges
that could graze anyone trying to secure themselves in the
hoist. Blood in the water would draw the sharks in a snap.

Urgency pumped through him, prodding him to speed
this up, but his training insisted on routine. *Eyes on the
line.* As they neared the side door, he passed over the controls to Smooth and grabbed for the cable.

"Slack . . ." Jimmy called the order to slow the cable.
He clamped the first woman's hand as she clambered up
the ramp. "Slack, slack." He hauled the second, then third
inside. "Stop slack. Survivors on the deck."

He reached to steady the stumbling brunette who had to be a performer, given her gold sequined dress. Sopping wet and gasping, she shoved a hank of hair from her face, mascara streaking her cheeks.

Smooth's megawatt smile shouted high-priced orthodontics. "Damn, she looks famous."

"Save the autograph hounding for later, and let's rustle up some blankets. We've got six more men and women to bring on board." Jimmy handed the pop diva over to his panty-peeler crew mate.

In quick succession, he scooped the remaining six in two runs, four people wearing costumes and two men in navy uniforms. Jimmy started to breathe easier as the last collapsed into the CV-22's belly.

"Colonel, we've got them all loaded and secured. No injuries. No sign of casualties. A quick head count, and we'll be ready to bounce." Good thing for Chuck and the other unaccounted-for soldiers, this had gone quickly. They should be back on track to reach Turkey for their NSA briefing by nightfall.

A collective exhale echoed, before the Colonel whistled low and long, "Thank God. Bob Hope would be so pissed."

Smooth grinned, although his eyes didn't stray from the barely legal diva; no surprise, since the guy never let a female pass without falling for her. "Your age is showing, Colonel. Bob Hope would be over a hundred."

Lieutenant Colonel Scanlon growled. "Hope's the father of the USO. Stop blaspheming a legend, or I'll turn Vapor loose on you. You don't want him rewiring your car so the horn honks every time you put on the turn signal."

Jimmy allowed himself a laugh now that the crisis had passed without so much as a shark nibble. Humor carried them through hell in this job, one of many reasons he preferred to crew with the squadron-renowned joker.

Maybe this day wouldn't turn into dog shit after all.

They would make a quick landing on the aircraft carrier, drop off their extra cargo, and be on their way, closer to finding Chuck.

His laughter faded. Back to business. "Sir, still running a visual, and I don't see any more in the water. Smooth's asking the survivors, just to be sure."

Smooth straightened, spinning fast back to Jimmy and holding up one finger. "We're missing one. A woman."

Damn it. Jimmy peered into the mist of sea spray below. Any of those curling waves could be shielding her— if she hadn't already drowned or met up with a shark.

"Okay, everybody," the colonel ordered, "eyeballs out. Let's find her. Vapor, work the infrared and see if you can spot a heat source. I'm gonna start a slow circle around what's left of the boat."

Jimmy braced a hand and planted his feet as the aircraft banked. Half the speedboat stuck from the water, smoke billowing, stealing what little visibility he had left. A crack cut through the air a second before the damaged boat exploded into a watery bonfire.

The CV-22 shuddered. Their new passengers shrieked. He zeroed in on the vision below. Flames flicked upward like a demonic hand shooting a fiery bird at the heavens. The orange red glow domed out over the water and illuminated a small figure struggling to stay afloat.

Bare arms smacked the water, long hair trailing behind the woman. Smoldering scraps of metal showered down around her.

A deadly shadow undulated below the surface a few feet away.

His focus narrowed, frustration at the possible cost of this delay taking a backseat to the life-threatening emergency at hand. "Got a visual. There is someone down there, alive." Her head and shoulders bobbed then disappeared from sight, her hair swooping after her. "Crap, she just went under. Colonel, come twenty degrees right, and you should see her."

"Copy all." The craft cranked hard and fast, the colonel's drawl growing thicker. "I saw her for a second before a wave hit her. Anyone else got another visual? Smooth? Hotwire?"

"I keep catching glimpses. She isn't gonna make it unless . . ." Focus gelled into determination.

Jimmy patted the flattened LPU—life preserver unit— draped over him. He would inflate it once he reached her. "I'm going in. Smooth, get ready to haul us up."

He stared out the yawning opening at the thirty-foot jump. Not much of a drop except . . . Hell, he hated heights even more than he hated sharks. Some might think that strange for a flier, but he'd learned from his dead sister to meet fears head-on, fists flying even to the end.

Jimmy took three steps back, keeping his eyes locked on the speck of humanity bobbing in the ocean below. He gasped in air tinged with the scent of hydraulic fluid and sprinted toward the load ramp. His combat boots pounded metal then air. No kicking free shoes for a nice little dip. Warriors went into the water in full gear.

"Ahhhhh . . ." He hurtled through the battering wind and sea spray. "Fuck."

She'd damn well better still be alive.

* * *

Chloe Nelson refused to die. The Mediterranean Sea, however, seemed determined to override her wishes.

She grappled through the wall of water slamming over her. A week of swimming lessons at the YMCA as a kid hadn't prepared her for the open high seas. Her head breaking free, she gasped for air, her eyes stinging. She choked on a salty gulp and prayed hard, really hard that those rescue folks in the hovering aircraft wouldn't abandon her while she worked her way clear of the debris.

The *whump, whump, whump* of the blades overhead churned waves faster around her, making it impossible to grab the harness they'd lowered for the rest of her group.

Now she couldn't see the thing, much less strap herself inside.

Could this be some kind of twisted justice for stepping so far outside her comfort zone as a classical musician? Never had she expected that years of nose-to-the-grindstone training would result in a gig as a backup singer wearing sequins, fringe and do-me-sailor pumps.

Those rhinestone-studded shoes were currently spiraling their way to the bottom of the Mediterranean. Chloe pedaled her bare feet faster underwater, determined to get out of there before she drowned or a shark made her his Happy Meal.

Something grazed her upper thigh.

She screamed, then choked on more water. Were there really sharks in this coastal region of Turkey? Too bad she hadn't taken an occasional break from practicing to watch the Discovery Channel. She battled the current, even as her instincts told her to hold still. Who could stay calm enough in a situation like this to punch a shark in the nose?

Chloe flailed a half spin and found . . .

Not a shark. Her muscles went limp. She faced a helmeted person, a man, with big shoulders and a powerful sidestroke that kept him well afloat despite the roiling sea. The "Halleluiah Chorus" chimed through her head.

He extended a gloved hand for her, his mouth moving, but she couldn't hear as another swoosh tugged her away. She fought forward, stretched her arm, wiggled her fingers.

Finally she gripped warm, strong help.

Even the simple support of linked fingers gave her the edge she needed to move closer. He yanked her nearer still, until his arm banded around her waist.

"Hold on to me," he shouted over the combined roar of the engines, wind, and waves.

Dark brown eyes peered back at her, intense, as if he could bind her up and free with just the strength of his gaze. She wished it were that simple.

"I'll bet that's easy"—her teeth chattered almost as fast as her rolling thoughts while she struggled not to push him under—"for most of the panting and soaking-wet women who throw themselves at you, but me?" She gasped in air, spat water, couldn't stop talking even though he probably didn't hear her. "I'm having a tough time right now."

She pummeled harder with her feet as he towed her toward the dangling line, the same cable that had eluded her earlier. The harness swayed in front of them, and he plucked it from the air as easily as coaxing a note from a violin.

Water crested and splashed over his helmet, stealing him from sight. She bit back a cry, held tight, and kicked faster to keep up her end of this swimming deal. She hadn't survived a kidney transplant last year just to lose her life now.

His head popped through again, his square jaw clenched tight.

God, she'd brought this man into danger because of her own ineptitude. "What do I do?"

"Nothing. I've got it." His hands slid over her with brisk efficiency, tucking the seat between her legs, dropping the sash over her shoulder and under her other arm. He sat across from her, securing his harness, and grabbed the metal pole between them.

How was this awkward tangle of limbs going to work?

"Lock your legs around my waist."

"Excuse me?" She choked on another briny swallow.

Okay, this was a life-or-death sort of thing. She would cuddle up to an angry grizzly bear right now if he could get her out of here.

She wrapped her thighs around the military guy's hips and locked her ankles. The cable pulled taut, then jerked. Her stomach lurched as they surged from the water. They spun in midair. She looked down, and her equilibrium went to hell in a handbasket.

Then she saw the sharks.

Every-freaking-where.

Even where she'd been swimming seconds before. She couldn't stop herself from thrashing as she rocked backward. Her fingers twisted in his wet flight suit. The wind whipped clean through her skimpy costume.

"Be still," he hollered. One arm still gripping the pole extending into the cable, he palmed the small of her back and flattened her to him. "Reach up and hold the treble hook."

She stared at the helmet, the jut of his jaw just inches away. She was flipping out over seeing the sharks after the fact, yet he'd knowingly jumped into the middle of them for her.

"Sorry," she bellowed back. She suppressed the instinctive need to wriggle and surrendered control. "I was taught not to plaster myself against strangers while half-naked."

"Believe me . . ." His eyes locked on hers, his voice suddenly clear in their private pocket of space. "The last thing I'm thinking about now is what we're wearing, Ariel."

Ariel? Oh, Little Mermaid. *Geez.*

"Fair enough." She relaxed against his chest, the waters churning all the faster below as they twirled on the thin wire.

Her champagne silk outfit turned clammy against her skin. At least the costume had held together. She sure hoped someone had a warm blanket up there. All flames from the explosion aside, she was freezing her tush off.

Explosion. Now that she was almost safe, the magnitude of how close she'd come to dying punched her. Hard. Concerns about her scantily clothed body didn't matter one whit. She was lucky to have cheated death. Again. Damn it all, she'd taken on this stint with the USO as a payback to the dead soldier who'd donated her kidney so Chloe could live.

The cable jerked to a stop just shy of the ramp. She stifled a scream and clamped her legs tighter around him. His wet uniform rasped against her bare calves. "At least I'm not afraid of heights. That would really suck."

He grunted.

The cable eased into motion again, drawing them inside, and just that fast, they were both standing on blessedly dry metal. Now she couldn't make herself let go of this guy who'd jumped into a shark pit. She gasped in air heavy with the scent of musky male and something akin to engine oil. She soaked up the heat of him because she must still be cold, otherwise why would her teeth chatter? The *whump, whump, whump* of the rotors synched up with his heart under her ear.

A blanket draped over her shoulders, and she forced herself to step deeper into the cavernous cargo hold full of equipment, soldiers, and soaked USO crew members. Adrenaline tingled away, almost as if dripping from her toes like the salt water pooling around her feet.

Her rescue guy grasped her arm. "Are you hurt?"

"Only my fashion sense." She found her footing and grabbed for the blanket sliding from her shoulders. "I noticed nobody else is wearing sequins to thc beach this year."

No wonder everyone was staring at her. Especially the towering man who'd hauled her tookus out of the sea.

Like he would be as interested if she wore her regular wardrobe of white shirts and khaki, khaki, and more khaki, varied only by the donning of her black formal wear for orchestral performing. She wondered what he would do if she flashed him her favored Vulcan salute along with a salutation of *Live long and prosper.*

And God, her thoughts were rambling. Must be shock in the aftermath of what she'd been through. How totally awkward. She needed to find a seat. Then people would look elsewhere.

She frowned. They weren't just staring. They were gaping.

Had she suffered a costume malfunction? She didn't normally need to think about wardrobe hazards in floor-length black taffeta or velvet, but she wasn't used to regulating showy getups that were vintage Cher.

Chloe clenched her fists, restraining the impulse to flatten her hands to her chest and check on "the girls"; now wouldn't that really get everyone gawking? She snuck a quick peek south instead as she leaned to scoop her blanket from the metal grate.

Her breasts were still tucked securely in the sequin-speckled costume. She blinked once, twice, and sure enough, her eyesight didn't lie. Oh damn.

"The girls" were safely constrained inside sopping-wet, *transparent* silk.

Two

Marta Surac killed her first man at thirteen.

Thirty years later as she writhed to the pulsing electronic techno beat, she still didn't feel guilty. She wouldn't have even wasted a thought on the past except for the popping of a cork in her new pub.

She plunged her hands in her hair, raising her arms higher until her bracelets hitched on her elbow. She pumped her hips closer to her young military dance partner. His eyes swept down her with an appreciation that didn't affect her in any way other than the power it provided. Marta stared right back, smiling, because this trained soldier didn't know she'd already taken down one of his own tonight.

He could be next, if she gave the word.

Glasses clinked while people at a nearby table toasted with the freshly decanted wine. She swayed faster in frenetic synch with the strobing lights and flashing thirty-year-old memory.

Her uncle had ripped off her clothes, unzipped his pants, and straddled her in the dank storage room behind her father's tavern. She'd learned how to defend herself after watching her family for years. She'd taken a corkscrew and jammed it into the bastard's back, pushing, twisting until she found his heart.

Quite symbolic, now that she thought of it, teasing her breasts against the soldier's chest. Didn't the American military men who frequented her bars call "the act" screwing? Uncle Radko had been trying to screw her, and she simply got to him first.

Dimly registering the American's hands sliding to her hips, she eyed the blue-tiled entrance to her newest pub on Istanbul's Nevizade Street. This crossroad of world cultures offered the perfect place to expand her international network. The boy keeping step until sweat sheened his face might be here for pleasure, but for her, it was always about business.

The door opened, and her senses tightened. Two familiar men pushed through the haze of unfiltered cigarette smoke that perpetually hovered in the air, returning to give the report she'd been anticipating. She made eye contact. *Stop. Wait.*

Music faded, a slower Turkish folk tune spinning up. She eased free of her dance partner.

"Thank you for a lovely time. Your drinks will be on the house this evening, so stay, party. It is early still," Marta offered up to soothe any rejected feelings. These boys always cheered over free alcohol. "I hope you enjoy your temporary leave."

Weaving around couples and tables already packed with locals and tourists even before sunset, she strode toward the duo waiting by the bar. She nodded, and Baris and Erol followed. Both were strong, ambitious, and best of all, amoral.

Her high-heeled Manolos clicked along the wood floor as the hallway narrowed in the renovated old building. Sconces on the walls vibrated from the music up front.

She selected the key on her charm bracelet and unlocked her office. "Come in and close the door behind you."

After the door snicked shut, Baris passed her a videodisc labeled only with a number. "It's done."

"Of course it is." She never doubted her orders would be followed. She evoked that sort of quiet fear. But she understood the wisdom of stroking their male egos. "I only hire the best."

Since Uncle Radko, she had taken more lives. Of course now she rarely wielded the corkscrew, gun, drugs, garrote, or whatever weapon the occasion warranted. She paid others. Not because of a lack of stomach for the task, but rather because she could afford it.

Marta sidestepped an oversized chaise covered with gold tasseled pillows on her way to the minibar and opened the false bottom of a cigar box. She thumbed the disc in her hand one last time before storing it away with the others. The captured image stayed imprinted on her mind as well as the DVD, since she'd been there when they taped beating the American soldier.

Now his lifeless body lay in a back alley.

The soldier hadn't proven as helpful as others they'd taken, and certainly not as valuable as another she still held. What world-altering secrets a tangle of gray matter could carry.

Baris pressed deeper into the room, his partner holding back. "We placed an empty condom wrapper with his fingerprints inside his wallet as you ordered, and a woman's strand of hair on his uniform."

"Perfect. We held him such a short time, they probably haven't even reported him missing yet." She'd quickly determined he would be worthless. She locked away the discs, positioning the wooden box precisely beside the brass cigar clippers. "That should provide a timeline for the missing hours between when he left his drinking friends and his death hours later."

Authorities would conclude he picked up a woman or prostitute, then met with muggers on his way back through the bustling Nevizade Street, narrow and crowded with pubs. Tables spilled out onto the stone road, pick-pockets were rampant.

Marta flattened her palm to the carved lid on the cigar container depicting a windswept sultan. No news media would see the recording. This little scene would be played for his fellow American aviator who she still held, a man she'd taken a week ago from a base in southern Turkey. Her remaining captive appeared more stubborn but also potentially more valuable.

She'd already kept him long enough that he could never be released without jeopardizing her anonymity; still, she had hopes of prying information free. She could afford one more week to work on him. His body's reappearance would simply require more creativity to hide his injuries. That also gave her more latitude to toy with him.

Erol and Baris started toward the paneled door, which reminded her of the rest of her agenda for the night.

"Baris," she called. "Stay with me awhile?"

She phrased it as a question even as she knew he wouldn't say no. The lure of laying the boss would be too appealing. Not a great hardship for him, either, because she knew full well she didn't look her age.

Erol's eyes snapped with jealousy, quickly hidden. He would have his turn, but he didn't need to know that yet. The employee backed out the door, leaving Baris alone with her. She waved him over to the chaise.

"Sit." She poured a glass half-full of raki mixed with water and placed it on a mosaic-covered side table. "You've worked hard today. You deserve to celebrate."

"I only did my job."

Marta opened the carved box, the regular lid this time. The scent of expensive tobacco swelled upward. She plucked a cigar free while scooping up the clippers and snipped the end as precisely as removing a fingertip.

She passed Baris the first-rate Cuban smoke and a lighter before sitting on the edge of her desk.

He hesitated. "Aren't you going to have one, too?"

"No, you go ahead." Leaning back on her hands, she inched her knees apart, not too far, just enough to pull her short skirt taut. "My turn to celebrate will come soon."

He lit the cigar and inhaled a puff. "How lucky we will celebrate together then."

Ah, boys. Always so full of promises and pride, but she wanted him to stay, so she kept that thought to herself. "You proved yourself loyal and efficient. I value that."

In her early days, she would have enjoyed the power over men, when she still savored the thrill of the kill. She knew better now. Emotions affected business, and control was everything, which brought her back to the dark-haired male in front of her. After her mother had learned about Uncle Radko, she'd taught her daughter about the power gained from sex. A power best wielded without the distraction of emotions and the mind-numbing joys any other woman might foolishly find with a strong man between her thighs.

Marta arched to sit upright, straining the buttons of her satin blouse. She slipped one open, then a second, enough for a peek at the crimson lace of her bra that matched the hint of panties. "Let's see how efficient you really are."

Baris drew hard on the cigar, but his eyes never left her.

Power. Here, with him, and a different sort of control than she had over her high-value American target. "I have an important job for you down in Adana."

"I am honored at your trust." Smoke swirled around his bearded face.

She had learned an important thing about her prisoner in the basement below. He might be proficient at his military job, but he was not as perfectly invincible as he thought. Already he'd let a name slip, just a whisper on a

groan. Only his first name, but still she had her people
looking into it while she gave him his final week.

Tossing aside the cigar clippers, Marta took in Baris's
dilating pupils and handsome face. Not that it mattered to
her if she screwed an ugly underling.

No thrill. No highs *or* lows. Thanks to years of careful
practice, tonight she would only exercise the power to
take her games to the next level.

★ MEDITERRANEAN SEA:
USS *THEODORE ROOSEVELT*

As the sun dipped into the horizon, Chloe had never been
more grateful for level flooring in her life.

She stepped down the side hatch steps of the CV-22
onto the overcrowded deck of the aircraft carrier where
she was supposed to have made an ocean approach full of
fanfare. She plucked at her now-dry, saltwater-stiff costume. The silk may have been see-through earlier, but
thank goodness the fabric dried quickly.

Some sailors in yellow jerseys hustled everyone off the
plane and over to a designated safe area on the packed
flight deck. Navy personnel in uniforms and numerous
colored jerseys raced around in concert with one another,
a synchronicity that could turn dangerous in a heartbeat.

She'd been warned during a preperformance briefing
about the hazards of being mowed down by prop wash or
swept overboard by jet exhaust. Not to mention the possibility of getting sucked in and spat out by an engine. The
whole day was scary—and exciting.

Who'd have thought she would ever land in a plane on
a navy ship? The thrill of the wind whipping, the roar of a
fighter jet landing on a tiny patch of metal almost managed to wipe away the fear from nearly dying today.

Perhaps the near-death moment had reminded her to
savor every second of this adventure she'd undertaken.

She'd spent so much of her life yearning to experience the world outside hospitals and practice halls. She'd gotten a bellyful today.

She should make tracks to the backstage area, but the hubbub was so flipping amazing. Aircraft parked close together with their wings folded up like massive metal bugs. Sailors mingled with entertainment legends.

How cool to be a part of this, thanks to her connection with Livia Cicero, a big-time Italian pop star currently signing autographs for a cluster of drooling swabbies. Last winter Livia had come to America to make her cross-over breakthrough. She'd performed at an Atlanta Falcons halftime show along with Chloe's orchestra. When Livia spoke to the crowd about her upcoming USO engagement, Chloe finally had her answer to how she could offer tribute to the soldier who'd saved her life with an organ donation.

Now she was only an hour away from beginning her week of performances for the troops. The sailors and soldiers on the USS *Theodore Roosevelt* off the coast of Turkey were expecting a show, and by God, apparently the USO intended to deliver in spite of the fact that half their cast had nearly been blown up.

That reminded her how this day could have turned out so differently. Her gaze gravitated toward the air force aviators who'd rescued them. The four-man crew strode down the stairs leading from the side hatch with matching desert tan flight suits and cocky struts. She slipped out of the line of performers to get a better look at the guys who'd saved her life.

And of course the fab four all wore cool shades.

She recalled reading in some article once that fliers' eyes were light-sensitive from too much time tooling around the skies among all those unfiltered UV rays. But somehow she knew that, even if they weren't, these self-proclaimed zipper-suited sky gods would shade their peeps all the same. Their choice of eyewear, however, revealed interesting details about these jet jocks.

The first guy wore classic Ray Ban aviators, signature of the more seasoned, older sort. Sure enough, as he drew closer, she could see he was the boss who'd checked on them all after they'd strapped into their seats.

Moving on to number two, he was someone she hadn't seen during the flight: ominous tinted wraparounds and a shaved bald head. His badass look was tempered by a huge smile and booming laugh.

Third up, the guy who'd flirted with every female, wore tortoiseshell squared-off shades, compliments of Christian Dior eyewear, if she wasn't mistaken. Given the way his flight bag was all beat up with a dented thermos sticking out, the expensive glasses—ones apparently picked to match his golden brown hair—must be a gift from a woman.

Finally, her eyes settled on the man who'd pulled her from the water. This flyboy wore sport performance sunglasses, rimless and looking like something from the next century. Her gaze lingered on him. How could she not be curious about a person who'd jumped into shark-infested waters to save her?

Now that he'd removed his helmet, she could see his angular face more clearly. Dark-haired with a standard military fade cut, he walked away from his aircraft with a lean, whipcord power. She couldn't see his eyes but remembered the dark and vibrant energy from when he'd been inches away from her.

Chloe figured she had at least fifteen free minutes to thank the guy before the show started. Who knew if she would ever see him again, and all embarrassment aside, she owed him a huge debt. She padded across the hot metal deck in the borrowed shoes the navy had supplied upon landing. The acres-big boat sat so still and impervious to the churning sea she could have sworn she walked on dry land.

She stopped beside the airman who'd pulled her out of the water, and yeah, she couldn't help but think of the soldier whose kidney now rested inside her. She really would have to keep a rein on the whole hero-worship vibe.

"Hi, I didn't get a chance to properly introduce myself before with the whole sharks and dunking deal." She thrust out her hand. "I'm Chloe Nelson."

"Captain Jimmy Gage," he clasped her hand, his flight glove rasping against her tender skin.

When he didn't so much as crack a smile or say anything more, she rushed to fill in the awkward silence. "Thank you for saving my life." She'd said those words so many times to different doctors, and she was grateful. "I don't know how I'll ever be able to repay you."

"No thanks necessary. It's all in the job description." His sports glasses hid any hint of emotion, as if to provide an extra layer of invincibility.

She struggled for something else to say, not ready to sound the final note on a sonata that didn't feel played out. "What's with all the different jersey colors on the navy folks? So far, I've seen yellow, purple, white, blue, red, and green."

He shuffled from boot to boot, his head cocking toward his crew mates as if eager to leave before he finally settled into a military stance that shouted duty and mannerly protocol. "Each color stands for the different job held. That makes it easier to find the right person in the overpacked crush."

"Interesting." Oooo-kay. Brilliant reply. Her summa cum laude diploma wasn't anywhere in sight today. She rubbed her hands along her arms. "The wind's really whipping."

"Do you need a fresh blanket?"

Blanket? If only she'd managed to secure one faster in the airplane. Her skin warmed from more than the setting sun.

"I'm all dry. You can use that megastar boom mic of yours," she tapped the helmet/headset dangling from his grip, "to let everyone know my wet T-shirt peep show is over, and it doesn't look like rain. Livia Cicero has already generated enough hype from her posters. Those guys don't need to see the intimate Livia for real up close and exposed."

She glanced over, and sure enough, the Italian diva's cluster of admirers had swelled near the USO's signature banner. A pair of backup dancers—Steven and Melanie, a girlfriend/boyfriend duo—circulated to keep the crowd happy while waiting. Unless Livia did some speed-signing, the show wouldn't get started on time.

Jimmy Gage ducked his head into her line of sight, his shoulders blocking the view of the star and her fan club. "Did you need anything else, ma'am?"

Ma'am? She'd been the Little Mermaid earlier.

She wasn't sure what she'd expected in speaking to him. A polite exchange and a quick laugh, maybe? He'd been so steady and reassuring earlier. Now it seemed her hottie savior had cooled off. "Nope, just had to say thank you for saving my life and covering me up before everyone in the plane saw my rack."

A tic twitched in the corner of his eye. Because she'd said *rack*? "Ah, come on. You have to admit it was a serious tension buster after what we'd been through."

"What *you've* been through." He nodded his head slowly, his features tightening. "Right. You'll have to pardon me if I'm not finding the whole peep show quite so mood-lifting."

Okay then. Way to go throwing a wet blanket over the rest of the day. "Well, uh, fair enough. I have to hit the stage now. Gotta warm up my background singer doo-wops."

She started to turn when an even heavier wet blanket—metaphorically speaking—hit her. How could she have forgotten such an all-important detail? Just because some flyboy crossed her path?

Chloe faced him again, wind tangling curls she still hadn't figured out how to tame. "I really"—*really*—"hate to ask this. But after the show, could you help me navigate this place and find the ship's doctor?"

His irritability morphed to alert attention. "Why didn't you tell us straight up you'd been hurt during the explosion? We'll find the ship's doc right now. The show can do without you."

"No, no, really. I'm not hurt. I, uh . . ." God, it was hard enough talking to a new doctor about something as personal, as intrinsically private, as her organ transplant surgery. She definitely couldn't share it with this standoffish stranger, even if he'd saved her life. "I have bad allergies, and if I don't take care of them by tonight, I won't be able to sing tomorrow. I packed plenty of medication," antirejection drugs and an assortment of others, "in my luggage, which has all been sent to our lodgings onshore. I had enough for a couple of days stashed in my purse, but my bag is now either ashes or at the bottom of the sea."

"You have allergies?" He peered at her over the top of his shades, irritation returning clear as day.

She liked the sunglasses in place better than his unshaded eyes, after all. "Never mind. If you're too busy to help me, I'll ask someone else."

"Not a problem." He held up a hand with a beleaguered sigh. "I'll be waiting for you after the show."

It felt disloyal to be torqued off at the guy who'd just saved her life, but Jimmy Gage was one uptight dude.

She couldn't have stopped the words bubbling out if she'd tried. She didn't try. "Well, who shot your cat?"

"Shot my cat?"

"Who pissed you off? I'm really sorry to be such a bother."

"A bother? A *bother*?" He stepped closer, his scowling eyebrows sinking below the top of his sunglasses.

Silently, she held her ground, refusing to be afraid.

Besides, it wasn't like he could hurt her with so many witnesses around.

"Listen, Shirley Temple," he batted aside a blond curl snaking on the wind toward his face, "my crew and I are a little short on time right now because you and your show people just had to have a fancy escort and fanfare. You couldn't simply arrive covertly and do your performance." He was practically nose to nose with her, the scent of aftershave, salty water, and something unmistakably masculine teasing her nose. "We're in the Middle East. It's dangerous. People could have died out there today because you and your group put yourselves—and thereby us—in unnecessary danger."

She started to shoot right back at him that how they arrived wasn't *her* decision. And she'd given up a prime performance in Atlanta to be here on this boat, entertaining troops like him who put their lives on the line for their country. She deserved thanks, not—

Except she wasn't here for gratitude. She'd traveled across the globe to repay a debt to another soldier who'd saved her life with a donor card. In honor of that dead servicewoman's sacrifice, Chloe would keep her angry words to herself.

She scavenged for her dignified conductor's calm and hoped it wasn't totally negated by her go-go getup. "I apologize on behalf of us all for any risks or scheduling problems we caused. Thank you again for what you did for me earlier and for escorting us safely to the USS *Roosevelt*."

She turned and walked away. Not that she had any idea where the performers were supposed to gather backstage. But she would hook up with Livia over by the stage rather than lose face by wandering around asking for directions. And she absolutely would not look back to see if Captain Jimmy Gage was watching her walk away.

Forget him. In spite of his offer, she would find someone else to direct her to the ship's doctor for her medicine. Chloe turned her attention to the stage and her upcoming performance.

She only had to get through the next three hours, and then she would never have to worry about crossing paths with Jimmy Gage again.

THREE

★──

Jimmy gripped the steel bars and clanked down the ship ladder for his flight debriefing belowdecks. The distant sound of music above offered a reminder of how he'd lost it with Chloe Nelson.

On a normal day, he would have been able to keep his anger in check. Yeah, he'd meant what he said about resenting how they'd all been put at risk for the sake of a showy arrival. And hell yeah, he knew he'd been curt because this mess with Chuck reminded him of his own unresolved crap from Afghanistan, the way he'd failed Socrates. But most of all, his brain roiled with thoughts of what even the smallest delay could cost Chuck. If his own rescue had come a few hours later, he would have been headless.

No one would die on his watch ever again.

Jimmy's boots thudded against the metal floor. He simply hadn't been able to scavenge much sympathy for Chloe Nelson's allergies. Not with what Chuck must be going through. And especially not after how he'd seen his sister fight a crippling battle with leukemia with such a fearless spirit. He'd dedicated his air force career to carrying on that same spirit.

He may have promised to help Chloe after her show, but he didn't have the time or inclination to dissect why he found the cranky mermaid look so damn sexy.

Jimmy strode deeper into the belly of the ship. What a freaking mess with all the pipes and wires running across an already too-low ceiling. Even if he asked for directions, sailors had a different name for everything, like how they called the ceiling the overhead.

Then there was that funky smell: eau d'aviation fuel and military surplus store. Every space below was jampacked and musty. Being in a cramped plane was one thing, since it only lasted a few hours, but to live that way for months on end? Definitely different strokes for different folks.

He turned down a passageway and stopped short before slamming into a hulking SEAL. "'Scuse me."

"No worries, sir." The special ops warrior disappeared around a corner.

Jimmy looked left, then right, about ready to flip a coin. He could have sworn the map pointed him this way. He turned around and went back through an opened hatch.

Success.

He charged ahead into the small metal cavern that would serve as their secured meeting space, the first to arrive. After his flight debrief, he would hook Chloe up with a doctor and label this one of life's odd encounters.

His boots thunked metal as he made his way across the room. A hand clamped on his shoulder. He looked back to find Vapor—with a big smile on his ugly mug.

"Shit, Vapor, you've really got to stop sneaking up like that, or I'm gonna have to rename you Casper."

"All those names you like to come up with for me, and

you still can't find a decent biker one." Vapor thumbed up toward the music. "So, are you looking to tap that?"

No need to badger Vince by asking who he meant. Jimmy knew his chitchat with Chloe Nelson wouldn't have gone unnoticed. "No mixing business with pleasure."

"Since when?"

"Since about five fucking minutes ago."

"Someone missed his morning java."

Jimmy scanned the room for somewhere to sit. By himself. He often wondered if the furniture in these places was put in while the boat was under construction and never replaced. Everything looked the same: sturdy metal painted gray.

Smooth ducked into the room and toward the simmering pot on a corner table. "Maybe he's holding out for the star, the Cicero lady."

Cicero? He thought of her signing autographs, aloof in a sultry way, her hair somehow looking deliberately tousled even though she'd been dunked in the ocean. Not his type. Too . . . Just too.

Something about Chloe struck him as more real. *Irritating*, but real.

He eyed the coffeepot. Sludge sounded good right about now.

Vapor pulled up alongside him, mumbling, "Where are the doughnuts? Don't they know aviators need doughnuts? It's a ritual, for God's sake. This break with tradition could doom our next flight."

"Go look for them out there. Your nose must be failing you." Jimmy pointed past the flat screen monitor suspended from the ceiling toward the door. Once he found food, Vapor would be too occupied to harp on the backup singer. The guy never seemed to get full.

The squadron commander filled the hatch, not scowling exactly, but certainly not smiling. "Can we quit the Match.com meets *Top Chef* routine long enough to take care of some minor international security issues?" Lieu-tenant Colonel Scanlon pushed deeper into the room. "Our contact from the National Security Agency has flown over from Turkey to update us on the latest about the boat explosion. A fighter ferrying him in from Incirlik Air Base landed on the deck while you were busy chatting up the showgirl."

Putting Chloe Nelson into the past wouldn't be as sim-ple to accomplish if his crew kept this up.

Scanlon hefted his flight bag on a long, narrow table in front of a row of chairs and pulled out a file. "I don't know about you, but I would like to get Agent Nunez's take on why we had to interrupt our mission for some deep-sea fishing."

Silence hung heavy while they took their seats. Jimmy could overlook the boss man's grouchiness. They all did. Scanlon's wife had died only six months ago. He wasn't a ray of sunshine, but he was getting the job done at a time in his life when no one would have blamed him for reach-ing for a bottle of antidepressants.

Vapor scrubbed his bald head. "I was kinda hoping the boat incident could be blamed on one of those swabbies setting off a cherry bomb in the head."

The boss sat scrolling through messages on his Black-Berry while talking. "A mechanical failure would be the best case scenario, gentlemen."

Vapor pinched off a piece of the Styrofoam on his cup and pitched it into his empty drink. "Too bad their engine mechanics didn't have me to help work out the kinks on their new model."

Nobody liked to mention the big *T* word, but being on guard against terrorism was a part of their daily life, espe-cially in this region of the world.

Jimmy cracked his knuckles. "Or it was a bomb. There are plenty of people on the south side of the Med who don't like us." And how ironic was that for him, given he actually had distant relatives from the area? Relatives who could end up popping him if things on this op soured. "Sorta hard to sift through all the crazies. I am assuming no Peoples' Brotherhood of American Haters has taken responsibility, so really, it's just all a guess. I say we carry on like there are bad guys out there and really watch our six."

Smooth tapped his boot in time with the throbbing pulse of the music from above. "True that, true that. The day has been a big bite in the ass, and to add insult to injury, we're missing all those smokin'-hot babes in the show. If it started raining on those costumes—"

"Watch your mouth, Romeo." The words fell out of Jimmy's mouth before he could stop and think how they would only fuel more talk about him and the backup singer.

Footsteps rattling out in the corridor saved him from further razzing.

The clanking grew louder, closer, until the open hatch filled with a female ensign standing beside the other new-comer, who was not in uniform.

A gray-haired man who looked to be local and about sixty years old waited in the opening. His dark clothing appeared to be some kind of groundskeeper's garb, complete with dirt staining the cuffs of his loose-fitting pants.

The ensign swept a hand into the room. "Here we are, Agent Nunez."

Agent? Jimmy straightened in his chair, his eyes following the old Turkish man while the ensign continued talking.

"We've set up the video equipment you requested. I'll be right outside in the hall if you need anything else."

"Thank you, Ensign," a distinctly American accent came from the guy's mouth. He walked into the room confidently, briskly, carrying a laptop computer under his arm.

The ensign stepped out and closed the hatch behind her, sealing them in with the "gardener," who was apparently Agent Nunez.

"Pardon my appearance, gentlemen, I came in straight out of the field." He cocked a silver brow. "Literally and figuratively. I've been collecting data in and around Incirlik, where three of the soldiers disappeared."

The more the man spoke, the more the years peeled away from his appearance. Wrinkles relaxed from his face, and his movements were quick and efficient as he connected his laptop to the projector. Nunez had either gone prematurely gray or dyed his hair, because the man before them now couldn't be older than forty.

This guy was good.

Nunez fired up the screen with a blazing white light, the slide changer gripped in his dirt-stained fist. "As you know, service members in the Middle East and Eastern Europe have been going missing, eleven to date." Slides clicked with official military photos, somber faces from different services. All in uniform with an American flag in the background. "Seven bodies were recovered, and four were listed as still MIA or AWOL."

No way in hell was Chuck AWOL. Even the suggestion made Jimmy fighting mad. He forced his hands to stay loose while he listened to the agent.

"Those numbers have changed."

Oh shit.

A new slide came onto the screen of a Turkish side street. "We found a dead army sergeant an hour ago in an alley, made to appear like a bar hookup with a prostitute gone wrong."

Not Chuck. Thank God. But still someone's friend or son.

"The other three are still missing. We don't believe these are random terrorist kidnappings but rather an organized network attempting to gain top secret operational and technological information. There is also a chance that they are attempting to turn some of those captured into spies for their side."

Nunez clicked a button, and Chuck Tanaka's photo

filled the screen. "Lucky for us, Captain Tanaka is assigned to your dark ops test squadron."

Jimmy forced his eyes to stay front, even as his fists went numb from clenching.

"Thanks to the nanosensor your unit implanted under his skin for testing, we've been able to narrow the search to this region and begin gathering preliminary data. The sensor monitoring his biometrics shows he's still alive." The agent paused long enough for a collective exhalation of relief.

"Thanks to the information periodically transmitted via low-power signal to cell phone towers, to satellites, and finally to a control center, we've been able to discern the captain has been drugged, and we know what those drugs are. Sadly, the low power of the nanosensor and the experimental nature leaves our information far from perfect."

A few more weeks, and they could have had that tracking device perfected, damn it.

Nunez clicked the PowerPoint slide to a small grid on a map. "We have his location narrowed down to a five-mile area. Contact with the sensor is spotty without a GPS-quality position indicator. Are there any questions thus far?"

Lieutenant Colonel Scanlon stroked a thumb over his BlackBerry. "We're with you so far. Please continue."

"Thank you, Colonel," Nunez answered, appropriately dropping the *lieutenant* part of the commander's rank in conversation, a protocol quirk of military lingo.

Nunez pushed a button on the podium, and the slide changed to an expanded map of Turkey. "With CIA paramilitary operatives already in place and your newly acquired CV-22 tilt-rotor, we plan to combine your latest aerial surveillance technology and the ground intelligence. We're confident we can trace the enemy's chain of command and launch a rescue mission."

Scanlon slid aside his BlackBerry with the barest hint

of impatience. "With all due respect, you're not telling us anything we don't already know. I sense you've got another shoe to drop in your presentation, Agent Nunez."

"Right you are, Colonel." The image on the screen shifted to an image of the USO boarding a C-17 back in the States. "The explosion today threw a monkey wrench in our plans. The troupe was supposed to make a one-show stop at Incirlik Air Base before heading on to Iraq and Afghanistan. Now, however, due to raised security concerns, they will be staying at Incirlik until authorities can trace the source of the explosion."

He clicked to the next slide, a promotional photo featuring a lineup of females performing. Chloe Nelson's blond mess of curls shone like a beacon from the back row. "Waiting for the USO group to leave Turkey risks too much time for Captain Tanaka, and as of now, no one is willing to cancel the tour altogether."

Jimmy could see what was coming like an unavoidable crash before Nunez even continued.

"I propose your crew continues to act as their official escort to Turkey, to provide protection for them on that newly extended leg of their trip." The crash landing just kept powering closer and closer. "This also offers an even more plausible cover story for your stay in Turkey."

Impact.

The music swelled overhead as if to taunt him.

So much for adios to the Little Mermaid.

* * *

Four hours later, Agent Mike Nunez sat strapped in the back of the CV-22 with the USO troupe, the plane bound for Turkey. His groundskeeper persona was now dead to him.

No grieving necessary, though. He'd died more times than he could count. That was his job.

He changed names and identities for undercover ops so often, his body had become a hull to be retooled for each assignment. A hull with one helluva brain packed with intelligence and the skills to keep himself alive for the next rebirth.

Right now, he only needed the brain. The body could hang out in the camo they'd loaned him after he took a quick shower to get rid of the gray coloring sprayed on his hair.

He wasn't overly enthused about his exposure to the USO troupe as he sat with them in the aircraft's cargo hold, but ultimately he had confidence in his ability to change his appearance enough that anyone in this cavernous hold could walk past his next persona—Miguel Carvalho—and not recognize him as the dude sitting here now.

But he wasn't depending only on his own skills.

The four aviators he'd met today could make or break his mission: an air force team from a small dark ops test squadron only a select few even knew existed. The shit these avionics pioneers created and flew was so damn spooky, even their own wives didn't know where they went or what they did with aircraft, weaponry, defense, surveillance, and sensors that blew even his mind. They tried it all. Most of the technology they used would never be known to the world.

They reported only to the air force chief of staff.

But for the next week, at least, they would be reporting to him. He needed their "toys." He just hoped they weren't so accustomed to running rogue they couldn't pull with the rest of the team in a crunch. Another reason he preferred to depend only on himself.

Savoring this rare solitary moment, Nunez pulled out his secure reading tablet and inserted his ID CAC—common access card—into a slot on the top and tapped in his code. The screen lit up secure green while the CV-22 engines droned. He began reviewing reports and intelligence assessments he would need before stepping on the streets of Turkey as Miguel Carvalho, a bored banking

heir from Spain. He had three bars on his target list near
the NATO base. All three had been the last known site for
soldiers who'd later disappeared.

Chatter from the crew over his headset distantly registered in his brain as he worked. Jimmy Gage's flat mid-
western accent growled low.

"If it was a bomb on the boat, who was the target? I
find that so much more pertinent than who did it."

Vapor's clipped Chicago tones interrupted. "And why
would that be more interesting, my friend? Is there something on that boat that intrigues you, the busty cage
dancer, perhaps?"

"Backup singer," Gage snapped.

Half smiling, Nunez scrolled through the latest update
on his data, searching for . . . he wasn't sure what. But he
would feel it when he saw it. He needed to study every
aspect of the three locales, because life threw enough surprises his way on its own.

Smooth strode past him in the cargo hold, pressing a
hand to his headset. "I hope no one associated with the
USO group is involved."

Vapor keyed up the mic. "I say there is no way the
USO babes are involved in anything. Where would they
hide weapons in those skimpy outfits? Although, once
they get wet, those costumes are as dangerous as a stun
gun. Wouldn't you say, Jimmy?"

The squadron commander cleared his throat. "I have a
better question. How about we pay attention to flying this
airplane? What do you think about that?"

Nunez shot a quick look at the women working to re-
pair their hair and makeup while dealing with the con-
straints of their seats. At least they couldn't hear what was
being said. He tuned out the voices and focused on work.

He thumbed the track ball down, down, down through
the maze of data. Paused. Scrolled back up a couple of
pages and stopped. Went back and read the list of employees on that fourth bar again.

Anya Surac.

He knew he hadn't seen it before. Still, something about it niggled at him. He scanned through the list of all the bars again, even ones farther up in northern Turkey, looking for . . .

Then he saw it. *Marta* A. Surac. She was on their persons of interest list, given that she owned establishments in two of the areas where American service members had gone missing. But so did a lot of other investors.

The bar where this Anya worked was a couple of kilometers farther away from the NATO air base than some others on his list but still within his radius of interest. He stared at the display so long his labyrinth screen saver popped up. An image of a tile meditation path on a cathedral floor bounced around the monitor in time with his ping-ponging thoughts.

The common last name could be coincidental. One woman owned a bar, another with the same surname worked as a waitress in another bar, both in Turkey. It was possible in a country that large, but it was still worth investigating more on this Anya Surac.

Could be a relative. Could be no connection at all.

Or it could be the same person.

Regardless, as Miguel Carvalho he would be meeting this Marta-Anya Surac—whoever she really was—very soon.

The speakers in the back of the plane hummed to life with instructions to prepare for landing. Nunez powered down his computer and stowed it away. Eyes closing, he rested his back, thunking against metal vibrating from the engine drone.

In the time it took the plane to touch down, Mike Nunez disappeared and became Miguel Carvalho.

FOUR

Chloe mentally prepped for her next show backstage while the moon outside the open hangar door competed with the dome of runway lights. She held her arms up while a costume mistress repaired a loose string of sequins.

They'd spent most of the day sleeping in their new quarters at the NATO base in southern Turkey, east of Adana, in the middle of farmland, farmland, and more farmland that they'd flown over in Jimmy Gage's airplane. She still couldn't believe the luck. Or bad luck rather.

After the performance on the aircraft carrier, she'd found someone else to locate the ship's doctor and felt quite proud of herself for avoiding more conflict with Jimmy. Then she'd been escorted back to Jimmy Gage's plane, which made total sense now that she thought about it, since their boat had blown up. Still, she'd managed to avoid seeing him for the whole flight.

Or had he been avoiding her?

And why was she still ruminating over one bristly exchange? Starting now, she was done thinking about Jimmy Gage and instead focusing on the scheduling changes.

The USO cast and crew wouldn't be staying in the historic accommodations in nearby Adana after all. They would be lodging on base where their security could be better monitored. After all, they'd been reassured, the Turkish Armed Forces were the second largest in NATO, after the U.S.

In all likelihood, the boat had simply suffered a regrettable malfunction. However, extra precautions needed to be made, including delaying their departure to Iraq.

Huge—freaking huge—military planes roared overhead, almost drowning out the comedian onstage. Her info packet told her that C-17s transported cargo in and out of Iraq. One of the crews originally from South Carolina would be taking the USO troupe the rest of the way, once they received the security thumbs-up. A seven-day tour now stretched to at least ten days. One television comic had already begged off the remainder of the tour, citing scheduling conflicts.

A double fence surrounded the base with American guards on the inside and Turkish guards on the outside. Even this far from an obvious threat, they prepared for anything. Normal? Or had the boat incident propelled the military to beef up the security force? And if so, that made Jimmy's words about the danger in this area sting all the more.

Livia Cicero hooked arms with her just offstage while the comic finished up his routine. "*Mia cara*, you need to relax. We are all okay. Threats on our lives are part of show business. I'm actually more concerned about the acoustical nightmare of performing in that metal warehouse."

"It's called a hangar. And thanks, but you're not helping." Chloe inched closer to accommodate the lighting guys hoisting heavy equipment to make way for the next act while the stage manager, Greg, called directions into his headset.

"I had this stalker once who was obsessed with collecting my leftover latte cups and matching my lipstick shades." She shuddered, gathering her sleek black hair into a barrette. "I don't even want to think about what he did with all those tubes of Pouty Pink the police found on him."

Chloe admired the woman's gutsy ability to shrug off something so scary. "Definitely creepy. But honestly, I'm over what happened earlier." Mostly, anyway. It was probably just mechanical failure, but she still wouldn't be opening any unmarked packages. "It's the performing part. It wasn't as easy as I expected on the aircraft carrier. I have a performance background from childhood, so it should have been a cakewalk."

"It is . . . how do you say it?" She gestured with long fingers tipped by a French manicure that had somehow survived their impromptu swim yesterday. "Apples and pears."

"Apples and oranges."

"Right. Different fruits, whatever." She tapped her Roman nose. "My point is that this is a different arena, and you are a bit more out there physically than when it is just your music. Loosen up. You will find the audience feeds you."

"I understand that in theory, but I have always lost myself in my music. It became more of a trancelike experience." She didn't want to mention that, yes, she thought there was a world of difference between conducting a symphony and strutting her badonkadonk.

"Ah, you had your back to the audience or your face buried in sheet music while you immersed yourself in the sounds, whereas this type of performing requires eye contact." Livia fluttered her lashes at a passing security guard wearing camo and carrying a big-butt gun slung over his shoulder.

"I hadn't thought of it that way." Apparently her badonkadonk had been on display after all. "You could have a point. I tried to look at the horizon, and it didn't work for me."

"Because you were not connecting with people and their emotions. Listen to that." She tipped her face, her lashes fluttering closed as the crowd applauded for the comedian bowing his way offstage. Her eyes slowly opened. "For now, choose one person. That will feel less overwhelming until you are more comfortable scanning the crowd."

Winking as she passed, Livia sprinted onstage to *her* applause and whistles.

This show versus her musical world? Definitely apples and pears. Because best she could recall, performances of Beethoven's greatest hits usually didn't receive catcalls.

Her cue came from the stage manager she'd only met the day before on the aircraft carrier. Chloe strode out with the other two backup singers and a line of dancers, waving and smiling until she felt creases forming in the caked makeup. Every swish of her costume around her upper thighs reminded her of how much she had on display.

She jogged to her microphone, scanning the crowd, searching the faces for one to lock onto that would help her zone out the rest. A nice, pimply faced eighteen-year-old seaman would remind her of the patriotic service she offered here. After all, she had a debt to repay.

Her gaze gravitated toward the front and a small patch of uniforms that differed from the rest. The cluster of solid tan took shape into aviators in desert flight suits. *His* crew.

They hadn't left.

The music swelled around her with a comforting familiarity. Stage lights bathed her in soothing heat.

Brown eyes hit her with something hotter.

Now that that the sun had set, Jimmy Gage kept his sunglasses hooked in the neck of his flight suit. She could have sworn he seemed to be watching her intently from three rows back with his applauding buddies. Or maybe she'd indulged in some subconscious wishful thinking, because she was still pissed off at him and liked the idea that she hadn't been so easily dismissed after all.

Of course now that she thought about it, pissed off could be channeled into fired up, which would infuse energy into her performance. Yep, she'd found her face. Definitely not pimply or eighteen, but at least she didn't have to worry about him getting the wrong idea and asking for her phone number.

The first song segued into the second, and wow, Livia was right, the rest of the world did fade away. Chloe leaned in closer to the microphone. And no, damn it, the sensation had nothing to do with *who* she stared at. For that matter, looking at *him* made it all the easier to pour herself into the forget-his-ass tune spinning up.

The jaunty beat of the music drew her in. The grinding emotions of the melody and lyrics pumped through her veins as clearly as across her vocal chords. Her college degrees may have been in piano performance and orchestral conducting, but she'd taken and enjoyed her fair share of voice classes. Somewhere along the line, she'd forgotten the joy of this part of her career.

A few more stanzas, and she would be able to stare at Jimmy Gage without even really seeing him at all, not that he was smiling anyway. Or even looking at her.

His attention seemed to be firmly planted on the guy a row ahead of him. A guy who was pushing through to the next row, closer to the front, with no signs of stopping. Her heart pounded harder than the percussion section.

She forced herself not to miss a beat, even as Jimmy plowed forward to grab the collar of the man trying to climb onstage.

★ THE OASIS NIGHTCLUB, ADANA, TURKEY

Nunez climbed the final three steps into the five-star nightclub toward the door host. "*Hola, mi amigo,*" he said only to receive a blank look, so he swapped to accented English. "How are you, my friend?"

The muscle-bound snob in a suit as slick as his pulled back hair and fedora assessed him with a dismissive sniff. No doubt calculating the make and cost of his Canali suit and Rolex. "Can I help you?"

"Yes, you may." Nunez fiddled with a gold cuff link, which actually housed a hidden camera that recorded movies complete with sound to a flash drive hidden inside his jacket liner. The door dude also wore a coat in spite of the warm weather. Seemed everyone had something to hide tonight.

Nunez casually strolled around the portico for a better shot of the doorman's face beneath the hat. "I was hoping to have a good raki tonight, and I heard this was the place."

The door host eyed the Versace necktie and hesitated an instant before sniffing again. "Sorry, the club is full. I can't let you in until some people leave."

Nunez reached for his money clip with a wad of lira and peeled off one at a time until he saw the glint in the overpaid fascist's eyes.

He palmed them and offered his hand. "Could you take another look and see if perhaps you've miscounted the crowd?"

The ponytailed guard pocketed the cash and opened the door with another *sniff, sniff.* Probably a cokehead. "Have a nice time, sir, and be careful with your raki. It is tough on the uninitiated."

Nunez nodded and entered the smoky bar.

He angled sideways to avoid the couple making out against the wall by the coat check station. No morals police here.

Turkey was a democratic, secular, constitutional republic. While 99 percent of the population was Muslim, the country adhered to its secular makeup, which included banning by law head cover in government buildings, schools, and universities, for both males and females. And the scantily clad ladies here bore that out.

The secular slant of the government also allowed for free-flowing alcohol, a freedom being exercised to the fullest tonight, given the sound of clinking glasses mingling with the techno beat of European rock.

Of the bars on his list, he'd opted for Miguel Carvalho to start with the one employing the mystery woman, a decision reinforced by how little information existed on her and the fact that so far none of the other agents on the ground had been able to locate a second woman with a similar name. He'd only been able to find one grainy photo on file of Marta A. Surac in an old case file looking into drug trafficking. Given the date on the photo and the woman's appearance, she must be in her forties. Not much to go on, but something at least.

He swept past the red velvet drapes into the main barroom, ignoring the avaricious female eyes checking out the new meat. He was here for one particular woman.

The low-lying cloud of smoke mixed with too many colognes hit him in a wave that lured him deeper into this world of excesses. Tables spread across half the space. Luminaires cast shadows over faces he needed to record. He made his way over the packed dance floor vibrating from frenetic bodies and overloud music.

A brass barstool gave him the best vantage point to peruse the room and begin spreading his cash like carrion to draw the vultures. He checked out a steady stream of waitresses with plunging silk necklines defying gravity to stay in place.

Eleven and a half minutes in, he spotted a possible Marta-Anya match just as the DJ dimmed the lights and spun up a Livia Cicero ballad. The waitress's long blond hair gathered back in a clasp shone like a beacon among the predominantly dark-haired locals, although her dusky skin and brown eyes with an exotic tilt hinted at a bottle of hair bleach. He tracked her progress, logging details.

Why couldn't anyone find more than a single photo? Even other records were confusing as hell. Anya Surac here. Marta A. Surac, forty-three, reported elsewhere. She seemed to have fallen out of thin air, and there were no records of her traveling.

Odd, but not totally out of the realm of possibility. No passports were required in the EU, so she could be from any multitude of small villages that at best reported births in church records—if at all. Furthermore, if her background was shady, there could be name changes involved to further complicate matters.

The one grainy photo on file of Marta A. Surac resembled the Anya woman. In the dim lighting, she appeared to be younger than the woman in the photo, but he couldn't be sure without a closer look.

An army lieutenant grabbed her ass. Apparently tonight *lieutenant* was Greek for "fucking moron."

Nunez started forward.

Marta-Anya spun on her spike heel, ponytail slicing the air. Her hand flashed with a streak of metal. She stabbed a steak knife into the wooden table half an inch away from the luminaire. Slowly, precisely, she eased away and gestured to the soldier's uneaten meal with a smile as if it were common practice to embed eating utensils in varnished mahogany.

Nunez leaned back in his chair and watched the show. The lady in red did *not* need his help.

Three other men in uniform at the table whistled and applauded. She nodded regally and strode away, no swish to her steps or the silk dress. Nothing but efficiency and speed. With those looks, her speed, and her ass—uh, sass—she no doubt raked in generous tips.

He studied her as she drew closer and her face became clearer . . . Definitely not in her forties. More like mid-twenties. He scrutinized her features for any signs of plastic surgery and found none. Adding years for a disguise was easy. Shaving years off for a disguise, however, he'd always been able to see through.

Damn.

So he was dealing with two different women. The older Surac woman who was his suspect and this younger woman who might or might not be tied in. Without question, they bore a striking resemblance to each other, even with the age difference. The similarity of names certainly upped the chances that they were related.

She walked right past him and leaned on the bar to ask for another round of drinks in Turkish. He did a double take. She was short. He wouldn't have guessed it from the way she'd reined in that table with such massive chutzpah. Maybe five foot two. She arched up on her toes to place the order.

"Nice job," he said in Spanish, since that was his cover country.

She frowned at him and shook her head uncomprehendingly.

"Nice job?" he swapped to carefully accented English. "Handling those soldiers"—he glanced at her brass name tag pinned to her dress—"Anya."

He could speak passable Turkish and understood it fluently, but he wanted to keep that bit of information to himself.

"Oh, that was nothing," she answered in heavily accented English while counting bills before shoving them in her apron pocket.

That was nothing? Looked impressive to him. Impressive enough to keep even him on guard around her. There weren't many who could accomplish that after so long spent watching his back.

"Would you like another drink?"

"Where did you learn to defend yourself so effectively?"

She peered back over her shoulder through narrowed eyes. "Are you looking for a demonstration? I have another knife within reach, although I grow weary from how long I carry trays. I might miss and cut off a finger."

"But I didn't touch you."

"There are many ways to touch a person that are equally as . . ." Her brow furrowed as she apparently searched for the right word. "Disrespectful."

Her grasp of English seemed quite extensive for a Turkish barmaid. Except she didn't look Turkish, more Russian. But again, appearances could be deceiving.

"No disrespect meant. In fact, that move of yours earned my complete respect."

She sniffed. "I must return to work or I am fired. Do you want a drink or not?"

He passed her his empty glass along with two folded bills, triple what the drink should cost. "Raki."

Raki was the national drink of Turkey, also called *aslan sütü* or lion's milk because of how it turned cloudy white when mixed with water. She took the money without comment or thanks.

"Not much of a talker, are you?"

"I am much of a worker."

"You seemed fine with speaking to those guys over there—as long as they kept their hands to themselves. Maybe I should wear a uniform next time." Like Chuck Tanaka.

"I was only taking their order as I have done yours. Now I need to return to work." She flipped the money between her fingers before sliding it into her apron pouch. She reached across the bar, snagged his drink, and centered it on a napkin. "Have a nice evening."

He extended an arm, blocking her exit. "How much would it cost to cover your wages for an hour so we could talk?"

"I do not talk to patrons." Her eyes flicked to a small paring knife lying behind the bar in a pile of sliced limes.

Didn't need to tell him twice. "Fair enough then. I will just have to monopolize your time placing drink orders until I am roaring drunk."

"Orders are always welcome." She pushed aside his arm as easily as she brushed off his advance.

He studied her brisk stride away and felt an unwelcome arousal inside him. That sort of distraction on the job meant death.

While she wasn't the Marta A. Surac on their suspect list, he couldn't ignore the possible connection. She was all the more suspicious for her easy capacity for violence she showed with the knife, and then there was her unflappable self-assurance. Yeah, he would definitely be hanging out here for a while longer, throwing around dough to cement his cover.

Except a quiet voice whispered in his head that he had just joined the ranks of the fucking morons.

FIVE

Fuck, that hurt.

Jimmy ducked to avoid another swing, his jaw still throbbing. One soldier trying to make his way up on the stage had swelled into an all-out brawl involving most of the first three rows. How had the dumb ass expected to make it past the shoulder-to-shoulder wall of security, easily identifiable in their cammos and blue berets?

Officers and senior NCOs pulled at the barely-old-enough-to-shave contingent pummeling out their pent-up energy. Jimmy had his eyes set on scooping up Chloe and getting her away from this chaos with her glittery heels and negligible costume intact. This woman sure had an uncanny knack for landing in the middle of trouble.

Jimmy dodged a blow and delivered a gut punch that reverberated up his arm. He didn't even want to think about how much damage the frenzy of a stomping mob could inflict on someone as fragile as Chloe. She looked so damn pale and delicate up there, it stroked all his protective instincts.

He could subdue these clowns, inflicting minimal damage, but that would take time. Reaching Chloe pronto limited how long he could waste on defensive moves.

Jimmy hurdled over two tussling bodies crashing into chairs. In some distant part of his brain, he registered that his crew mates had joined in to break up the brawl. Or maybe they were battling through to drag him out before he wrecked himself for flight duties. Except he had never been downed in a bar fight, and he didn't intend to start today.

He vaulted onstage and made his way toward the cluster of screaming performers—male and female—jamming up the exit into the wings. He latched his gaze on Chloe's mass of blond curls piled on top of her head and pushed toward her.

Ducking a shoulder into her stomach, he hefted her up. Not much of a heft, actually. She was lighter, frailer feeling, when she wasn't waterlogged.

A security cop headed toward them with his M-4 carbine drawn. "Halt. Put her down."

Great. They thought he was one of the hormonal whackos.

Chloe waved, angling her head to the side. "It's okay. He's helping me."

The cop nodded and rushed past them toward the fray. Jimmy pressed ahead, out of the hangar and onto the moonlit tarmac.

She jostled along on his shoulder. "You can thank me for not selling you out to that cop for fun."

Seemed she'd used up all her gratitude earlier. "And you can thank me for saving your ass again."

He smacked a flattened palm on her butt—only to steady her of course. And to stop the tantalizing brush of her breasts across his back.

"Ouch, you Cro-Magnon." She smacked his butt right back. "Put me down."

"You were wriggling. I was only keeping you from falling off." Of course, if she touched him like that again, he might just drop her.

He sidestepped a rolling cart and plopped her back on her own damn feet. "Are you all right?"

Her piled curls slid precariously to one side, but the woman herself looked plenty steady as she gazed up at him with assessing eyes.

"I wasn't the one in a fistfight. How are you?" She reached toward the corner of his mouth.

He flinched away. "I'm fine."

"Sorry. Didn't mean to insult your masculinity." She folded her arms over her chest defensively. "I appreciate that you're concerned, but I was actually okay. One of these days I really would like to save my own tookus."

"You're going to need something more than a couple of killer mics swinging around like a nunchaku." Now that he had her face-to-face, that brought another irritation to mind. "I assume your allergies are under control? I notice you're not sneezing. I waited around after your first show for a half hour to take you to the doctor."

"I found a security cop who was *happy* to help me, thank you very much."

"Good." He stepped between her and a stream of people pouring from the mosh pit. "See if you can stay out of trouble for a while."

"How many close calls can a person have? I already feel like I'm wearing a red shirt."

"Red shirt?" He struggled to follow her tangential logic. God, she gave him a headache. "Like the aircraft carrier crews?"

"No. Like in a *Star Trek* episode. I take it you're not a Trekkie."

Not so much. "I rarely watch television."

"Figures," she mumbled. "In *Star Trek*, the characters wearing a red shirt variation of the uniform always ended up dead. Well, except for Scotty, of course, and . . . Never mind. You're obviously not a card-carrying member of the Geek Club."

The tilt of her snooty nose made it clear she hadn't paid him a compliment.

Before he could answer, she looked toward the stage and frowned. "I hope everyone's okay. Surely this trip will be smooth sailing from now on."

Was she insulting their security? If so, she'd gone too far. He started to remind her who'd rescued her perky ass twice now, but the handcuffed men in uniform being escorted away didn't exactly speak well for his side.

Where the hell was Nunez? Jimmy eyed Chloe—a long way down, since she barely reached his chin. Too bad she couldn't transfer some of that moxie into muscle. "I'll stay here with you until we're sure everything's safe."

She opened her mouth to argue.

He held up his index finger, stopping shy of touching her mouth. "If you leave now, you'll only be in the way. Let security do their job in calming the crowd."

"Fine. You're right." She puffed a sigh, hot and steamy along his skin.

He curled his finger closed and lowered his arm to his side. How long would he have to stand here with her?

She looked away, her hand fluttering up to sweep back her askew hair bun. "Where did you learn all those moves out there? Was it some kind of judo wrestling?"

He welcomed the distraction of a safe, neutral topic. "You've got the country right, different Japanese technique though. Aikido, which focuses on self-defense without harming the attacker. And I throw in an occasional good old American bar-fight punch when absolutely necessary."

"Is martial arts standard air force survival training now?"

"I pulled some time in Japan. I took a few classes."

Actually, he'd mastered a number of martial art forms because, hey, if you planned to throw your sorry mug into every brawl, it made sense to have that mug well-defended.

"A few classes? Yeah, right." A tiny smile tugged at a corner of her mouth. "And I really didn't watch the *Star Trek* 'Trouble with Tribbles' episode twenty-seven times."

Tribbles? "What can I say? I'm Mars, god of war." He thumped his chest.

"A Roman mythology reference? That's not what I would have expected from you."

"If I'm not mistaken, you just called me a dumb jet jock." Did she think he crawled straight out of the primordial ooze into the cockpit? Little did she know that to make major in the air force these days required a master's degree. "We flyboys do read a book without pictures every now and then."

"Sorry." Her gaze dipped away, and she plucked at a stray string on the hem of her costume. "So the whole 'I am Mars, god of war' thing . . . Does that pickup line actually work on women?"

"You would be surprised." Although it appeared it didn't stand a chance of gaining traction with her. Not that he wanted it to. Back to that subject change. "Actually, the word *martial* comes from Mars. So in essence, *martial arts* means the art of Mars."

"Damn," Vapor appeared beside him, the big guy moving as quietly as—well—vapor. "Next thing you know he'll be pulling out the pocket-sized copy of Sun Tzu's *The Art of War* he carries around in his flight suit."

"Hey pal, don't you have a rubber chicken or whoopee cushion to go play with?"

"Nah, I'm good." Vapor scrubbed a hand over his shaved head with that aw-gosh-golly-and-shucks shit he pulled to romance women. Nobody would guess right now that he'd once been a hard-core biker. "Sorry about the ruckus over there, ma'am. I can help you find your quarters if you would like to leave."

Chloe backed away from them both. "Actually, I should check in with the stage manager to see if we're finishing the show. I'll be careful to stay clear of trouble."

Vapor scratched his shiny head. "Isn't the stage manager the dweeby guy dressed all in black like Dieter from those old *Saturday Night Live* episodes? If so, he's in the head hyperventilating."

Chloe winced.

Vapor winked at her as she stepped farther away. "Just call if you need me."

Good. She had a new protector now. Even one up to speed on old TV pop culture references. Given the rumors about Vapor's teenage days on the street, he could handle anything, anywhere. Bodyguard duty over and done.

Jimmy eyed his friend. Eyed Chloe.

Next thing he knew, Jimmy called out to Chloe, "If you're really serious about protecting yourself when no one's around, I can teach you some basic self-defense moves."

She raised a hand over her shoulder and waved some kind of noncommittal response that set his teeth on edge with frustration at himself as much as her.

Why the hell didn't he just walk away from this woman? For that matter, Vince—his whole damn crew— should be staying away from her and anyone else until they found Chuck. The implanted chip showed he was still alive, but that could change at any minute.

Given all the missing airmen and recent incidents, it did, in fact, seem they were all wearing red shirts.

★ DOWNTOWN ISTANBUL

Marta Surac slammed the door shut on the basement cell.

The damp smell of mold and fear saturated each

breath. How sad she did not have time to savor this moment of power as she raced back and forth between bars,
dealing with her current captive and scoping out future
possibilities.

However, the continued success of her operation depended on keeping her captures widespread, and she'd
already pushed as far as she dared in this country.

Her heels clicked a slow tattoo on the cement floor as
Baris ended his "interview" with the airman. The jeans
the flyboy had worn to the bar were now stained with
blood. So far they'd only found out a smattering about
him. Just his first name, Chuck, and that he was a pilot. In
fact, the scarcity of information available led her to believe his missions were classified.

Even the drugs did not work beyond babblings of
childhood games. He'd obviously been trained in avoidance techniques and possessed a strong will. But she had
so many other options for her captives.

Chuck's face was swollen and bruised beyond recognition, but she'd studied him early on and determined him
to be of some Polynesian descent, although his accent was
100 percent American.

"Baris, enough. Leave us now." Rarely did she have to
participate in interrogations anymore, but this gentleman
was proving difficult. She had another mission in mind for
Baris later, anyway.

Her hulking employee cracked his knuckles and eyed
her with a possessiveness she would deal with later.
These animals she employed always angled for sex after
a session.

But first . . .

"Close the door behind you."

Their guest didn't pose any threat to her, thanks to the
shackles that secured his wrists and ankles to the chair,
which was bolted to the floor. She pulled her hands from
behind her back and placed a water bottle on the table
beside Airman Chuck. In her other hand, she held a key, a

ruby ring glinting as red as the blood trickling from the corner of his lips.

Marta unlocked his left hand, the broken one. "Have a drink."

He eyed the bottle suspiciously.

She twisted the cap, the seal hissing. "It has not even been opened, so it's safe to drink."

He grasped the plastic bottle and brought it to his mouth. His shaking grip sloshed water until he finally managed to steady the opening between his teeth. He drained a third in a single swig before swiping his wrist across his face, leaving a smear of blood.

She circled his chair, lingering longest in front. "You are wise to question whether the drink has been tampered with. They will use any means possible to achieve their goal."

"Not just they," he rasped. "You, too."

She nodded. "Of course. You show your intelligence again. Your brain and strength make for quite a combination in holding out against our methods of persuasion. Your military has trained you well in resistance techniques."

Both a challenge and a frustration for her. She had a buyer in mind for the type of information she believed Chuck held, a buyer pressuring her for more U.S. military secrets. She'd upped her number of kidnappings recently in hopes of obtaining the nugget that would bring the payoff dangled in front of her. That kind of money would allow her to transplant her network into Southeast Asia.

He took another swallow of water, eying her silently then placing the bottle back on the small wooden table.

"A smart, strong man such as yourself must realize this can only end two ways. Either you give us what we need on your own terms and you live, or we will coerce some portion of information from you, and you will lose what little control you have over your situation before you die."

He did not show even a flicker to indicate he'd heard her. He must have deep secrets to guard.

A thrill tickled low in her belly. Apparently she could still feel after all, because this man's unusual strength brought a rush of pleasure. Breaking him suddenly became about more than the money she could garner from selling his information.

He reached for the bottled water, his teeth gritted as he forced himself not to shake.

She whipped her hand from her pocket, flicked the switchblade, and stabbed the wood a centimeter away from his fingers. The knife vibrated in her grip with understated menace.

"You drink when I tell you to drink."

★ INCIRLIK AIR BASE

Nunez entered the hangar that housed the CV-22, his eyes blurry from the bar's smoke but his mind still clear, thanks to the experimental drugs he'd popped to combat the effects of the alcohol. Sure, there were times he winced at taking unapproved meds for his job, but at least he wasn't a total guinea pig like the guys who'd run the first round of testing on the pills.

That made him think of the four dudes in front of him and how much crap they tried out, not knowing if their asses would be blown up.

He'd worked for three hours reviewing video feed from his hidden camera, searching for some clue to give him a better handle on the bar and the Surac woman. Shit out of luck so far. Once his eyes started to blur, he'd decided to check in on the air crew because . . . Well, he needed to do something after a frustrating two days of no progress and no answers.

The crew of four gathered around a table set up next to the airplane. The flat surface was lined with laptops and a spaghetti jumble of wires running from the computers into random open panels on the airplane. They seemed to be calibrating or testing something. Probably the advanced sensor suite they hoped to use to find Chuck Tanaka.

"Is there a problem here, gentlemen?" Tearing the plane apart sure didn't look like a good sign, and damn it all, he needed their technology.

Vince Deluca poked his bald head out from behind a cluster of wires and cables, a doughnut in hand. "Nice duds, Nunez. Are you pimpin' on the side?"

"I'll be taking a personal day when the bill for this wardrobe hits the boss's desk." He stepped deeper into the hangar and tried to make sense of how these test aviators thrust their hands into the tangle of wires and cables. "This mess you've got here looks worse than when my mom's Christmas lights come out of storage. Is something wrong?"

Jimmy Gage stepped from around the line of laptops. Word had it, he pounded his body relentlessly in the weight room and on the basketball court since his four-month captivity. Captain Invincible could do it all. That kind of arrogance could make or break the op. "We're just tweaking the sensors and conducting continuity checks. Looks like everything is up and running. No ill effects from our rough ride in."

"Felt smooth to me," Nunez said and meant it. "I never would have guessed this wasn't your primary plane. How many test drives do you get in something like this before they clear you to take it out for a spin solo?"

Lieutenant Colonel Scanlon glanced up, looking over the rims of his Buddy Holly glasses. "You don't want to know."

"So you test dudes really can fly anything."

The commander nodded. "That's the point of the training. We're writing the tech manual on new aircraft and equipment no one's flown yet. Makes sense we need to be able to step inside anything and figure out how to make it do that flying thing."

Gage jerked a thumb toward Vince Deluca. "Vapor here is famous back at test pilot school. An instructor came in and dropped a dash one—that's the flight manual—for an A-7 attack plane they flew back in the dark ages. Then he told him to be ready bright and early for a live weapons release, flown in formation with two other planes. Next morning, Vapor clocks in, bags under his eyes. But he fired up that engine, rolled the baby out to the runway, and flew his mission flawlessly. When he landed, the ground guys noticed something off in the way he was sitting."

Vapor shrugged massive shoulders. "Yeah, yeah, who the hell thinks to read about how to slide the seat backward and forward? I had to eat my knees for the whole flight."

Nunez leaned a hip against the table. "You could have asked for help."

The line of crewdogs eyed him as if he'd blasphemed.

Smooth backed away, hands up. "That would have been as bad as stopping for directions. Can't be cutting off the *cajones* that way, or someone may get a leg up on you with the ladies."

"Point made." Nunez kept his perch by the table while the crew went back to their stations.

He'd understood in theory that these men were scientists and engineers as well as aviators, but seeing was a whole other matter. Sure, he played with high-tech gadgets in the field, but so much of his job involved the human factor of going undercover. How much of his field work could be outsourced to their technology?

They shrugged off the risk with jokes and posturing. But how many of them would die to make that technology available?

Gage reaffixed a metal panel onto the plane with exaggerated concentration. "So, Nunez, what's the scoop on the fight that broke out?"

"That's the million dollar question. Tough to decipher

exactly how it began. No one's claiming responsibility, so we don't know yet if there's a connection with the explosion on the boat. We've got guys tracing bomb parts and working the underwater recovery mission to gather more evidence."

Smooth clicked through computer keys without even looking their way. "Probably just horny guys out of control."

"Quite possibly," Nunez answered, unconvinced. "We're as sure as we can be for now. Any particular reason you want to know, Gage?"

"Just curious." He gave the panel a final fist-thump. "Once you've got Chuck's locale better pinpointed, we'll close in with surveillance."

Nunez bypassed the nearly empty coffeepot and box of doughnuts to stride down the line of equipment. "You can really see through walls with this thing?"

"Absolutely," the commander answered without hesitation. "We worked the kinks out of this particular piece of equipment during the surge over in Iraq. With miniature munitions we developed, you could take out a lone sniper in a room and not even knock the knickknacks off the mantel."

Gage leaned forward with intense eyes. "This one time, some Iraqi policemen were kidnapped and hustled off into a particularly bad neighborhood in Sadr City. We trolled over the area until we found a whole bunch of bodies crammed into one room in this walled compound. There were eleven missing policemen and eleven warm bodies in there. We called in the cavalry on the ground, told them where the other bodies in the house were, and turned them loose. They got those guys out of there before anyone had a chance to roll out the torture table."

The commander stroked a computer screen with reverence. "The inventor of this system saved at least eleven families a lot of pain. I would say this thing has already proved it was worth the money."

Nunez looked to the undercurrents of their fireside storytelling. "And that was the first time you used it? In combat while the enemy shot at you?"

"Sure," Gage answered, adrenaline all but crackling in his eyes.

"You work the kinks out in operation." Nunez twisted the camera button on his jacket, praying like crazy the thing wouldn't explode into flames. "I so didn't need to hear that."

The commander nudged his black-rimmed glasses in place. "Agent Nunez, sometimes there's a push to deliver, and we have to go with our gut."

"What if it had gone the other way?"

Gage grinned. "Our guts are pretty fucking good."

Nunez hoped for Chuck Tanaka's sake that Jimmy Gage could back up that cockiness.

SIX

Eyes closed, Chloe eased down the cinderblock hall wall to sit on the floor and savor the sensation of undiluted Boston Philharmonic pouring through her iPod earbuds. Oh yeah. Just what she needed to pass the time as she waited for Livia to finish her rehearsal in the base basketball court allocated for their use.

Hanging around seemed to be the status quo lately. They were still waiting for the go-ahead to resume their tour. At least they had practices to pass the time, even private rehearsal rooms. The event director had worked her tail off this morning for shows they weren't even certain they would present.

For a hijacked moment in the deserted back corridor, Chloe indulged in a Mozart fix. She hadn't expected to miss her job this much, since she would be singing. It had always been about the music for her, the one thing sporadic bouts of poor health couldn't leach away.

Don't go there. Just let the waterfall of notes obliterate all else. Her hands gravitated by instinct to "conduct." Peace melted her muscles.

Then it tingled away. Someone was here, in the remote passageway. The tile floor underneath her went ice cold.

The sense of being eyeballed crescendoed in time with the music. She jolted to her feet, her eyes snapping open, muscles tensed.

Jimmy lounged against the wall by a Turkish tapestry. Even wearing air force sweatpants and a T-shirt, he carried that unmistakable confidence. So much for chalking his charisma up to the uniform.

She thumbed her iPod off and pulled out the earbuds. Muffled music from the gymnasium vibrated through the wall as Livia nailed high C.

"Jamming?" He crossed one Nike-shod foot over the other.

"Not exactly 'Rock Me Amadeus,' but yeah, I have Mozart plugged in today."

"You're a classical buff?" He sounded surprised.

"An orchestra conductor in Atlanta."

His brows shot high. "No shit?"

His total shock was a little insulting. Did he really consider her a ditz? Then she recalled his irritation when she'd assumed Jimmy "Mars, god of war" Gage wouldn't be the type to study up on Roman mythology. Apparently they'd both made some erroneous assumptions about each other.

"No shit. Classical music is my life, whether it be through conducting or playing the piano or even singing."

"So that's why you were doing the . . ." He waved his hands in a not-half-bad imitation of her conducting a three-four beat.

She stared down at her motionless fingers with their nails trimmed short for playing the piano. "It's instinctive when I listen." Enough of the chitchat. Her years of intense health concerns had left her with a deep-seated need not to waste precious time on picayune crap like pissing contests. "What brings you here?"

"My job."

"Duh. I meant *here*, to see *me*."

"Self-defense class for our local mayhem-prone Mozart groupie."

She'd heard his invitation as she'd walked away after the concert fight, but she hadn't thought he meant it. "You were serious about that?"

"Serious as the next riot you'll probably land in the middle of."

She resisted the urge to roll her eyes and reached for her earbuds. "Thanks all the same, but I think I'll just invest in a can of mace."

In a flash so fast she barely registered the blur of his sweat suit in motion, Jimmy looped his arms around her torso and neck, hauling her back flat against his front. What the hell?

Her iPod dropped from her restrained hand. She wriggled to get free. Unsuccessfully. His arms locked her tighter against the hard-muscled length of him. The roots of her hair began to tingle.

She stilled, half-afraid to move and stir those tingles into a body-wide wave.

His head lowered, his mouth beside her ear. "How effective do you think that mace is going to be right now?"

Warm breath steamed over the sensitive skin along her earlobe, farther to her cheek, until she shivered. Her lashes fluttered closed in utter frustration, humiliation even. How disturbing to be so acutely attracted to someone she wasn't even sure she liked.

"Let go, please," she whispered, hating the slight bobble in her voice.

"I was simply trying to prove my point." His arms slid away. He wasn't cheesy about it, no copping a feel, but the simple brush of movement still jangled her already off-kilter nerves.

"People who insist on being right all the time are really annoying."

"That will give you the perfect motivation to be a good student so you can kick my ass. Unless there's some reason you're afraid of the challenge?"

Did this guy take mind game classes in between saving the world? Regardless, his blasted psychology was effective. She was a fighter. "Where do we start?"

He swept a hand ahead of him, his ever-stoic face betraying no emotion. "This way, maestro."

"*Maestra*, for females." She deserved to indulge in just a little condescension, damn it.

"Right, definitely *maestra* then. Get ready to rock out, Sun Tzu style." He charged down the hall with confident strides she had to double-time to match.

★ ADANA, TURKEY

Nunez baked in the afternoon sun even without a suit jacket and tie. Nothing new. A large portion of his job included sitting around and waiting as inconspicuously as possible.

At least the food rocked at the tiny café across from the nightclub. Sitting at an outdoor table, he tore off another bite of his Lamb Adana—a cross between a gyro and his mother's meatloaf—while skimming through a local newspaper. All of which provided the perfect vantage point to catch sight of Ms. Surac when she reported for work.

Over the past couple of days, he'd been rotating through the local bars on his list but still hadn't connected with the Oasis's cagey waitress again or found out anything more about the older Surac woman. He turned a page on the paper and paused mid-flip. Oh yeah. Good things came to those who waited. Anya approached the club, winding around pedestrians picking their way through vendor stalls. She strode down the cobblestone street, blond hair catching on the air with each gliding step.

Her steps faltered. She frowned, looking around and hitching her purse more securely on her shoulder. Her face tipped to the wind as if she could scent danger.

Then she looked straight at him.

Instincts such as hers were golden. Or deadly. He stared right back, allowing himself a small smile. Her exotic dark eyes widened. He didn't even bother deluding himself. The static between them crackled with raw lust.

He reached for his money clip and tossed double the cost of the meal on the table. He wove through traffic at a slow jog, his eyes on the target.

The door fascist descended the steps and blocked his path, leaving Anya free to bustle past and up the marble steps. She cast a quick glance at him over her shoulder.

Nunez didn't even bother smiling this time, just stared back. He could have sworn he detected vulnerability in her eyes, but he'd grown too jaded. All he could see was her marked resemblance to the older woman in the photo of his suspect. That she would be here, at a bar under suspicion, couldn't be coincidence.

The door dude crowded his space and defused the static. Did this guy ever sleep? Yet another sign the man was a cokehead or doing some other brand of speed, which made him unpredictable.

There was no pushing past him without creating a scene. She opened the door herself, small price to pay for a clean getaway.

"We're closed." Mr. Slick's sunglasses shielded his condescending look today. The guy clearly clocked double duty as a doorman and bouncer.

The Terminator with a fedora and a Valentino suit.

"I'll wait." Nunez didn't budge.

Neither did the doorman. "Be careful of pickpockets. They prey on those who loiter."

A stare-down later, the doorman sniffed and turned away, back to his post, offering a quick flash of his braided ponytail and 9 mm tucked in the small of his back. He parked his uptight ass on a wrought-iron bench, snagging a newspaper from beside him.

Nunez studied the door closing behind Anya Surac, half registering the cacophony of car horns on the pedestrian-packed street. Wafting scents of roasting kabobs in a nearby stall presented a far greater distraction, since this mission left more time for drinking and little for eating. He eyed the vendors lining the street.

"Crash and burn, my friend," a male voice rode the smell of cigar smoke. "Crash and burn. Your lady does not seem interested."

Nunez pivoted fast and found the man standing in a nearby doorway. Now that guy's accent was easy enough to place. The dude hailed from somewhere around Greece. Nunez catalogued the piece of info before moving closer for details—a man in his fifties, graying curls, thick brows, and an even thicker stogie.

The stranger nodded a dismissal to the glorified bouncer. Nunez's mental antennae went on alert, hands sliding up to ride on his belt, within reach of his own concealed weapon. "The tougher they are, the greater the victory."

"True. True." The man stubbed out his cigar on the sole of his Barker Black ostrich-capped shoes. A downright sacrilege. "You throw around much money."

Nunez fed the guy a noncommittal, "I believe in enjoying life."

Wait for it. Wait . . . for . . . it.

The man thrust out his hand. "Spiros Kutros."

Nunez's antennae homed in. Kutros, a man who claimed distant kinship to a defunct Mediterranean royal family. And an investor in this very club.

Interesting. "Miguel Carvalho."

"Carvalho? Ah, I have heard of you."

Of course he had. The NSA and CIA built a variety of covers, sometimes years in advance, planting reports, photos, and gossip for times when an undercover agent had to launch a sting quickly, without the luxury of months to build trust. Stepping into Miguel Carvalho's "life" had been simple.

Kutros flashed perfect teeth that only the very wealthy around here could afford. "That waitress, she is a hot one."

"Do you have a prior claim?"

"None. I prefer my women to be like . . . How do the Americans say? . . . Like my whiskey, smooth and easy."

Was it a coincidence that he mentioned America so early on? "Ah, but the bite sneaks up on a man faster that way. At least I know what I'm in for with ones like that."

"To each his own, my friend."

Miguel would want a woman like her. But what did Mike want? He never took the time to consider relationships. Any sort of real connection had been discouraged the second his family entered the witness protection program.

He'd enjoyed plenty of sex but not entanglements. And always with women who shared his lack of expectations. There were plenty of female agents in his shoes, needing physical release between undercover assignments.

"So," Kutros spoke through puffs of smoke, "you are alone on your vacation?"

"Who says I am on vacation?"

"If you are not on vacation, your employer must be very frustrated."

"Who said I need a job?"

Kutros threw his head back and laughed until his amusement turned into a raspy cough. "My kind of person."

"I take that to mean you do not have a job calling you?"

"Investments to oversee." Kutros pulled out a new cigar and pointed it toward the club. "Not a bad job checking the alcohol and service, eh?"

"You're a lucky man."

"That I am." Kutros extended the cigar. "Welcome to Turkey."

Mike took the Cuban smoke he knew sold for four hundred dollars. Connection made. "Thank you, my friend."

SEVEN

★ ―――――――――――――――――――――――――――――――

What the hell had he gotten himself into?

Jimmy swung open the door to an exercise room full of blue mats and no people. If the threat around here was real, did he truly expect Chloe to fight her way free with a crash course in kickboxing a guy in the stones?

Two seconds into disproving her mace theory, he realized this was a bad idea. He'd never been attracted to someone who irritated him before, and the feeling chapped his hide.

Damn it, excuses were for the weak.

Get this lesson over, and move on.

He powered deeper into the musky room, echoes from an intramural volleyball match thundering on the other side of the partition. The universal feel of the space wrapped around him with a comforting familiarity, and he couldn't resist a vertical leap to touch the basketball rim.

Chloe's laughter rocketed around the metal rafters at the slam dunk pantomime.

He cat-footed his landing and shrugged. "Sorry—habit, I guess."

"That's like me trying to conduct the music on my iPod."

"Pretty much." He jockeyed forward with a boxer's bounce.

She stood waiting on the mat, her khakis and flowing white shirt casual enough for her to move around. "Ready whenever you are, Sugar Ray."

Eyes off the exposed line of her jaw. Her jaw, for crying out loud. A curve with creamy soft skin he could still feel imprinted on his wrist.

He shook off the distraction. "If you're serious about learning self-defense—and I think all women should be—when you get back to Atlanta, consider taking a course in Krav Maga for women. You have to know Atlanta isn't exactly the safest city in the world."

"Krav Maga?" She gathered her curls in her fist and looped the length into some kind of loose knot behind her neck.

"Krav Maga is the official self-defense of the Israeli forces." He settled into explanation, into the zone, more comfortable in this instructor role. "It's a take no quarter, practical style."

"I thought you were into defense with the least damage to the attacker."

"In my case, the enemy has valuable information, and I want to keep them alive. If you're in a fight, I doubt the person downing you holds top secret info about enemy forces." How much would it have taken to bring Chuck down? At what point would he crack? The thin layer of camaraderie he'd felt with Chloe evaporated. "But learning that takes intense training. For now, we're going to cover some quick and easy techniques."

"Self-defense 101 for dummies."

He ignored the quip. "First tip, use anything around

you for a weapon: a rock, a pencil, an umbrella. Smash hard things on bone and pointy things into softer areas."

"The old 'hold keys between the fingers' principle. Right. I'm not a total dunce when it comes to being safe. I read all those safety tips forwarded over the Internet."

"The Internet, huh?" How naïve could she be? "Then I guess we're done here."

"Watch it, pal, or I'll come after you with my conductor's baton." The glint in her eyes mixed impish fun and wicked revenge.

He was wading into deep waters here. Back to the instructor role. "And if you do decide to use that conductor's stick, the most vulnerable strike points are the eyes, nose, throat, groin, and knees."

"I thought all guys were on alert for the old knee to the groin defense." She shifted her weight from foot to foot, eying him with an intensity that suggested she wouldn't pass up an opportunity to have him singing soprano.

"That's why you have to be certain of success if you try it. Another option: squeeze the guy's testicles until he passes out or pukes." Even the thought made him queasy. Images of overrevved soldiers launching on the stage toward a pale-faced Chloe made him sicker. "If you're fighting a woman, pinch the inside of her thigh as tightly as you can. It works on a man, too."

"Pinching?" She tapped her index finger and thumb together, already eying his thigh as if assessing whether she should give it a try right now. "That seems too easy."

"Hurts like hell." Even trained in martial arts, he'd used the old pinchers during an escape attempt in Afghanistan. He'd downed the guard until the sadistic bastard hurled, then commandeered his gun and made it out the window to a crappy ass side street before being caught.

In retribution, his captors had strapped him to a metal table and hooked him up to a car battery.

He shoved aside the nightmare and the remembered

burn it brought. Sensory recall sucked. "Sure, there are other moves that could be more debilitating, but they're also more complicated. When that adrenaline's flooding your system, it can be difficult to remember intricate moves unless you've been highly trained."

"Since I don't have time to earn a black belt, I take it there won't be any high-flying kicks."

"Exactly."

"Well, damn." She hitched her hands on her hips, full breasts straining against her shirt. "I always wanted to be Kung Fu Barbie."

Why couldn't she grasp how serious the stakes were here? He was trying to help keep her safe. Couldn't she understand how vulnerable she was? Even with the crash course, her odds sucked against a seriously trained opponent.

"I prefer Street-Smart Barbie." Jimmy snapped his fingers repeatedly. "Now, let's move along. Your attacker may have captured you from behind, immobilizing your hands. That leaves just your legs and feet free."

Jimmy settled behind her and slid his arms around her waist. "Raise your foot as far as possible and boot your attacker in the knee. Once you've done that, let your foot slide downward to ram his instep."

Her breasts grazed his hands. Her bottom nestled against him. Her scent, something flowery and intensely feminine, teased his nose.

Ah, hell.

He continued his instructions through gritted teeth and willed his body not to respond. He would just think about emergency procedures. As a flight tester, he had numerous planes to pick from. Today he would go with emergency procedures for the T-37, a trainer and appropriate choice, since he was in uncharted territory with this woman.

How to recover from a spin?
Throttles—idle.
Rudder and ailerons—neutral.

Stick—abruptly full aft and hold.
Rudder—

His buckling knee shouted a warning to his testosterone-fogged brain a second too late. Chloe's foot nailed his instep. Pain shot up his thigh as he struggled to keep his balance. A roar from the crowd next door rivaled his mental yelp of pain.

He swallowed back a grunt and held tight, managing to keep them both on their feet. "You're a fast learner."

"The upside to being a prodigy." She glanced back over her shoulder at him.

Her smile lit up the room like a blinding flash to night-vision goggles, and he resented the feeling. Big time. He tightened his hold and resolve. He swept his foot behind her knees and downed Chloe before that smile of hers could blast him out of the sky.

Jimmy followed her to the mat in a textbook-perfect pin, dancing right into danger with this woman against his better judgment. "It doesn't pay to get too cocky, Baby Einstein."

He couldn't tell if he'd stunned her quiet or just knocked the wind out of her, but she just stared up at him with wide green eyes, her blond curls a riotous fan spread over the mat. Jimmy cupped the back of her neck, his hand moving instinctively, much like how he jumped for the rim without thinking . . . or how she conducted her iPod music.

Chloe didn't pull away.

She inhaled gusty little breaths that puffed peppermint into the sparse space between them. "Why did you do that?"

"The tables can turn fast, and the stakes are too high around here." He would be wise to remember his own advice. Like now. He should get off of her. And he would.

Just not yet.

Confusion flickered through her eyes, pretty much the

same thing batting around inside him. His eyes settled on her lips, plump and moist and just begging to be—

The double doors clicked open.

Jimmy jumped off Chloe just as she sat up, an inch away from head-butting his chin.

"Whoops," a male voice from the entrance broke the moment. "Sorry, sir."

Jimmy pulled away in time to see a pair of young airmen backing out. Chloe flattened her palms to the mat for balance, her pupils wide.

Living in the moment was one thing. Outright recklessness was another altogether. His instincts told him he needed to get away from Chloe before his control snapped.

He rolled to his feet again. "I have to hit the bunk for a power nap. I'm flying later."

Flying? Chloe steadied herself with one hand, while her mind raced to catch up with what had just happened between them—or rather what hadn't happened. "Are you leaving Incirlik?"

His face blanked. "No."

"Why would you fly here, and at night? Is something wrong?" She stood up, her brain filled with all the dangers in the Middle East that he'd harped on so often. She wanted to believe his concerns were skewed because of his military experiences. They were in Turkey, after all, not Afghanistan or Iraq.

But still.

She swayed on her feet. His hand shot out to steady her, fingers landing right over her transplant scar. She jerked back instinctively.

His eyes shuttered. "We're flying a demo of the new aircraft for the local military, showing off night moves. What are your plans for tomorrow?"

The abrupt subject change let her know loud and clear her questions were unwelcome. "Security cleared us for sightseeing around the base and into that city close by . . . uh . . ."

"Adana?" He sounded irritated again. "You're leaving the security of the base to pick up a few souvenirs? Have you forgotten someone may have tried to blow you up back on that boat?"

"Apparently the security people here feel they have that well in hand. We can go to Adana as long as we have a security escort." She stared back at him.

"Have you not listened to anything I've said? Good God, woman, I feel like I'm beating my head against a wall."

"I hear that happens quite often to hardheaded people."

His jaw flexed. "I don't know what's going on with you, but you have got a serious chip on your shoulder." He raised his hands in surrender, backing a step. "Forget it. Lesson over. I'm out of here."

"Wait," she gripped his arm, "I don't get this, get you. Security tells me it's fine to leave the base. I do what they advise, and you rip my head off. How am I in the wrong here?"

"I have a more conservative approach when it comes to things like risking your life."

Yeah, she knew she was prickly after a lifetime spent being fearful of risks and danger. "Why bother with things like self-defense if I'm going to spend my life in a bubble?"

"Do whatever you want. You're an adult, and I can't stop you. Good luck, and I sincerely hope you'll enjoy an uneventful day of shopping for little ivory camels."

She watched him plow through the door, his fist hammering the metal bar. Her body swirled with a mishmash of feelings: anger, attraction, frustration. Not surprising. But she hadn't expected the flash of sympathy. What a dark way to live, always searching for threats around every corner, always expecting the worst, a mind-set she'd worked so hard to overcome.

Because she knew firsthand the dangers of sinking too far into darker emotions.

* * *

Some people feared the dark. Chuck Tanaka embraced those increasingly rare opaque moments when no one touched him.

He rolled from his back to his side on concrete as cold and unforgiving as his captors. The chain on his ankle shackle rattled in time with the muted music thrumming above him. A groan slipped between his cracked lips and echoed in the damp cement cell that reeked of cigar smoke wafting from the guard outside his door.

Which battered part of his body summoned the sound? Who the hell knew? He'd gone past pain two days into captivity.

Now he focused on one thing: keeping his brain locked away from the sadistic bastards who'd been working him over.

And the she-demon. She worried him more than those two goons. She utilized mind games with a skill that scared the crap out of him. Early in his stay, he'd heard screams from the next room. The only screams lately had been his own.

He didn't expect to live. Even if somehow, beyond the odds, he was rescued, he could feel himself bleeding out inside. Still, he fought the Grim Reaper to give the tracking chip a chance to work, to lead someone here to break up this twisted woman's operation.

The device would continue to transmit, even if he died, but the reading would show he wasn't alive, rendering their search less urgent. Someone else could be taken. If by chance he could hang on long enough to tell them what he'd seen . . .

His focus faded. He grazed his fingers over the back of his shoulder where the flight surgeon had embedded the tracking device. How much abuse could the microchip withstand? What a way to field-test the thing. The bitch's clowns had put it through every pace with their fists.

He couldn't keep on with his nonanswer policy. He needed something else to help him hang on.

Try to think. Work up plausible misinformation in advance. Pray the chip keeps working.

He heard the tap, tap, tap of high heels advancing in the hall. Bile burned his raw throat. Light flooded his cell.

Chuck pushed against the cement floor and forced his body into an upright position, keeping his eyes off the battery they'd placed in the corner yesterday as taunting evidence of how far they were willing to go. He sagged back against the wall, but by God, he was sitting.

The door creaked wider to reveal the nameless woman. His devil sure as shit did wear Prada.

She wore a bloodred dress with leopard shoes like this was some fucking fashion show. She flicked her blond hair over her shoulders and advanced into the room, stopping short of his bare feet that ached with at least three broken toes.

She raised her hand, her ruby ring glinting along with a small ring of keys dangling from her fist. "Time to go for a ride."

Ah hell. Game over.

He'd been ready, even hoping for death more than once. But now that the time had come to cowboy up and die like a man, he prayed he had it in him. "What? No TLC? Damn. So you're finally ready to dump my dead body."

A slight smile curved her painted lips. "You're not lucky enough to die yet."

A flicker of hope warmed his chilled insides. "Aren't you full of cheer today?"

"You are either very stupid or very smart." She leaned to reach inside her purse, exposing the valley between her breasts. "I suspect the latter, but my friends and I can overcome that."

"Lady," the chuckle rumbling over his cracked ribs surprised him as much as it seemed to shock her, "I'm seven poundings past hurt."

Her brown eyes flicked toward the car battery in the corner. "I thought your military trained you well enough to know there are many more ways left for me to work with you."

Yeah, he knew, all right. He'd just been hoping she didn't. "I guess that means you're not taking me out for pizza and a brewski."

"Correct." She pulled out a small box, flicked it open, and pulled out a syringe.

What the—

She slid the needle into his arm. Coolness flooded the vein, and he didn't even know what to fight against.

Some kind of truth serum? Or a lethal cocktail? He battled the darkness for once, confused for the first time by her behavior.

Why had she been so gentle with the shot?

EIGHT

★

The nocturnal city skyline splayed out beyond Jimmy's windscreen. He manned the stick as the primary pilot tonight with Vince riding shotgun, the control panel spread in front of them. Chuck waited somewhere down there, if only the tracking chip could give them a more precise locale than the five-mile radius "somewhere in downtown Istanbul." But the developmental device wasn't large enough to work as an actual GPS.

At least the reads on Chuck's vitals reassured them he lived. Although his heart rate spiked so high sometimes they knew bad shit was going down on a regular basis. Chuck wasn't vacationing on the Riviera.

The weight of what their brother-in-arms must be suffering thickened the air with his presence.

If only tonight could bring Chuck's rescue, but they didn't have enough data and couldn't risk tipping their hand. So they flew this flight in preparation as an orientation sortie. Jimmy maintained a higher altitude to aid the cloak of darkness, which made the low-power chip tougher to pinpoint. However, if anyone could milk more info out of the transmitter, the colonel would succeed.

Lieutenant Colonel Scanlon worked in the cargo bay, undoubtedly hunched over the makeshift console monitoring the tracking controls. Once they completely fielded the gear—months into the future—it would be installed in aircraft flight decks.

For now, the prototype was strapped in back with its mishmash of orange wires distinguishing it from permanent parts of the plane. Jimmy had lost count of how many orange-wired aircraft he'd flown on a wing and a prayer that everything would work as advertised.

No night-vision goggles this time, given how close they were to the wash of city lights. Instead, they would rely on the FLIR, the forward looking infrared camera.

Vapor thumbed the interphone mic. "Remember the time Chuck saved Jimmy's ass in the Officers' Club bar at Nellis, when those fighter pilots swarmed around the pool table playing crud?"

The radio crackled with the heavily accented voice of the air traffic controller. "Blackbird two-two, reset altimeter two-niner-niner-eight."

Jimmy keyed up the radio. "Copy, two-niner-niner-eight. Two-niner-niner-eight set pilot."

Vapor reset his altimeter and keyed up his interphone, "Set copilot."

Jimmy remembered that evening well. "When are they not in the club playing crud?"

Vapor chuckled low. "No dodging the story, my brother."

"Spill it," Smooth coaxed over the airwaves. "I haven't heard this one."

"Fine. I was minding my own business, drinking an Alabama slammer—"

"Hitting on a smoking-hot babe who flew F-15s," Vapor interjected.

"Yeah, whatever. This arrogant fighter dude from her

squadron was shooting off his mouth faster than those pool balls whipping across the table. I managed to press the mental mute button on most of his bullshit."

"But the kicker?"

"Hey, Vapor? Do you want to tell the story?" Jimmy waited until his pal sagged back. "He said that sometimes, late at night, he had to get his wife to remind him he's just a *normal* man."

Smooth whistled low.

Vapor shook his head. "I swear on my favorite dog's grave Jimmy levitated off the floor. Thank God Chuck tackled him fast enough for the rest of us to restrain him, or he would have beat the inflated ego right out of that jackass."

Jimmy adjusted the heading to correct for a wind shift. "Chuck always had the coolest head."

"Has," Lieutenant Colonel Scanlon barked through the headset. "Not had. No past tense."

Silence crackled over the airwaves. Vapor's jaw worked as if he was trying to come up with something lighthearted to say. Then his yap closed. Even the squadron's funny man couldn't inject a mood booster.

A warning warble came over the interphone.

Jimmy looked fast at the threat page of his display. "The optics detector seems to think someone is checking us over. Eyeballs out, crew."

"Roger, Hotwire," echoed in his ears in triplicate.

Probably a low threat, but someone *had* taken an interest in them. Hopefully just a stargazer with a set of binoculars, but still . . .

He made an executive decision. "Let's get the hell out of here. We don't need some terrorist using an erector set to launch any MANPADS." Every pilot respected—and feared—the lethal power of a low-tech Man Portable Air Defense System. Enough so he knew the time had come to cut short their mission, a bite in the butt, since it meant less time to gather info on Chuck.

Vapor nodded. "Roger that. Let's cloak up and move out."

Jimmy paged through a display and entered the initial command for another of their test projects, a no-shit cloaking device. "Outside lights are off. Missile defense systems are active. Sure wish we knew if this one actually works. Wouldn't it be sweet to test something at a nice quiet Stateside base before hanging our ass on its success?"

"Remember, gentlemen," the colonel's ever-steady voice of reason rumbled over his ears, "keep it calm. Tech order warnings are written in blood, since something drastic happened to bring that flaw to the fore. Cautions are written in stupidity. Let's not be dead *or* stupid at the end of the day."

Deeper they flew into the Turkish countryside, leaving Chuck behind in the skyline full of ornate spires enduring God only knew what.

Actually, Jimmy had a helluva decent inkling. His four months as a "guest" of the Afghani rebels had given him a fair taste. At first, he'd taken the punches as a sort of penance for Socrates' death. Later, he hadn't been able to form thoughts clearly enough to do more than survive the day in hopes of making it to the next one so maybe, just maybe he could live long enough to tell Sarah how her husband had died.

Apparently the bastards who'd taken him hadn't read the Geneva convention relative to the treatment of prisoners of war. At least he hadn't been raped like the guy in the cell next to him, although listening and being unable to help had presented a unique hell all its own.

When tasking came down from headquarters for his squadron to work this mission to rescue Chuck, Jimmy had known he would be on the crew. Chuck would need someone to talk to afterward. Sure, there would be military shrinks aplenty. Jimmy had done his requisite time on the couch, and yes, it had helped. He wouldn't have been functional otherwise. But the brotherhood was strong, and sharing experiences with someone who'd been there was an integral part of processing, especially given that so much of what they did was classified.

Like the whole "cloak of invisibility" deal right now.

And damn, in the past he would have considered that a Harry Potter kind of thing, but now the phrase sounded more like something from one of Chloe's *Star Trek* shows. And damn it again, that woman was invading his thoughts even from miles away.

"Fuck," the commander hissed over the airwaves.

Not a good sign. Lieutenant Colonel Scanlon never lost his calm. Jimmy homed his focus back in on the job where it belonged: on this flight. "Sir? Problem with the equipment?"

"The tracking chip is working fine. Perfectly, in fact."

His fist clenched around the stick. If Chuck's life support signal had faded . . . Shit. Now he couldn't even feel the stick in his hand anymore. "And?"

"Chuck's alive."

Jimmy exhaled long and hard. Then waited.

"The accelerometers from the chip show it's moving. *He*'s being moved."

Not stellar news for the good guys. All that work to pinpoint his locale would be for crap. They would be back to a "general vicinity" guess again once the signal steadied.

The past and present meshed. Chuck had saved him from a major ass beating that evening a year ago, and Jimmy hadn't been one bit thankful. He'd wanted to pound heads, needed to let off steam on the second anniversary of his capture by the Afghanis.

He'd lost more than his friend back in those desert mountains. The bastards had fried him numb. He wondered sometimes if maybe they'd scrambled his brain, like with some kind of electroshock therapy gone way bad.

Sure, he'd survived with all his body parts in working order, but they'd cooked away more than his sperm count.

They'd numbed him from the inside out.

The past was nipping his heels tonight with razor-sharp teeth that could slice through any numbness. He didn't even want to think about what twisted versions of Chuck's current hell and his past one that dreams might hold. All they could do was wait to get a fresh lock-in on a new locale, then work the intel angle.

More damned waiting.

Shut-eye was definitely out of the question. He couldn't do anything more about Chuck at that moment, a reality he had to accept. Meanwhile, he needed to channel all that pent-up energy somewhere, or he would explode.

An image of Chloe popped to mind, full force if not fully welcome. He glanced at his watch. If debrief stayed on schedule, he should just be able to make it in time to join her damned shopping trip. Maybe he could funnel some of his frustrated need to rescue Chuck into watching Chloe's ass.

If nothing else, he'd learned Chloe Nelson had a way of firing him up from zero to eighty in sixty seconds flat. Right now, aggravating or not, he needed the distraction she could offer.

* * *

Nunez clinked glasses with Kutros and banged back his seventh shot of raki.

He hoped the pills those test guys swore by worked for the long haul, because he was pushing them to the limits tonight. The local brew packed a potent punch.

He pretended to be drunk like the semiroyal beside him and raked in the info. The other two bars had proved fruitless thus far. Nunez's CIA paramilitary operatives in the area had even used some of that air force–tested technology for seeing through walls. Nothing suspicious had come up at the other clubs. They would sweep the Oasis tonight to check out the back office and search for underground holdings.

Intelligence already indicated Kutros had a finger in everything from drugs to smuggling arms into the Middle East. It wasn't a far leap to believe he would pound secrets from service members.

"You are a good sort, Carvalho. Good sort. Hold your liquor good, too." Kutros jabbed his cigar stub in the air, the tip glowing in the dimly lit club.

The older man wavered toward the bottle, the glass clinking against the rim as he poured another round. Kutros reached once, twice, again before finally getting hold of his drink. He knocked back the raki with a wince. Closed his eyes.

And fell flat on his face on the table.

Nunez pried the glass from the unconscious man's grip and thunked it on the table with extra force in hopes of waking the drunk, but no luck. Kutros was out cold. No more info coming out of him tonight. And if ever Nunez had needed to push a case forward . . .

His instincts told him the Surac woman held answers, and he'd come here tonight to find them—not because of he wanted another look at *her*. He'd dealt with attraction on the job before. What made her draw so tenacious? Could that be part of a well-honed act to lure in unsuspecting servicemen for the Marta woman, who might or might not be a relative?

His gaze zeroed in on Anya, not that he'd let her out of his sight for the whole night, even though she'd managed to somehow avoid ever being his server. Her avoidance spoke louder than any sly look.

She slid out of sight, ducking behind the bar then rising. She carried her purse and a lightweight sweater over her arm.

He bolted from his table, slapping down a stack of bills. He hit the exit in time to catch sight of her rounding a corner. Luck was with him. Even the door dude was busy hassling some poor sap who'd shown up in an off-the-rack suit.

Nunez made tracks around the corner onto a narrow side street. There. He spotted her. She walked quickly under a line of iron balconies, her silky dress and hair glinting from the streetlamps, making her an easy target for anyone.

Doors and windows stayed open in deference to the heat. Sounds of an argument drifted from one house, a crying baby in another, many televisions. The street might be teeming with life indoors, but he doubted anybody would help her. This was a hear nothing, see nothing neighborhood.

Nunez fell in step alongside her. "Remember me?"

"No." She charged ahead without so much as a glance his way.

"I think you do." Was he not worth her time because he didn't wear a uniform?

"I think you are an arrogant man, and I know I am a woman with a gun in her purse pointed at you."

Impressive. "You have a good grasp of English so understand, I do not plan to give you any reason to use that gun. In fact, I want to see you safely home."

She stayed silent, her heels still clicking away on the cobblestone path. But she didn't ditch him.

Or shoot him.

"Where did you learn to speak English so well?"

"I must to work."

He angled closer. "Although your accent is a little thick."

"Then ask for someone else to serve you when you come to the club."

Thick, but sexy. "I can't seem to place it. Where did you say you're from?"

"I did not say."

Stopping under a small archway, she reached into her

simple—but top-quality—leather bag. He tensed, ready to take her down at the least sign she intended to plug a hole in his heart. With a flicker of a smile, she pulled free . . . her keys.

"Good night." She twisted a key in the lock and disappeared inside the narrow building sandwiched between an unending string of others like it. Time-worn paint on stucco. Battered brick.

Places that held shadows and secrets.

* * *

Anya bolted all four of the locks behind her before breathing in the relative safety of her home. She clicked on the lights as she strode deeper into her apartment, not that it took her long to reach the kitchen, but the space was all hers.

The press of so many bodies while she worked threatened her oxygen supply. Being a Surac seemed to come with a hefty dose of claustrophobia.

Apparently masochism, too, since she chose to make her living in a bar like prior generations. Men admired her legs, enough so to leave larger tips. She pulled out her roll of bills and tossed them aside before placing her leather purse on the table, her knife clanking against wood.

Once upon a youth long lost, she had dreamed of leaving weapons behind and growing flowers. How fanciful was that? She'd imagined surrounding herself with floral perfume to erase the stench of her amoral family.

And the solitude. That appealed most, whether found in a contained hothouse or in vast fields of farmed posies. Instead, she made do with a window box of leggy buttercups.

She had no trade experience except bartending, and after so much time passed, she was left with no choice but to follow in the family tradition. She liked to think she'd maintained the spirit of an isolationist, no relationships, connections, or feelings.

Life was simpler that way. No joy, no pain.

Pleasure? That consisted of survival and sleep. Until this one man upset the balance.

He didn't stare at her legs. He looked into her eyes and stirred something deep in her belly. Desire. Which also meant danger.

She'd learned early from Aunt Marta that sex killed.

NINE

★_____

What a killer trip to the mall.

Hopefully not literally.

Chloe eyed their bodyguard as she slid into a musty seat in the military bus slated to take them to nearby Adana. A guard stood by the driver, an AK-47 gripped in both hands. How could Livia lounge so nonchalantly a seat behind, just filing her nails?

Was it really worth the risk for sightseeing and a shopping trip just to buy a few tapestry drink coasters? But then how much could happen in the seven miles—or twelve kilometers as they said around here—until they reached Adana, the fifth most populous city in Turkey?

She needed to get a grip on more than the seat in front of her and quit falling back into her old fearful scripts. She'd come to this region aware of the risks, determined to enjoy life even if that meant mentally shutting out the automatic weapons that were a staple around here.

Besides, she had her nifty new self-defense skills at her

disposal, thanks to Jimmy Gage. Of course, even thinking about him sent her senses strumming with memories of tangling together on the mat.

The bus bucked forward. Just as fast, the vehicle jerked to a halt. Chloe's knees whacked the seat ahead of her. The guard snapped to attention. The door swung open and the guard backed away.

Jimmy bounded up the steps as if materializing from her thoughts. "Got room for one more?"

The uniformed driver nodded. "There are still a few places near the back, sir."

What was he doing here? Hadn't he said it was too dangerous? Was he leaping to her defense again?

For a guy who kept pushing her away, he sure seemed to follow her a lot.

Jimmy loped down the aisle toward her, his eyes fixed on her yet shuttered. She fidgeted in the cracked vinyl seat. She wasn't totally naïve. She had experience with guys, not a lot, since chronic illness had often left her with little except her music. Still, she'd been out with enough men that she shouldn't be this unsettled by a guy she barely knew.

But, "Roll Over Beethoven," Jimmy looked hot. Low-slung jeans fit his lazy stride to a *T*. He sat beside her without even asking.

She scooched toward the window, trying to escape the heat of warm denim against her washed-thin khakis. "You're really taking a dangerous risk leaving the base for some frivolous sightseeing."

"You're a regular comedian. The USO should sign you on to do stand-up." He unhooked his sunglasses from his shirt and slid them on.

"I would have brought you a little ivory camel if you'd just asked."

"I was afraid you'd bring a tusk instead and implant it in one of my vulnerable strike points."

"Definite possibility." The back-and-forth snipping was

actually starting to become perversely energizing. "Seriously, what are you doing here? Was your flight last night canceled?"

"Nope." He crossed his arms over his chest, scowl set.

Chloe jabbed a thumb toward the front of the bus. "I already have a very competent bodyguard."

"Uh-huh."

"I also have nifty new kung fu moves at my disposal. I'll be able to handle Romulans and purse snatchers with ease." She cut the air with her hands while Livia listened in none-too-subtly from the seat behind.

He peered at her over the top of his sunglasses. Chloe steeled her face, not in any way ready to let him see how much he confused her. No doubt ego boy had enough notches on his bedpost without adding her to the count.

"Well, Captain, just so we're clear, you're coming for yourself, of your own volition. I'm not taking any crap from you if you get your wallet jacked."

"Understood." Jimmy unclipped his BlackBerry from his waistband and began scrolling through mail as if she didn't exist, as if his leg wasn't still pressed up against hers, blasting muscled heat straight through her khakis.

Quiet settled but for the engine's grumble and the raspy *swoosh*, *swoosh* of Livia's nail file. The bus lumbered past the rows of flags at the NATO base. She'd read in her *Touring Turkey* book about the legend behind the Turkish flag, that in battle, the shapes were seen reflected in a pool of warriors' blood. Once outside the front gate, Chloe hitched her elbow on the window to soak up the mountainous countryside, rather than risk looking at Jimmy and have him snap at her about something else.

Or keep ignoring her.

The rolling landscape was dotted with flat-roofed houses. She'd also read in her tourism book that locals slept there to escape spring and summer heat.

Jimmy stayed silent, tapping a message on his BlackBerry, his somber mood darn near palpable. Something about his face struck her as different: not irritated as usual but something else.

She fidgeted in her seat. "Is everything okay? Are *you* okay?"

"Fine."

"Did something happen last night during your flight?"

"I'm alive, so everything must have gone just fine."

"Not the benchmark for success I like to put on my workday."

A dry smile tugged at his mouth as he kept typing on his tiny keypad. "We aren't singing 'Happy Birthday, Mr. President' for standing ovations."

Okay, he'd just stepped over the line in dissing her profession. Regardless of what he'd done for her, she didn't have to put up with rudeness. "There are plenty of other empty seats if you want peace and quiet before your souvenir junket. I hear they have bins of the glass blue 'eyes' for jewelry to ward off bad moods."

He tucked aside the BlackBerry and settled his undivided attention on her. "I didn't come along for souvenirs. I'm here for you."

Livia shifted in her seat, the vinyl upholstery squeaking. "Wow, flyboy, you're a charmer when you want to be."

Chloe looked between the two of them. A sliver of jealousy flashed through her. Silly on her part, certainly. Still, Chloe couldn't help comparing her own khakis and well-washed T-shirt from a Renaissance festival to the diva pop star's hip-hugging hot pink capris and silk butterfly tunic edged in gold beads.

How could a girl not come up feeling a little lacking?

Livia tapped the back of their seat with her nail file. "So, Captain Gage, what do they call you? All of you gentlemen have such interesting play names for each others."

"Play names?" That brought him upright in his seat. "We take our call signs—or go bys—seriously."

"Call signs." She filed her nails again, a cluster of silver rings flashing in the sunlight as her hand worked. "Tell me more."

"We come by our call signs in a number of ways." He removed his sports sunglasses and hooked them back on the neck of his polo shirt. "Most get the nickname after completing specialty trainings. We have a party with a keg and ceremony. In other cases, somebody stumbles on one by doing something especially, uh, memorable, and the label sticks."

"How did you decide on your name?" Chloe asked.

"We don't decide on our own." He hitched an ankle on one knee, his foot jostling in time to a tune only he could hear. "It's given to us. The call sign may be a simple play on someone's name, like Lieutenant Ryder would be Easy."

The camo-wearing driver stretched up in his seat, peering back at them in the large mirror over his windshield. "Or there's the ever-famous Colonel Pat 'My' Johnson."

Livia frowned in confusion, while Chloe shook her head. "Very mature, gentlemen."

The driver chuckled as he settled back behind the wheel, taking the sharp turn on the dusty road toward increasingly large clusters of houses near a small mosque. "Carry on, Captain."

Jimmy included the growing crowd in his story as his arm slid along the back of Chloe's seat. "Names also come from personalities, like how our flight engineer is a ladies' man, thus his call sign, Smooth."

The touch of his fingers along the rim of her T-shirt sleeve felt mighty darn smooth to her. Chloe inched closer to the dirty window. "I heard your friends call you Hotwire. Seems pretty accurate a personality tag to me with your temper and all."

Livia pursed her lips in a flirty little moue. "You appear very level to me, Captain Hotwire."

"My call sign can be taken two ways. I have a mechanical engineering degree or more likely, because I have a tendency to land in the nearest fight."

Well, that explained a lot, maybe even explained the sparks she'd thought she felt between them on the exercise mat. He was merely a volatile guy, and she happened to be the person in the room.

She should be relieved. She *was* relieved, damn it.

★ ★ ★

Jimmy stepped off the bus onto a steaming cobblestone street in historic Adana. Spices filled market baskets, scenting the air with memories of his grandmother's kitchen. But he was here today for something other than reminiscing about past family vacations to Turkey. He'd come to watch out for Chloe and take his mind off of Chuck's recent locale change that he couldn't seem to do a damned thing about.

He'd been here often enough in the past on work and family trips to be familiar with the mingling remnants of the Byzantine and Ottoman Empires. He didn't need to do the tourist gig with a map and Turkish spoons—or camels. Little did many of the sightseers know that some of these street vendors mixed local wares with goods from the air base.

Even though he wanted to avoid downtown for a number of safety reasons, he had to admit that seeing the area through Chloe's wide eyes brought back some of the newness he'd felt during his first visit at eight. They'd all come to meet his grandmother's relatives, before the family finances were overstretched by his sister Jenny's cancer treatments, back during a time when he could look at women without worrying about how fragile they could be.

He pushed back that thought before it sent his mood farther down the crapper. Focus on the moment: watching, protecting.

So many cultural eras and politics and religions came together in one place. Bebekli Kilise—the Catholic Church of Babies—sprawled at the city's center while spires of mosques spiked toward the sky. All those beautiful sites provided too many places to hide.

Chloe shot ahead to a food stall packed with candies and cakey sweets before he could stop her.

"Damn it, Speed Racer, slow down."

She didn't seem to have heard. He gripped Livia's arm and sprinted to catch up with Chloe before she got mugged—or worse.

Chloe fished in her purse and pulled out the local tender. She pointed to a pyramid of baklava and held up three fingers, then added a bag of individually wrapped Turkish delights.

His mouth watered, reminding him of practical concerns. He hadn't eaten anything except that shitty boxed meal during his flight. Many thought of baklava as a Greek dessert, but it belonged to Turkey as well.

"*Teşekkür ederim*," Chloe thanked the vendor and surprised the hell out of Jimmy.

Not many bothered to wade through their Turkish phrase book. The language wasn't more difficult to pick up than Spanish or French.

Chloe passed a baklava to Jimmy with a prim smile. "Thank you for the escort." Before he could respond, she'd turned to Livia. "And for you."

"Do you know how many stomach crunches and miles on the exercise bike that will cost me?"

"I declare this Calories Be Damned Day." Chloe bit into her baklava.

Her groan shot straight to his groin.

Livia nibbled a corner as if to make Chloe happy, then wrapped the napkin around the rest and tucked it into her large pink leather bag. "I am going to hang with the hunky guard for the day and pretend he is my boy toy. You kids feel free to run off on your own."

Kids? He had at least five years on her.

Livia sashayed past a wobbly bicyclist and three honking cars. Once she reached the guard, Jimmy returned his attention to Chloe.

Beside her, children played in a circle, bouncing an overlarge ball with their feet and heads. Chloe had focused her attention on a street band.

Musicians with ouds, some reed instruments, and a tambourine evoked the past with folk music while adults and children danced along with unmistakable artistry and a timeless appeal. Slowly, people from the crowd joined the dancers on the strewn wool carpets. The free-flowing movements appeared easy enough, with no set parameters other than hold hands overhead, snap fingers, sway shoulders, and twirl.

Chloe swayed beside him, edging closer and closer. Her feet and hands moved in time, mimicking, picking up the gist of the freestyle movement. She laughed. Just a simple sound, but it jolted straight through him.

She clasped his hand and backed toward the dancers. He shook his head.

Chloe held tighter. "Scared of looking silly?"

She'd thrown down the gauntlet.

"Fear is for the weak." He nudged her deeper into the dancers, his feet synching up with hers.

Soon her hair was down and twirling around her while hands thump, thump, thumped on drums. He could swear the air smelled different, smoky from more than incense. Chloe took on a time warp quality. She could have been any woman, any time, all the way back to the Ottoman Empire. He continued to move with the music instinctively, but his attention stayed totally on Chloe. Her blond curls whipped past her face long enough for her gaze to hook on his briefly.

The music slowed, but the moment still vibrated through him as the crowd jostled by. Pulling himself back to the present was a helluva lot tougher than it should have been.

He took her hand in his again and backed her out of the

crowd, jostling against another person. Damn it, he should have been more aware of his surroundings.

Jimmy glanced over his shoulder. "Excuse me."

He looked straight at the face of Agent Mike Nunez.

"*Excusa.*" The agent nodded and strode forward in clothes that appeared to cost more than a month of captain's pay.

O-kay. He knew better than to ask. Their jobs operated on a need-to-know basis.

He shot a quick glance at Chloe as she waved her thanks to the musicians. She didn't seem to have noticed Agent Nunez while the dancers melded back into the pedestrians.

Jimmy gripped her arm. "Come on, Gypsy Rose. We're going to find some real food."

"Why, thank you for that polite luncheon invitation, sir. I would be delighted to join you."

Ignoring her dig, he drew her to his side. Because she felt damn good, sure. But also because the crush of activity made him nervous.

All bustled around with seemingly benign activity, but threats came in deceptive packages these days. He took in the haggling at a fish stand, the sizzle of meat as a vendor sliced away at a haunch. Kids laughed at a puppet show at his nine o'clock, while a group of mothers looked on, some in veils, others in traditional western garb.

He gauged the pace and direction of Nunez and chose the opposite. He jabbed a finger toward a street-side café with an open grill so he could be sure his food was made fresh.

She smiled up at him. "Thanks again for *asking*. Yes, I would love to eat there."

Sighing, he stopped. "Where would you like to go?"

"You pick."

Here he was, trying to find an outside café with the best vantage point for keeping an eye out for possible trouble, and she was busting his chops. Jimmy gripped her elbow and steered her through the increasing throng to a wrought-iron table near a bookseller's stand.

He held out her chair with exaggerated manners.

She took her seat with a flourish. "I'm delighted to be dining with such a scintillating conversationalist."

"I'm a bodyguard today. Not some hired gigolo from an escort service."

"I'll do most of the talking, then. At least we can't argue that way." She propped her elbow on the table, and her chin fell to rest on her fist.

He liked her fingers with their short, unpolished nails. Sure, he realized she must keep them trimmed to play the piano, but still, those industrious hands enticed him a lot more than Livia Cicero's for-show-only hot pink manicure.

Chloe's eyes sparkled in the afternoon sun as she took in the surroundings. "This is exactly the sort of atmosphere I wanted to experience when I volunteered for this gig. God, that music was amazing."

Jimmy claimed the seat that kept his back to the painted brick wall so he could watch without worrying about what went on behind him. "I hadn't realized you're a trained dancer, too. No wonder you were a quick study with the self-defense moves."

"I've never taken a single dance lesson. I just let the music resonate through me, and the next thing I knew, I was joining in."

An image of her abandon while dancing sparked in his mind and shot straight to his groin with an unexpected force.

She picked up her menu, scanning. "I probably looked like Snoopy from those Charlie Brown movies, dancing like a goof."

Something about the way she said it tugged at him. He could have sworn there was a vulnerability in her half laugh that didn't quite fit with her outward bravado. He couldn't bring himself to roll out the easy quip. A part of him wanted to tell her that for the first time he understood that touchy-feely phrase about dancing like no one was looking.

And the rest of him kept thinking about his sister, of how easily somebody vibrantly, fearlessly alive could be taken away.

A waitress approached their table, putting their conversation on hold. He started to pick up the menu again, then scanned the other diners instead. He knew all the local dishes. The more important factor would be choosing the one best prepared here.

He looked past a table of locals eating summer vegetables and fruits to a group of tourists tearing into a loaf of Turkish bread. He started to move on, but something prickled at his brain and he scanned back to a woman in a burka. What bothered him about her? Even though the head-to-toe dark garb for females wasn't required in this predominantly Muslim region, there were plenty who wore it.

He studied the shoulders that seemed overly large for a woman. The walk, rather than the softer swaying steps of a female, more the stride of . . . a *man*.

Jimmy reached for Chloe. Searched for a cop to alert. And all too damned late.

The man in the burka whipped up his hand holding a plunger detonator and shouted his battle cry of death.

TEN

Chloe stifled a scream. Jimmy slammed into her at the same moment the blast exploded through the café. Her thoughts shattered into pieces as jagged as the windows spitting glass everywhere.

Ear-numbing thunder. Falling debris. Shrieks.

Fear.

Shock waves rolled over her. Jimmy's arms tightened around her, his shoulders curving protectively. A creak sounded overhead.

"Son of a bitch," Jimmy growled in her ear, rolling her to the right. "Cover your face."

The tasseled awning crashed to the ground an inch away.

Gravel bit into her arms and knees. Blood made a sticky paste on her pant leg. Her muscles bunched so tight, she couldn't move even if her pounding heart wasn't scaring her motionless. The explosion on the boat had been bad. Really bad. But this . . . this was hell.

With the possibility of an encore.

She forced her gritty eyes open and found a severed leg sticking from the rubble. How odd to notice the man had lost his shoe as well as a limb.

Someone screamed again and again, hurting her ears, scratching her throat. Ohmigod, the sound came from her, and she couldn't stop, couldn't stop her convulsed muscles from twitching as she stared at that shoeless foot with a tiny hole in the heel of the sock.

Wading through the layers of horror, she realized Jimmy had his arms around her waist, rubbing his hands along her back and waist, soothing a shush, shush, shush in her ears. She couldn't hope to recapture calm, but shutting up to breathe would be a reasonable start.

"I'm okay, I'm okay, I'm okay," she chanted, her words eventually slowing enough to stave off hyperventilation.

"Of course you are. I never doubted it." He squeezed her waist, his eyes sweeping over her. "I'm going to assess the situation, but I'm not leaving. I'll keep your back and you keep mine until we're sure everything's safe."

His cool logic calmed her.

A muggy breeze full of soot swept over her midriff where her shirt had bunched and twisted. She eased up, tugging her shirt down over her waist again. She started to kneel and—*whoa*. She so didn't need to look at that two-inch piece of glass sticking out of her calf. Seeing the imbedded shard made it hurt even worse.

"Are you sure you're all right?" Jimmy didn't look back at her, his attention still locked in surveillance mode, except to her, it seemed impossible to discern anything in the chaotic mass of screaming people. There could be more attackers in the crush of humanity, and no one would know.

They had to leave. Jimmy didn't need to know about her leg.

"I'm fine," she managed in a halfway normal voice, no

small feat. Chloe snatched a cloth napkin from the rubble beside the toppled table.

One hand gripping a gun, Jimmy reached behind him with the other to touch her. A gun?

She didn't have time to wonder why he'd packed heat for sightseeing. Chloe set her teeth and will and yanked the piece of glass out. Fast. A whimper must have slid past her lips.

"Chloe?"

"Nothing. Just a wimpy moment." She tied the napkin tightly around the pulsing wound. "Focus on keeping us alive while I unearth my courage from my stomach."

He chuckled low, a welcome sound.

She searched the mayhem for a way out, a pocket of safety in a world where she no longer trusted the seeming status quo. Cars screeched to a halt. Carrying a new threat? People rushed to phones. To call for help or signal another wave of attacks?

Law enforcement hoofed toward the scene, but she feared everyone except the man beside her. "What now?"

"We leave. The guard has Livia and the others. As far as I'm concerned, I would rather not wait around for a possible repeat."

Amen to that.

Chloe fit her hand in his, and he pulled her to her feet. He glanced at her makeshift bandage. A frown flickered over his face.

She nudged him. "It's a scrape. Let's go."

He tucked her close to his side and shouldered through the frantic hordes, keeping his head low. They broke free onto a narrow street beside the bistro. Stragglers ran toward and away from the explosion while vendors tossed their wares into wagons. A police car sling-shotted past, siren blaring. Homeowners closed doors and trundled shutters up tight.

Three turns later, he slowed to a stop in a quiet housing

division. She sagged against the stone wall, panting. The mayhem from the attack echoed softly in the distance, along with sirens.

Jimmy planted a hand beside her head, shielding her with his body while checking around them. "Are you sure I didn't hurt you when I slammed you to the ground? What about your leg?"

"You saved my life. Again. Do you think I'm going to complain about scraped palms and a scratch on my leg?" Now wasn't the time to tell him she'd hit the ground pretty damn hard on her surgery incision. She was probably okay, but just to be safe, she would check in with the doctor when they got back to the base.

"You're sure?" He tore his gaze off the street.

"I'm going to be fine." And she would. She knew how to take care of herself.

"Thank God." He hauled her against his chest. "Chloe, you could have died back there."

He squeezed her a bit too hard, but she stifled the wince. The solid strength of his arms, the musky scent of him, the vibrant beat of his heart felt damn good right now. She tipped her face up to breathe, bringing her lips right up to his as he looked down at her.

Jimmy sealed his mouth to hers hard, fast, and God, he tasted even better than he looked. She stayed still for a second then fisted his polo shirt. He tangled his fingers in her hair, deeper, deeper still, much like she wanted to burrow as close as she could to him.

Chloe moaned a "Yes" against his mouth. She needed this kiss, the bold rasp of his tongue against hers as she yanked him nearer.

Her fingers twisted tighter in his shirt . . . ohmigod . . . becoming sticky with blood. *His.*

She jerked back to check him over, the mood broken, even if her nerves still hummed. "Jimmy?"

The wind ruffled through his already tousled hair. Nicks and small cuts dotted one cheek, and his forearm appeared abraded from the cement. It could have been so much worse, and it would have been her fault.

He'd been right. She shouldn't have left the base. "I'm so sorry for not listening to you."

Jimmy pinched the bridge of his nose. "I'm the one who should apologize. This isn't exactly the time or place for a kiss. Or chitchat."

His hand fell away, and his face shut down. "We need to find a taxi and get back to the base."

"Of course." Each painful step pulsed more blood from the slice in her leg until her sock became grossly squishy. "Should we go to the police station and make a statement? We might have something useful to offer."

"We'll give our statements to the base security. Trust me." His voice went darker than his scowl. "You don't want to see the inside of a Turkish interrogation room."

Chloe knew a haunted soul when she saw one, and she reached out to him. The forbidding look on his face stopped her cold.

He hailed a taxi—a rusty little piece of shit, but at least the POS's engine hummed—and jerked the door open. He guided her inside with brusque hands and dove in after her, sealing them inside with an ancient driver and the smell of garlicky olive oil.

Sliding his gun unobtrusively on his knee, covered by his broad palm, Jimmy gave instructions to the driver she couldn't understand, even with her limited phrase book knowledge. How did he know the language so well? Yet another confusing mystery about this man who snapped at her one moment, saved her life another, and kissed her senseless the next.

He settled back in his seat, not in the least relaxed as he looked out the windows. "Do you want to tell me about that big scar I saw on your side when we were lying on the ground back there at the café? It looked pretty serious."

Her thoughts scrambled to that frightening second

when he'd tackled her, held her around the waist. She seemed to recall her shirt had rucked up during the fall. She was always careful about keeping her scar concealed, but she must have been too distracted, given the circumstances.

Did she want to talk about it? "Not really."

He nodded toward her makeshift napkin tourniquet. "Just like you don't want to tell me you cut your leg."

"Hey," she snapped back. "I understand you're frustrated because we left the base today—"

"That's an understatement." His mouth went tight in a sign she was beginning to recognize as Jimmy trying to hold back his anger. "You are the most pigheaded, reckless human being I have ever met in my life. Don't you even give a shit about living?"

"Of course I do." She may have come to accept the probability of death during her teen years, but she'd never stopped wanting to live. "Sadly, I'm not a fortune-teller to know somebody would try to blow me up today, and apparently, the base's security team lacks your ability to see into the future as well. I feel very confident they want me to keep breathing as much as I do."

"Well, you sure couldn't tell it by the choices you've been making." He twisted in his seat to check out a pair of motorbikes close on their tail.

"You were right, okay? Totally right. I shouldn't have left the base. You can lord it over me all you want." And it hadn't escaped her notice that they still weren't home free yet.

The bikes whipped past and around a corner.

He relaxed back in his seat, his muscles still tensed, biceps straining against the sleeves of his polo shirt. "I don't want to gloat. I want you to stop taking your life for granted. We are not in the U.S. of A. right now, and I'm not always going to be around to protect you."

"Who are you to judge me? You don't even know me." Tears of frustration stung. He didn't know her because she hadn't let him, and once she did, he would let her down just like all the other men she'd dared let get close.

"Damn straight I don't know you, but for some reason, I can't seem to drag my sorry ass away from you." He skimmed his fingers gently along her side again. "Chloe, what happened to you?"

She bit back the words. It wasn't his business.

His fingers lingered, just a light touch but somehow tender, intimate. "I've come to your rescue three times now. I'm calling in the marker."

She jerked away. "That's not fair."

"If you expect life to be fair, you'd better prepare yourself for one long suck fest." He stared her down for a whole block before raising a hand in surrender. "Never mind. Keep your secrets."

The fight flooded out of her, such a rare occurrence it surprised the hell out of her. But it wasn't every day a girl almost got blown up. Jimmy, too, for that matter, and it would have been her fault. She owed him her life. He deserved at least the truth, even as her stomach clenched.

Chloe sagged back in her seat. "I had a kidney transplant."

She watched his reaction. She watched as—just like every other man she'd told about her condition—his face closed up, and he looked away.

* * *

A transplant patient.

Charging through security measures at Incirlik Air Base on his way to a vaulted meeting room, he still worked to process what Chloe had said in the taxi. Tough to do with the taste of her still on his mouth, her flowery scent still in his senses, the feel of her soft body under his still imprinted.

Her revelation had knocked him on his ass at a time he was still reeling from the explosion and how close she'd come to getting blown up. After the way he'd lost his sister to cancer, he couldn't help but be rocked by the similarities in their chronic health battles.

It was the last thing he'd expected to hear from sexy, full-on Chloe Nelson, but it explained that vulnerable vibe he kept getting from her. The one that kept luring him to drag her off somewhere safe.

Jimmy flashed his ID to the guard and passed over his cell phone and BlackBerry. No electronics were allowed where he was going. The guard nodded him through the metal detector.

Not that they'd talked about her transplant in any detail, since she'd clammed up for the rest of the taxi ride. She made it clear that while he may have gotten his answer, he wasn't prying anything more from her.

And what *did* he want?

An outlet? Jimmy was deep-down pissed off at whoever'd set the explosion, at the bastards who'd taken Chuck, at life for dealing his sister and Chloe a raw hand, and at himself for not knowing how to handle what she'd told him.

His boots echoed down the long, chilly corridor, thundering as loud as his anger, anger directed at a crap ton of things. Problem was? He couldn't fix big-time health concerns. He didn't know who'd taken Chuck. And the guy responsible for the marketplace bombing currently had his guts splattered all over concrete.

At least Chloe's leg injury had been minor, requiring only four stitches. Currently she was safely ensconced in an office with base security police, giving her version of the afternoon's attack. Now he needed to meet up with Nunez for some sort of high security meeting in the vault.

A half hour after they'd bumped into each other at the market, the agent had sent a text message requesting this confab about the explosion—or rather *explosions*. Three other bombs had gone off throughout the day. Two at tourist sites and one right outside the front gate of the base, bursting the water pipes.

Too much was happening too fast for it to be unrelated.

He swiped his card through the third cipher lock and entered the windowless secure room. There was nowhere to hide anything in this bare room, not even some coffee to jolt his system.

Part of him hoped the agent had news on Chuck, and another part feared he did have news on Chuck. The bad kind.

Nunez sat in a stark steel chair at an even starker table. Today the agent looked like, well, an agent. Wearing a simple black suit, white shirt, dark tie, and expressionless face, he could have been a blank slate waiting to be filled with the next persona. "Only a few scrapes? You're lucky."

Jimmy straddled the seat across from the agent, the scab forming on his forearm tugging uncomfortably. "Just some ringing in my ears. I'm glad you were a few blocks away. Flying flack can spray a destructive distance." He shoved the image of Chloe's bleeding leg, the vision of her puckered scar to the back of his mind.

"Any more information on the other attacks?" Jimmy asked.

"Only that two of the bombs were set off by remote control. We believe those two bombers who died were unwilling participants." A single bead of sweat popped on Nunez's forehead, a virtual flood of emotion from a man who played life so close to the vest. "It looks like two women were plucked from a mental facility."

"The bastards."

Nunez thumbed away the droplet of perspiration. "I agree."

Silence felt a helluva lot heavier in a vault. Much like the quiet that echoed around inside him when he hit the sack at night and the enormity of all the secrets he had to protect swelled inside him, reminding him he had to be careful, even in sleep, not to let something slip.

At least he had his squadron buds, even more importantly his core crew, to shoot the shit with about their highly classified work. Unlike Nunez. The agent was out there alone in the middle of evil sons of bitches who tortured people and took advantage of society's most vulnerable.

Jimmy reviewed the afternoon that had now carved out a permanent cubby in his memory. "I know that the chances are slim anyone would have recognized you from the rescue day since you kept to yourself and wore a helmet the whole time. But best I could tell, no one made you. I watched for signs. Not that I think they would have recognized you anyway, given the whole *GQ* look."

Nunez's blasé expression broke for an instant. "What gave me away to you? I'd changed my clothes from earlier, not to mention my whole superspy demeanor."

Jimmy searched for a specific detail, something about the man's gestalt . . . and came up blank. He'd just known. "I honestly don't have an answer for you."

The agent's eyes blazed with an almost eerie intensity as he leaned forward. "I believe it's because you have an instinct for this side of the work that even most working the job don't possess."

"I appreciate the compliment."

Nunez quirked a brow. "I'm only stating a fact, and not necessarily a good one. That gift can be a curse. Happy oblivion is a whole lot easier."

"Ah, oblivion's—"

"For the weak. Right." They shared a laugh before the mood turned somber again. "I can use an extra pair of eyes, and bringing in someone else would take time."

Adrenaline tingled like a brush with an electrical outlet, simultaneously dangerous and stimulating.

"Bring someone in for what?"

"I've pegged a bar that appears to be a serious contender. Are you up for a drink and a possible kidnapping?"

The adrenaline now hummed through his veins like a nuclear power plant. "Is the Pope Catholic?"

"Good." Nunez's eyes lit with an answering excitement of the chase. "I'll get back to you with the details shortly. First—"

The vault door hissed open again, and Lieutenant Colonel Scanlon strode through.

Jimmy stood at attention. Clearly this wasn't your everyday, average shoot-the-shit session with the colonel in attendance.

Scanlon saluted and took his seat with the two men at the table. "At ease, Captain. Glad to see you're all right after today's attack."

"Me, too, sir." No one needed to state the obvious. Riots in the area boded poorly for getting Chuck out of there without detection or a major incident—if, in fact, this hunch even played out.

Nunez didn't require fancy video technology to command attention. "I've called you both here for a reason. Obviously we're always concerned for the well-being of any civilians on foreign soil. But gentlemen, if something happens to one of those USO performers . . ." His scowl went soulless. "I don't have to spell out the catastrophic fallout to international relations in an already shaky region."

Jimmy's arm itched at even the mention of the afternoon bombing and how close Chloe had come to dying. If someone was gunning for performers on the USO tour this aggressively, he wanted her on the first plane out.

Nunez continued, no fidgeting, just pure, intense focus. The man didn't even toy with the pen beside his hand. "I understand you've got your hands full with rescuing Chuck Tanaka; however, the agency still believes that your best cover for being here can be gained by protecting our USO personnel."

Jimmy thought of Livia Cicero's shout of outrage over

being confined after the bombing. At least Chloe finally seemed to grasp the serious nature of nearly being blown to bits. "The performers and crews are already in lockdown. No more jaunts out."

Scanlon cleaned his black-framed glasses. "Sending them home would be simplest."

"Certainly. If the USO would agree, and if the enemy wouldn't dance in the streets over the victory."

Scanlon slid his glasses back in place. "So give us our marching orders, Nunez."

"A twofold plan. Captain Gage is going to help me with a little field work."

That must be related to the drink and possible kidnapping Nunez had mentioned. What did that have to do with the colonel?

"I need you to pull some protective detail here. We have security beefed up, but Colonel, we would like for you to stick close to the Cicero woman."

Jimmy muffled a cough. He was going into the field, and the colonel was babysitting? Life was flipped on its ass today.

Scanlon didn't bat an eye. He did, however, clench his jaw. "How long?"

"As long as you're at Incirlik, for both her protection and to give us time to delve more into her background. She passed the security clearances necessary to participate in the production, but that doesn't mean they dug deep enough."

His eyes narrowed. "You're targeting her because she's not American?"

"Everyone is suspect, but yes, her loyalties are more likely to be divided than some of the others in the USO cast and crew. Having you around on a social basis will seem less obvious than a guard."

Scanlon scowled. "Why not just tell her the guard is for her protection?"

"We'll still have guards trailing her covertly in shifts,

but she is notorious for ditching security. Your extra assistance would be greatly appreciated."

The colonel whipped off his birth control glasses, pinched his nose, and muttered something that sounded much like a sarcastic "Great."

"Of course we understand there will be instances when you're busy with other duties, at which times our security will double."

Jimmy rocked his chair on two legs, enjoying the moment for some perverse reason. Could be this struck his funny bone on a day that had otherwise been pretty much dog shit. "Smooth would be glad to act like her boy toy."

"We don't want romantic entanglements mucking up the water."

Jimmy lowered his chair. "Sorry, Colonel, I tried."

Nunez seemed to weigh his next words carefully before stating, "In my opinion, Colonel Scanlon is the least likely to be distracted by her because of his recently widowed status, which is the very reason I chose him."

Awkward moment, for sure.

An image flashed to mind of the colonel at a squadron party with his wife days before she'd died. They'd appeared so into each other while dancing.

And there wasn't a thing any of them could do for him.

If he'd been a contemporary, Jimmy would have poured a few beers down his throat until the guy got maudlin and unloaded some of the grief clogging his insides. But due to the colonel's rank, contemporaries in the work field were sparse. What a stark existence for a person who'd spent the prior years of his career in a crew-bonding mentality.

Lieutenant Colonel Scanlon's expression stayed blank, even if his fists clenched. "Astute observation, Agent Nunez. Consider the job done."

ELEVEN

Chloe thumbed through the selections on her iPod, nothing else to do while she hung around in a recreation center room designated for the performers who chose to stick it out after the marketplace attack. Every rational instinct told her, "Time to hitch a ride home." They didn't even have water for showers because of the bombing at the front gate. Tenacity, the debt to that soldier, and a memory of a flyboy's kiss, however, kept her in Turkey.

Meanwhile, she'd traveled to an exotic country only to be entertained with foosball, a stack of board games, and her choice of three channels on the Armed Forces Network, currently spouting nonstop episodes of *Jeopardy.*

For eight hundred dollars, name sexual frustration in Turkey.

Alex, would that be: Who is kiss 'em and leave 'em Jimmy Gage?

She'd barely seen him since they'd been shuttled to military doctors to be checked over once everyone had regrouped at Incirlik Air Base. She would have assumed he was flying, except it seemed the colonel had plenty of free time on his hands to hang out with them, even if he brought along paperwork. She suspected the obvious.

Now that Jimmy knew about her transplant, he'd lost interest. She should have been used to this by now; in fact, she worked to keep men at bay rather than run the risk. But somehow Jimmy had gotten under her skin.

She blinked back tears, angry tears *not* hurt, and focused on studying the boss. Maybe he could give them some insights on the current security status. Although why was he even here?

Wouldn't he have preferred somewhere quieter than a room littered with USO personnel? Apparently not. He'd commandeered a table for himself, his laptop, and a stack of files.

A group of backstage techies stayed glued to the double jeopardy question while the band played cards. Their stage manager, Greg, wore noise-reducing headphones while tuning into a video of the last performance on his computer.

The boyfriend/girlfriend dance team stayed off to the side stretching, using a chair rail as a makeshift ballet bar while ignoring each other over some tiff. Of course Melanie and Steven weren't the only ones irritable, thanks to the water problem.

Livia Cicero paced, her leather ankle boots clicking on industrial tile. Her designer scarlet jumpsuit with her name sewn across the butt in gold and black thread drew the eyes of every male in the room.

"I cannot believe I am being held captive." She gripped the jeweled cell phone she'd been forbidden to turn on. "I came on this trip to entertain the soldiers and soak in the culture. Instead, I am only soaking in sweat."

Greg crossed the room with a smart, efficient walk, snatched up the remote control, and thumbed the volume down two notches. Did he own anything other than black turtlenecks and matching loose pants? "I heard they're hoping to have the water pipes fixed sometime tomorrow."

"Hoping?" Livia snagged a bottled water and twisted the cap. "We're going to need more perfume."

Greg closed up his computer. "I'll hunt down another box of the baby wipes they've been giving out."

Livia drained half her water bottle, visibly unimpressed.

Chloe unwound her iPod earbuds, not that she'd gotten to listen for more than sixty seconds at a stretch before Livia interrupted or the dance team sniped at each other. As a conductor, she was used to handling relationship dramas and diva theatrics. The performers deserved to be respected for their talent but otherwise needed to be treated as one of the crowd. "We've all been given the option of flying home anytime," she said to Livia.

"I fulfill my commitments." She turned on a spiky heel and faced the colonel. "Have you ever considered corrective eye surgery?"

"No," he answered without even pausing in his typing.

"Or new glasses?" Livia bent at the knees to get a better view of his specs, which seemed to involve a quick inventory of the man himself.

"These work fine." He tapped the bulky frames.

"They do have a certain retro appeal."

He pulled them off and turned them to the side for display. "They're air force issue and therefore free."

Scanlon slid them back on his face.

"Are you always so unsociable?"

He peered over the tops of the rims. "Are you always this rude?"

She flounced down into the chair next to him, her velour jumpsuit swishing in the silence. Livia flicked her nails repeatedly. "I am bored."

Chloe wasn't. Watching these two spark off each other was better than any iPod offerings or the three-station television. She stuffed her music away and hugged her knees in the uncomfy faux-leather chair. Over in the corner, even the boyfriend/girlfriend dance pair slowed their pliés and pouting to listen in.

Lieutenant Colonel Scanlon flipped to the next page in the file. "Did someone forget to pull the green M&M's out of your candy dish?"

Livia sniffed. "I don't eat chocolate."

A smile flickered along his mouth for the first time. "Not my point, diva."

Chloe sensed the "entertainment" was about to turn ugly. Livia Cicero was known in the tabloids for her dramatic meltdowns. Chloe wasn't sure why she liked this drama queen. Maybe because the woman embodied all the bold colors of life Chloe had longed for in her youth.

Regardless, Livia had unselfishly done her a favor by lining up the backup singer gig when no one would have blamed her for blowing off the request.

Chloe unfolded from her chair, scavenging for a way to stop the exchange before it went south. "Livia, come over here." Chloe gestured to the battered piano in the corner. Even the captain of the starship *Enterprise* got stuck playing peacemaker on occasion. "I'll run through some songs and scales so we can exercise our vocal chords. I can even record you with the new feature on my iPod. The piano may not be as top drawer as the grand they've got over in the rehearsal room, but they've kept this antique in tune."

"I wouldn't want to bother our colonel."

He peered over the top of his glasses. "Please. Sing."

"Since you asked so nicely." Livia patted his face.

Her hand lingered. She stalled in place, her smile fading to confusion. Even more telling, the colonel didn't move, either.

Livia dropped her hand and bolted to her feet, double-timing toward the ancient upright.

Chloe limbered her fingers with rapid scales along the ivories. The familiar feel of cool keys, the action of give and take under her touch, the routine rolled over her, more relaxing than meditation and a massage combined. Returning her hands to the middle, she paused and nodded to Livia.

The singer's voice hit pure and true from note one of the vocal warm-up. Note by note, everyone in the room began to abandon whatever else they'd been doing to listen in.

Professional respect swelled. Livia Cicero wasn't just a pretty pop star package. The woman's classical training couldn't be missed. Livia may have been gifted with an angel voice, but she'd unmistakably put in the time to hone her instrument.

Scales transitioned into songs, a mix of arias and popular tunes, finally a love ballad that had gained Livia recognition early in her career. Melanie and Steven even shrugged off their argument and swayed together.

The colonel shot to his feet, interrupting them. "Play something else."

Livia hitched a hand on her hip and thrust out her bottom lip. "Do I sound so horrible, or are you just anti-romance, Colonel?"

Chloe stared from one to the other in their standoff, the whole room silent. The Colonel wasn't irritated. He looked completely shell-shocked.

The song had struck an emotional chord for him, and *not* in a good way. Chloe had seen the same heartbroken look on her father's face after her mother died in a car wreck. This man had lost and lost big.

Livia's blasé mask slipped to reveal genuine compassion. "I'm sorry."

Apparently the diva wasn't as self-absorbed as she liked everyone to think.

He blinked once, the hint of emotion gone and replaced by cool composure. "It's all right."

Lieutenant Colonel Scanlon dropped back into his chair, losing himself in the work spread out over the table.

Chloe returned to simple scales again. Safer all the way around for everyone.

* * *

Jimmy Gage was onboard with the plan.

Nunez half-listened to Kutros while watching the airman work the bar with ease while Anya served drinks. Gage hadn't even hesitated when asked to sign on for some undercover help. The guy was a downright natural.

Thanks to listening devices the size of a grain of rice resting in the ear canal, he and Gage could hear each other and communicate freely in an emergency. Gage had spent the past four hours bragging to any woman who would listen about his high-profile military career, a fine line to walk, since the man really did possess secrets that could topple security in more than one country.

But he'd seen the guy train in the gym. Gage could take care of himself, part of what made him the perfect choice in a pinch. The pieces fit for using him rather than wasting time calling in an agency backup. If anyone in this place made their bread and butter off kidnapping American servicemen, Jimmy "Hotwire" Gage would be looking at the inside of a dark hood by the week's end.

Which reminded him he needed to nudge harder with Kutros. The untraceable finances and proximity to the locations of interest around Turkish bars made him a prominent suspect in the recent disappearances.

"Do you mind picking up the tab tonight, my friend? I am a little cash strapped." Nunez had plotted this next phase carefully, putting himself in line to be drawn into the underground network if Kutros had access to such a thing.

Kutros puffed on his cigar, blowing smoke through his nose in twin dragon trails. "Not a problem."

The scent of expensive tobacco almost managed to override the cloying cologne of the woman at the next table.

"My accountant will be wiring me money from Madrid soon," Nunez pushed to maintain his accent, more difficult for some reason with Gage around reminding him of his real world. "He simply has a few transactions to clear up first."

Kutros studied the inside of his glass of raki for three beats of the band's tambourine. In the dim flicker of the candle sconce, the man didn't appear as old. Closer to forty than fifty. "Do you need a place to stay? A loan? Just temporarily, of course."

"No, but *gracias*, I will keep your generous offer in mind."

"Ah, a prideful man."

"What can I say? I still feel compelled to fill my own bank account." Nunez stopped short of asking for a "job."

"I will keep my ears open for opportunities for you, my friend." His calculating eyes cleared, and he smiled. "Ah, look. There is your favorite waitress finishing her shift."

Nunez twisted in his seat, and sure enough, he was gifted with a mind-numbing view of Senorita Surac's backside hugged by silk as she swished past a sweaty bouncer evicting an overly rowdy soldier. Apparently the door jerk was falling down on the job tonight if they needed to call in the cavalry.

She sidestepped the sloshed soldier and continued toward the employees' exit. And shit, he'd let his interest in her be so well-known Kutros noticed? Nothing to do but go with it. Let the old man believe the attention was of a sexual nature.

Not completely untrue. "What can I say? I appreciate a beautiful woman."

"Women are expensive," he spoke and puffed at the same time. "But very much worth it. So what are you doing sitting here with me? Go catch her before she gets away."

He couldn't think of a plausible reason to say no. "I will see you tomorrow then?"

"Of course."

"*Gracias*."

Nunez wove around the clumps of military members and civilians, mingling for drinks, dancing, and under-the-table drugs. He'd long ago developed a level of numbness to the illegalities he had to overlook in order to keep his eye on the bigger picture.

He reached the "employees only" door just as his target clasped the knob. He covered her fingers with his, only for a second before skimming a single bangle on her wrist and letting his hand fall away. One touch was plenty potent.

The slight widening of her eyes indicated she concurred.

For an instant he allowed himself the pleasure of taking in the subtle softening of her face as she shed her work look. He'd only glimpsed this smooth openness once before on her way to clock in.

"The crowd is rowdy tonight." He nodded toward Jimmy Gage chugging shots and shouting requests at the band.

"That happens when new troops roll in," she answered neatly.

She faced him without brushing him aside for once. Progress. And he didn't have to fend off the sniffly door bully this time.

"You follow the military habits that closely?"

"I follow anything to do with my patrons that brings bigger tips." She patted the pocket of her whisper-thin apron, the lacy hem grazing along a perfectly shaped thigh. "I have rent to pay."

The more he thought about that night he'd walked her home, the more her hole-in-the-wall studio apartment bothered him. He would have expected her to live better if she was a part of some underground operation. Of course, she could also be one of those fanatics who donated every penny to "the cause."

It chafed Nunez relentlessly that he had yet to identify what the hell cause that might be or if she was even tied in. For all the military men disappearing, there should have been an identifying end result, a particular faction growing smarter or richer.

"Do you always walk home after work?"

"Why is that your business?"

Smart woman. But he was smarter, and damned if it didn't look like she was softening up for some conversation tonight. "I am trying to be chivalrous."

"Chiva-what?" Her forehead puckered. "This word I do not understand."

"Chivalrous. It means being courteous—"

The furrows deepened. Zero comprehension.

He searched for another word. "Being polite, helpful."

"Ah, helpful." When she smiled, her Slavic eyes narrowed nearly closed. Sexy. Sultry. "Can a woman be this . . . uh . . . chivalrous?"

"The word traditionally applies to the way a man acts to a woman."

She nodded, smile fading, eyes fully open and wary again. "Interesting word."

Sometimes he hated the freaky-weird ability he had of reading others' emotions. Right now he really hated it, because he knew without question chivalry was an alien concept to Anya Surac.

"I would like to call you a cab." Gage would be fine for ten minutes, and if he wasn't, Nunez would hear the duress word in his earpiece and come running.

"I do not have the money."

"You always walk home, even if you work the last shift?"

She nodded.

Anger kicked him in the gut, too hard, too fast, especially for a man who never lost it. "The bar closes at two o'clock in the fucking morning."

A smile tapered her eyes. "I believe your language is not chivalrous."

His language also was too Mike Nunez and not nearly Miguel Carvalho, a dangerous slip he wouldn't let happen again. "My apologies."

"Accepted." Her grin stayed this time.

He liked it . . . too much. He needed cool and level.

"Please let me make it up to you by walking you safely home." His ear set let him know Gage was wrapping things up for the night anyway.

Kutros was hitting on a hooker.

Nothing more held Nunez in the Oasis tonight, and something—someone—very compelling called him to leave. He waited on an answer that became more important than it should. She was a link to his case. A link to Chuck Tanaka.

She hitched her purse over her shoulder. "In the spirit of giving your chivalry a try, I accept."

TWELVE

Jimmy tried like hell to keep his steps even on the way to his base quarters, but there was no denying the truth. Antialcohol meds be damned, he had a buzz worthy of any frat rush.

He braced a hand on the corridor wall, the evening at the Oasis rolling through his mind as fast as the floor undulated beneath his feet. When he left, Nunez had still been at the bar waiting around for some waitress. Not a bad gig, getting to flirt with pretty women.

If it weren't for the fact any of those women might be out to slit your throat. Now, that was a sobering thought.

The tile floor steadied under him, and he picked up speed rounding a corner, the hall empty and silent other than the low drone of the television in the commons room. He welcomed the chance to help find their friend, and he wasn't exactly a novice at this sort of thing. He'd done plenty of "spooking around" in the military test world. Secret meetings with heads of state for briefings on new test projects. Traveling to other countries for additional meetings with generals overseas.

Patience paid off, and all things told, this op would move fast. Of course, Nunez had laid the groundwork over time, investigating other missing soldiers, until finally the break came with Chuck and his tracking device.

They were so close now, if the tracking info could be believed. Nunez assured him they had people on the ground searching Adana for human intel. Any day they could be launching a rescue.

He glanced inside and found Chloe, sitting alone, barely dressed.

She pulled a baby wipe from a container and swiped it along one arm, then over another. His pulse throbbed in his ears.

Okay, to be fair, she wore more clothes than the rock star chick usually draped over strategic body parts. But for Chloe, the shape-hugging white tank top and cut-off khaki shorts made for Daisy Duke–fantasy material that turned him inside out at a time when his defenses were seriously compromised.

Was it her dry wit or her sarcastic putdowns that drew him to her? Had to be her refreshing honesty that never failed to knock him flat. All that starch wrapped up in a pretty package. A pretty package with some serious issues he wasn't sure he could handle. A wise man would retreat and regroup. Mars, god of war, however, insisted retreat was for sissies.

His drunken feet carried him the rest of the way into the room. "Anything good showing on the Armed Forces Network?"

Chloe twisted at the waist to face him. She held up her hands. "Stay back. I'm in dire need of a date with a shower and my lavender soap. I smell like a compost heap doused in baby powder."

"I seriously doubt that."

Her eyes glinted, and not in a good way. She was still pissed over the way he'd pulled back in the cab after she told him about her kidney transplant. He'd been a jackass. He just wasn't sure he could do any better now.

He did know that against all better judgment, he wanted to be here with her now. He didn't want to think about Chuck and what could be happening to him. He didn't want to think about his own time as a POW.

Jimmy dropped onto the leather recliner by the sofa. Distance was good. Undoubtedly he smelled like a smoky bar and a vat of beer. He'd made use of the bathroom sink to wipe down as best he could. Not as clean as he would like when stepping into the room with Chloe, but a definite improvement over his sweaty self earlier. He couldn't go too far in self-sanitizing and send up a red flag here that he had access to the outside world.

Chloe rubbed a wipe along the back of her neck, nodding toward the coffee table. "You can commandeer the remote if your masculinity so dictates." She stood. "I'm going to bed."

"Stay," he said without looking at her. Who knew what his eyes might give away about the alcohol—or his past?

"I'm not a dog."

"*Please*, have a seat." He forced the words up his raw throat and risked a glance in her direction.

Confusion flickered across her face before she slowly eased back onto the sofa.

"Thanks." He snagged the control and rubbed his thumb over the buttons without changing channels. Damn straight there was something calming about a remote in his hand. "Having trouble sleeping?"

"Pretty much." She eyed him warily. "I feel rank. My sheets are musty. Inside is cooler but stuffy due to no cleaning. Outside, I just sweat more, which makes inside worse."

"I'm sorry your trip here has been less than stellar. Security should lighten up soon."

"I've been doing my own sightseeing on TV and with all these posters." She reached for the *Touring Turkey* book on the coffee table. "My guide doesn't have much personality, but the details are accurate."

He looked around the room, empty except for scattered furniture, a foosball table, and a magazine rack full of outdated periodicals and a few local newspapers. "Where are all your friends?"

"Everyone ran for cover when two of the dancers had a fight. Steven thinks Melanie's messing around on him, which is ironic, considering rumor has it *he's* cheating on *her*." She leaned forward, elbows on her knees. "But the highlight of the evening?"

"Your group gave an impromptu performance?"

"No, just Livia. She shaved her legs in the sink using a water bottle." A wicked grin lit her eyes. "Your colonel about had a seizure."

"Now, that would have made for some awesome vacation photos."

She pitched the book onto the cushion beside her and pointed to a framed poster of a castle on a small Mediterranean islet west of Adana. "I had planned to see that during my time in Turkey."

He didn't even need to bother reading the caption along the bottom. He'd visited the Maiden's Castle twice as a kid with his grandmother, a relentless tour guide when it came to showing off her homeland.

Chloe scooped up her small pile of wipes and tossed them into the metal can by the sofa. "Do you know the story of the Maiden's Castle?"

He tipped his head back on the oversized recliner and made himself far too comfortable taking a Chloe inventory. He knew he was a little drunk, or he wouldn't ogle her, but he'd used up his ability to put on a show at the bar.

His grandmother had shared the story long before they visited the place together, but he needed to hear Chloe's voice. "Tell me."

"The castle dates back to the twelfth century during the Byzantine era." She reached to the guidebook again and fanned pages with her thumb. "Legend holds that an Armenian king prayed for a daughter. Finally his prayer was answered, but a sorcerer cursed her. Her father was told she would die from a snakebite, so dear old dad built an impregnable castle to keep her safe."

"Looks to me like a person could swim out there." In fact, he knew so, since he'd done it.

"True. However, she died because a snake hid inside a basket of food."

She crossed her legs, tucking her bare feet under her knees and making all too visible the bandage on her leg, reminding him of how close she'd been to danger, of another insidious threat she would live with for the rest of her life as a transplant patient.

He pulled his focus back on her words rather than just the sound of her melodically husky voice.

"I researched the area before coming here, since there would be so little time for sightseeing."

"Maiden's Castle is a rather obscure choice."

"For me, it's not always about seeing the biggest or most popular landmark." She looked down, even though the floor sported nothing more interesting than industrial carpet in need of cleaning. "I believe the experience should speak to the tourist on a personal level."

"My grandmother loved that castle, too."

Her head popped up. "Your grandmother?"

"She was born here."

Chloe bristled. "Why did you let me babble on about the place if you already knew about it? I feel like an idiot."

"I just wanted to hear you talk."

Her eyes widened, and her mouth opened and closed a couple of times before she settled on "Oh."

"My grandmother told me once that she identified with the princess. She wanted to spread her wings beyond her home country. She fulfilled that dream by marrying a U.S. serviceman." He stretched his legs in front of him, getting a little too comfortable with her but at least she was giving him a respite from worrying about Chuck. "Do you feel some kind of connection with the princess, too? Was your father overprotective?"

"He certainly coddled me, especially after my mother died in a car accident. But truth be told, I felt like my illness kept me locked away from the world." She studied her clipped fingernails.

His woozy brain cleared. Fast. This wasn't about tourist spots any longer.

Chloe looked up, face defiant, challenging. "My kidney came from a brain-dead army soldier."

He pushed back thoughts of his sister and bone marrow transplants. Memories of how he'd failed her could freeze him up inside faster than dry ice. "What happened?"

"She survived an improvised explosive device at a checkpoint, even made it back to the States. But the damage was too extensive. That's all I'll ever know. The enormity of her sacrifice still boggles my mind. Such a gift she's given me, and I can't even thank her family."

"So you're here to say thank you. Good on ya." He nodded, once, with a military precision.

A bit of bravado leaked from her, and she blinked fast. "Thanks. It means a lot to me."

He felt lower than dirt after all, since he wanted nothing more than to run like hell from this conversation. "Why did you need a transplant?"

"I developed juvenile diabetes, type one. Over time, diabetes can damage the small blood vessels in the body, including the vessels in the kidneys. About thirty percent of people with type one will eventually have some degree of kidney disease."

"And you were in the percentage."

She might find comfort in the stats and numbers, but

he couldn't distance himself to look at her that analytically. He should have put his sorry buzzed butt in bed instead of thinking he could have a conversation with her about something so personal.

"I received my first transplant at sixteen."

"First?" *Shit.*

"Yes, I've had the surgery twice. My father donated one of his, and I did pretty well for eight years, and then the kidney started failing. We're still not sure why. After two years on dialysis, yes. I received the kidney from the brain dead soldier."

Her eyes watered for the first time since she'd begun her story. Hell, for the *only* time he could recall in a week that would have sent many ducking and running.

"There's no reason I can't continue to be here as long as I control my craving for baklava and take my meds. That was actually why I needed to see the ship's doctor."

"Not . . . allergies," he said, feeling like an idiot for not having taken her more seriously or seeing through her ruse.

"Right. I'm on the standard drugs: tacrolimus, mycophenolate and prednisone. As well as insulin for my diabetes." She wiggled her fingers toward him. "So, poof. Consider yourself cured of your protector disease."

"I just hope you're careful. You've already . . ." He stopped.

Her hands fell to her lap. "Already been through the rejection process once?"

He nodded, frustration, anger, and a god-awful helplessness roiling through him.

Chloe glided up onto her knees and leaned over the arm of the sofa. Before he could blink, she pressed a kiss to his lips, lingered, then sank back before he could do something dumb.

Like roll her flat under him on the sofa, cover her, shield her—take her.

"What was that for?"

"A thank-you."

"What the hell for?"

"For listening." She smiled, more of those tears hovering. "Not sprinting for the door."

Ah crap. That was exactly what he wanted to do.

* * *

Nunez studied the night shadows for hidden threats along the narrow cobblestone road where Anya lived.

She strode beside him, her heels click, click, clicking in time with the droplets of water plopping from an overworked ancient air conditioner jutting out of a window overhead. The scent of grilled kabobs and strong Turkish coffee filled the air even hours after the street vendors had closed down for the day. It pissed him off to think of Anya making this long walk alone every night.

Stopping in front of an orange stucco walk-up, she pulled her bulky key chain from her purse. A pink monkey in a tutu hung from the ring, along with a telescope rod, the kind that unfurled into a foot-long baton for ass whopping. "Thank you for the escort."

"You should have one every night."

"You should not worry about me." She patted her purse, keys jingling in her grip. "I have protection."

"Your gun?"

She leaned toward him and smiled. "I do not really have a gun."

"Ah, so you're packing mace in that bag?" He cocked a brow. "I'm scared."

"I carry my knife." Across from him, she leaned a hip against the iron railing as two men passed, conversing and laughing in another language. "A switchblade, I believe it is called in English."

His mind jetted back to the first time he'd seen her standing down the rowdy army contingent with a surprising strength emanating from her willowy body. "How does a woman become proficient with a switchblade?"

"My aunt taught me how to protect myself from non-chivalrous men."

"Unchivalrous," he corrected automatically, his brain still hitched on a single word that could mean nothing . . . or everything. *aunt*. "Do you live with her?"

"She lives elsewhere, running her own businesses."

"Businesses?" he prodded carefully, watching the play of streetlamps highlight the small tic over one exotic eye, nuances that spoke louder than her words.

"Taverns and nightclubs, like my parents used to run."

He lounged back against the iron railing along her steps, which afforded him a better view of the deep color of her lips, lips free of the artifice of makeup. Was she as guileless through and through? "Why not work for your aunt?"

"Does not every young person want to break free from their family and set up independence?"

"That they do." How damned ironic that he'd resented his parents for the secret childhood they'd forced him to live in the witness protection program, and yet now he spent most of his adulthood pretending to be another person.

"I learned much from my aunt, but the time came for me to leave upper Turkey and Aunt Marta."

Marta. The name he'd been seeking. Well, hell. Mystery solved. He would run a data search in hopes of confirming Anya was Marta's niece, but her words rang true.

"You lived with your aunt? What about your parents?" He studied the tiny stain just below her breasts, a tiny red blot that could be cherry juice.

She fidgeted with her keychain, twirling the ballerina monkey with nervous fingers, so he stayed silent rather than risk pressing her too hard. He would take his lead from whatever she said next.

"I lived with her during my teenage years after my mother and father died."

"I'm sorry about your parents."

"At least I had someone to look after me."

"Your aunt, who runs a tavern and nightclubs."

She eyed him suspiciously before shrugging, her keys rattling an impatient clink. "Yes. She just opened a new one in Istanbul and another up in Stuttgart, Germany . . ." Anya selected a key, looking ready to run. "Well, you get the point."

"The family business expands."

"I knew how to tap a keg before I could ride a bicycle." She dangled her keys in front of him, the tiny monkey in a tutu spinning. "When I was little, I wanted to be a ballerina, not a barmaid."

He weighed whether to believe everything she'd told him, especially when he could tell by the rapid, visible pulse in her wrist how much his questions bothered her. He watched that blue vein throb and tore apart her words for evidence.

There was still a chance Anya might be as innocent as she appeared—or she could be working for her aunt by broadening the network. Either way, he couldn't deny his fascination with a woman who hid her real self as effectively as he did, an intriguing quality in an already sexy woman.

A woman he intended to kiss within the next two seconds.

THIRTEEN

★ _____

Standing on her front stoop, Anya watched the shift in Miguel Carvalho's eyes and knew he intended to kiss her. And she intended to let him.

For the first time, she had the attention of a man with no ties to Aunt Marta, and that stirred her almost as much as the warmth of his mouth settling against hers.

He grasped a lock of hair that had escaped her clasp. He grazed his fingers along the length until his knuckles rested on her jaw.

Miguel attracted her. She could not deny his good looks.

How often she'd admired his dark hair that rested along his shirt collar, begging her fingers to test the texture. Silky seduction or raspy, coarse temptation? Now she knew.

Pure silken sensuality.

She deepened the kiss, noting every detail to remember later. The give of his mouth against hers. The warm sweep of that first taste of his tongue.

Their bodies barely brushed. Still, she caught a whiff of his musky aftershave, felt the muscles along his chest contract beneath his silk shirt. She sensed his restraint, and that touched her more firmly than any frenzied clench. Her fingers crawled up his arms to his shoulders, and she urged him closer.

The strength of his arms banded around her back, luring her to ignore everything else and follow that feeling of sensuality and safety. What a unique sensation: security. She could grow addicted, and he would be leaving soon.

Anya eased away from Miguel and the urge to take this further. She needed to stop and think. Her actions had serious repercussions. While he didn't have connections to her aunt, what did she know about this man? He spent too much money and drank. A lot. Not huge testaments to his character.

Except he also worried enough about a simple waitress to see her safely home.

"Thank you for walking with me." Her heart thrummed an argument with her decision to pull back, her lips still tender from the play of his mouth.

"My pleasure. I would have done so every day."

Except she had been avoiding him, until in a moment of weakness she accepted his offer of help. Just once she didn't want to be alone, seeing shadows shift around her, itching with the sense of being followed. She still was not certain letting him into her life was the right decision. She needed time to think, and she certainly could not think with him standing just two steps down from her, which put them at eye level, his gaze entreating her to stay.

His knuckles trailed her arm. "Are you working at the Oasis tomorrow?"

"I am on the late shift."

"So you go in later."

This sounded like the start of—

"Would you like to go out for an early supper before work?"

"I think I would," she spoke before she could reconsider.

"Then I will see you tomorrow."

She saw the promise in his eyes. She wanted to trust him, but she did not have much experience with people who valued their word. Of course, this whole new start away from Aunt Marta was about leaving the past behind.

Anya fumbled with her keys while Miguel kept his post on her steps, seeing her safely inside. A last-minute debate waged within her over the possibility of pulling him inside after all . . . But no. She knew better than to follow passionate impulses.

Closing the door after her, she let the encounter play out in her mind again. Not much time, all told. Probably a total of thirty minutes since she'd left the Oasis.

She wasn't sure what had brought about his change from distant chivalry to aggressive pursuer, but she didn't doubt her ability to read men. Miguel wanted her.

Her aunt had instructed her well. *Aunt Marta.* Even a thought of her formidable relative seemed to swell through the room like the woman's cloying cologne.

Anya hated the pinch of disloyalty but couldn't ignore it. She owed her aunt for housing and feeding her after she'd been orphaned at eleven. A time of disillusionment seared into her memory. Like the day she had learned her family made their living from something other than serving up drinks.

Her parents had been dead for a month when a boy at school had shoved her into the school bathroom. Other boys had been waiting. They'd taunted her, encircling her, shoving her from one to the other. Each tore at her clothes or stole a grope.

The message? Tell her aunt that a new family ruled the neighborhood. She hadn't been raped, thanks to the intervention of a teacher who'd heard the noise, but she'd felt violated all the same.

Face still streaked from her tears, she'd informed her

aunt. Rather than consolation, she'd received an initiation talk. Time to join the family business. Work for food. Run packages, because who would suspect a kid? Then as a teen, use her femininity to distract men into spilling information.

Her aunt had never explained how she was supposed to feel about that. The focus of discussions had always been on what the man wanted and never what she might want. She had bought into the family indoctrination for years. She had transported drugs and information. She had let men she did not admire into her bed just to have someone hold her. She had done everything Marta Surac asked, even at the expense of her heart.

Right up until the day her aunt had demanded she pull the trigger.

* * *

A light from the open door knifed across the dark cell, giving Chuck his first peek at his new "home" since those goons had tossed him in a couple of hours ago. From what his rattled brains could tell, it wasn't much different from the last cell, or the one before that. They moved him often now.

The cement wall had sure as shit hurt just as much as the others when his back slammed into it. His shoulder still throbbed, probably broken. He could feel blood from the scrape sticking to his shirt.

Right over the tracking device.

He hurt too much to care anymore. Chuck simply sat and waited. He no longer had enough control over his body or mind to do anything more. They'd broken him.

The woman—he'd actually heard someone call her Marta, a tiny nugget of information he couldn't do a thing with—strode across the room and knelt beside him, her pencil-thin skirt pulled tight around her thighs, her heels eye level from his vantage point sprawled on the floor.

Her perfume swamped his nose. Her round face and soulless eyes swam in and out of focus. She didn't bring water anymore.

He wanted her knife. To use on her and then himself. But one of her goons stood at the door with fists and gun in clear sight.

"I am beginning to doubt your usefulness, Airman Chuck."

B.F.D. Like that mattered to him now.

"Help me, and I will make sure your family has a body to bury. Continue on this ridiculous path, and no one will find the pieces of your corpse."

He didn't have any family. But he did have friends. His air force buds must have been working their asses off for the past two weeks . . . Had it really only been such a handful of days? He couldn't be sure, as he lost track of time, never sure how long he'd been unconscious.

How many programs would they have to reevaluate or scrap because they couldn't be sure if he'd cracked? Would he have a chance to let them know he hadn't spilled anything?

Would that stay true if Marta kept at him much longer?

"Your shoulder appears painful."

"No . . . shit . . . Sherlock."

She laughed, smoothing her hand over his back, along the bloody, torn shirt. "I like men with spirit. Maybe there's some life in you yet."

She frowned, pausing. Her fingers glided back to the split in the shirt and skin from where a jagged patch of wall had torn away his flesh. She prodded, gently, but still her touch stung his raw wound.

"What is this?" Her voice lost its phony-ass affectation of friendliness as her finger circled . . . right over his tracking device.

Damn.

Her knife flashed in the stark light of the overhead bulb. She pressed the steel tip into his shoulder and prodded. Fire scored his back. As the bitch continued her search, he bit down a shout to a groan.

Head cocked, she cradled her "prize." No squeamishness on her part. He wished he could say the same for himself as his stomach tumbled over itself in a death spiral.

She thumbed away blood until silver peeked through. "Interesting. I might have thought it just a piece of flak, but there is a symmetry and warmth to the piece." She lifted her hand. "I don't suppose you want to save us both some trouble and just tell me what it is?"

"It's . . . an identification chip." The lie rasped along his throat, raw from lack of water. He barely recognized his own voice anymore. "It allows my body to be identified if . . . I suffer an injury in combat," he gasped for air, "that destroys my face or prints." Would she accept his explanation?

"Very smart. I would press you for more, but you require so much work. My people can analyze this."

He could only hope whoever her "people" were, they wouldn't be able to detect the device's properties, such as broadcasting life support data. Which now had been halted. *His* people would think he'd died, and they didn't even have a way to search for his body. Resolve seeped from him, exhaustion filling the void.

His journey had finally finished.

FOURTEEN

Marta punched in the security code to the garage attached to the small holding house on the outskirts of Adana and drove inside.

She turned off the engine, slid her arm through a grocery sack, and snagged her purse that held the plastic container with her "find" from the airman's back. Still she could feel the warmth of the small silver chip between her fingers.

It's purpose, however, iced her.

Marta swung her legs out and hip-bumped the door closed again. The engineers on her payroll had informed her that the chip was some sort of high-tech tracking device like none they'd ever seen. All her work moving the captive from Istanbul to Adana may have been fruitless.

Of course, if the device worked perfectly, he would have already been found. Apparently its signal was low-power. The technicians she'd worked with in the past assured her they could either disarm it or boost the signal if she wished to lead those on the other end to her. Eventually she hoped this would bring her a pretty penny from a contact she'd cultivated in China.

For the moment, the device had been temporarily disarmed until she could revamp her plans, starting with sending Erol on an "errand." At least something could be gained from her decision to keep Chuck alive that one more week, a week now nearing its end.

She climbed two steps and tapped in the code for her second layer of security. Baris had his own assignment checking on Anya. How naïve that the girl just thought she could leave. No one left the family business. Anya had been fed and supported for years. She owed loyalty and help.

Marta avoided the wall mirror. Her looks wouldn't hold out forever. Although thanks to the whole American urban cougar phenom, she could draw younger men in for a while longer.

She entered the kitchen in what looked like an unassuming little haven for an unassuming family. Belowground, however, she kept her latest "guest" in a cellar tricked out for persuading prisoners. Erol sat at the small wooden table, licking chicken from his fingers as he feasted on a carcass.

Marta dumped the sack on the counter and sifted through the fresh fruit and bread to pluck free a new disposable phone. It was imperative she keep up a steady stream of untraceable communication with her people.

She slid the phone across the scarred wood table. "I have a job for you."

His eyes lit with avarice as he snatched the phone a second before it reached the edge. His frustration over Baris's preferential treatment in receiving assignments had been ill-disguised. Idiot. He really did not understand how to best wield his assets and power.

She opened her purse. "I need you to transport something."

His face crumpled with disappointment, quickly followed by anger. "I am being demoted to your delivery boy?"

"You are what I pay you to be," she snapped. Then she calmed. Men needed their egos stroked more often than their privates. "This little container is extremely valuable, and your mission will be quite dangerous. I will understand if you do not wish to undertake such a risky task."

His shoulders braced, his chin thrust. Predictable. "What will I be delivering?"

She resisted the urge to snap again. Why could they not simply follow orders? Always the questions, questions, questions. She had people in her operation willing to organize a suicide bombing attack, for heaven's sake. What she asked of Erol was positively benign in comparison to the irons she already had in the fire.

Marta held up the container and opened the lid to display the silver chip, about the size of an almond sliver. "I discovered this embedded in our captive's shoulder. My technicians reassure me it can still transmit a low power signal. We will turn it back on again at the right time. I will be moving our captive east, and you will be traveling with this package to the north to lead authorities astray."

Erol's first stop would be to meet up with one of her techie wizards who would increase the signal pulse that had apparently been hampered somehow by implantation. She already looked forward to the amount of money she could make from this piece of innovation on the black market. With more information gathered about the device, perhaps she could even launch a bidding war.

Wealth and power—she would never be without them again. Luckily for her, she'd discovered that brokering information internationally proved far more profitable than the small-time neighborhood power ploys her family had used for generations.

Meanwhile, leading military personnel around on a wild-goose chase as she tested their strengths and weaknesses would be quite fun. Not many things in her life brought entertainment. She would savor this.

Marta patted Erol's cheek, flashing him a glimpse of

her breasts in her low-cut satin jacket. He licked his lips in a disgusting display of his tongue. Why did men think that gesture was a turn-on?

Uncle Radko had done the same as the drunken fool lurched toward her, grabbed her, plastered his wet mouth against hers. Once he died, she had wanted to cut his tongue from his head. Instead, she'd stolen his cigar clipper to remind herself of the importance of power, of control.

"Soon, Erol. Soon." She held still and let him stare his fill while believing his turn with her would come after the mission.

In reality, he merely neared his turn to die.

He'd outlived his usefulness and proven to be an unreliable, weak employee. She preferred Baris, anyway. Odd, because she couldn't remember a time when she wanted one man over another, but these past few days had been different, somehow. A flicker of worry flamed through her, one she quickly snuffed. She could manage a simple case of hormones with the same efficiency she handled everything else.

First, she needed to move Baris as well before he spent too much time in close contact with the pretty Anya. Her charms were better used elsewhere. The girl thought she'd been so crafty in staging her escape. Little did she know, Marta had made sure that particular job opened with the best pay in order to lure Anya exactly where she needed to be: in place for Marta to investigate the security around a USO community. She already had a top bidder in Iran interested in attaining that information before the popular entertainment group left Turkey.

The time had come to launch her ultimate test.

* * *

"Damn it, I want to be on that flight." Jimmy restrained the urge to pound the mission planning table. Losing control wouldn't help make his case with Lieutenant Colonel Scanlon.

They'd finally gotten a solid lock on Chuck's tracking device, finally had a concrete mission to fly with a chance of rescue. Rescue, not just a body recovery.

He chose to believe the vital signs detector had merely shorted out, which channeled more power to the signal when it resumed. He filed the possibility away for future testing.

Right now, however, he could only think of locating Chuck.

Lieutenant Colonel Scanlon folded the mission chart in front of him. "We have enough pilots. Vapor and I can handle the stick. You're already tapped elsewhere, Captain."

"But if Chuck isn't even around here—"

"Nunez still thinks part of the network responsible for taking Chuck works out of the Oasis. That's the reason we started here in the first place."

Vapor snagged his helmet bag from the ground. "Hey, be grateful you're getting out of this place for a while. Maybe you can grab a shower. You're really getting ripe, pal."

Jimmy ignored Vince and stayed focused on the colonel. "Are you ordering me to stay, sir?"

"If that's what it takes, but I suspect that won't be necessary."

"Of course, sir."

"Jimmy"—the colonel rarely used first names, usually opting for the rank or call sign—"you're a hell of an officer, focused and talented, but you can't be everywhere at once. Push that drive too far, and you'll burn out before you become a general. And make no mistake, I predict a star in your future."

That was one fat-ass bone to wave under a guy's nose, but stars weren't going to keep his friend breathing.

"I just want Chuck found alive."

Scanlon clapped him on the shoulder. "You need to accept it may be too late. But damn it all, we *will* bring him home."

He wanted to believe that, except the thought of Socrates' empty grave told him the fallen didn't always make it home. Jimmy resigned himself to the inevitable. He wouldn't be on this flight. He had another mission to perform.

Still, his slacks and bogus silk shirt he had to wear itched a reminder of his more comfortable flight suit.

Jimmy powered down the corridor toward the glowing Exit sign. Outside he would hook up with a small contingent of Nunez's CIA paramilitary dudes wearing civvies and looking like airmen out on the town, too. They would watch his back and gather intel around him.

He cleared the doorway near the small lot of official buses. At the end of the row waited two rental cars, one for him and one for Nunez's men. He picked up his pace toward the cars. Heat enfolded him in an oppressive blanket.

A body rammed into his chest, someone short and curvy, with a whiff of baby powder.

"Chloe."

She stared up at him, squinting in the late afternoon sun. "You've been tough to locate lately."

He wouldn't exactly say he'd been hiding since their discussion about her transplant, because that would be wrong. He'd just been slammed with work. Right? "Why aren't you with the rest of your group?"

"I've been trying to find you for the past hour." She flattened her palm to stop him from forging past. "What's going on around here?"

"What do you mean?" he hedged, eying the parking lot where he expected his "drinking buddies" to show up soon.

"Everyone's in a frenzy. Plowing through the halls. Extra cops everywhere I turn." She waved her hand toward the military personnel weaving in an out, security high due to the threat and the impending flight. "Just look around."

Time to divert her attention. "They must have heard there's been a new shipment of baby wipes at the Base Exchange."

"Not amused." Her lips pulled tight. "I thought we reached an understanding last night that we would be honest with each other. I've held up my end of the deal telling you huge and private pieces of my life. Answer me this one question, please."

The last thing he needed now was to worry about her, too. Analysis of the navy speedboat wreckage indicated a bomb had been planted, making the military or the USO the target. While Nunez's time was being devoted to finding Chuck, the base security had a whole other mission looking into who might want to disrupt a peaceful group of entertainers.

Why didn't the higher-ups just cancel this ill-fated USO tour and send the people home? "People are busy with repairs. Water lines should be running again within a couple of hours."

"So I hear, but I'm not worried about my next bath. Damn it, Jimmy, I know you're avoiding my question. I'm worried about—"

The rest of her sentence played out in his mind and kicked him in the gut. "Me? Don't be. This is what I do, and I'm good at it."

"Crying shame you have such self-esteem issues." Her green eyes snapped with anger, and she had a right.

He was dodging her questions. He'd been dodging *her* rather than risk hurting her by saying the wrong thing.

"You have to realize I can't talk to a civilian about military business." He gripped her shoulders, her soft flesh giving beneath his hands.

Soft and vulnerable.

He stole a look over his shoulder at the fence separating the base from the threats in the outside world. How many pipe bombers or car bombers or suicide bombers waited for their shot at the U.S. stronghold on foreign soil?

Nunez's people were scrambling to discover any possible connection between the bomb in the marketplace and the stepped up violence against servicemen and servicewomen. In Jimmy's head the events had to be tied. Clearly, the suicide bombers had targeted the military in choosing a watering hole well known for its service member patronage, followed by an explosion outside Incirlik's front gate. Given that all the supposedly AWOL personnel had disappeared in this corner of the world—

Chloe snapped her fingers in front of his face until he looked down at her again. "Is there going to be another attack on the front gate? Is the power going to be blown next? Or the whole base? I believe I have a right to know that much."

"I don't have any reason to think so." He tightened his hold. "But I want to stress how important it is for you and your USO friends to stay on this side of the fence."

She met his eyes dead-on. "You're going to tell me to leave, aren't you?"

His fingers flexed on her shoulders, and before he could think, he pulled her in for a kiss. Yeah, he needed to feel her softness against him.

She tasted like toothpaste and something more, something unmistakably *her*. He knew intellectually that the upcoming mission had him pumped with adrenaline, which spiked his sex drive. But it was more than that. His arms tightened around her, wanting her, needing to keep her safe.

He suddenly remembered her scar and what it meant. He backed off. "Are you okay? Did I hurt you?"

His gaze dropped to her side, the place where he'd seen her transplant scar after the marketplace explosion.

She took his hand from her shoulder and drew it to her side, sliding it under her shirt to rest on a thin, puckered line of scar tissue.

He fought the urge to tug away. He hated himself for being a lowlife bastard and letting his own screwed-up business show around Chloe. For some reason he still didn't understand, he couldn't walk away from her.

"Jimmy, I know that some folks get freaked out by this. I don't agree with people who think that way, and I'm not even sure I can respect their feelings. However, I do accept it's a reality I have to live with, since this is the only way I *can* live."

Jimmy angled closer to her, dodging her eyes by resting his cheek against hers. "My sister had leukemia as a teenager." He swallowed hard. "She died while waiting for a bone marrow donor."

Her hands slid up to squeeze his arms. "I don't know what to say other than I'm so sorry."

"I shouldn't let it mess with my head around you."

"I can see how you would look at me and think of your sister given how we've both faced such major health problems."

He lifted his head and locked eyes with her. "You've only got a part of that right. Jenny's death may have left me with baggage about protecting women, but when I look at you, my thoughts are anything but brotherly."

He let all the heat he was feeling shine through—no barriers there and no chance of acting on it out here. Chloe's eyes widened in surprise, then answering heat. Strong. Tempting.

Dangerous to his concentration.

He broke away. "I really have to go."

A tentative smile tugged at her mouth in time with the confusion now flickering across her face. "Go save the world."

"Catch ya later, maestra." Jimmy dodged around her before he could be tempted to stick around, because, well, now that he looked, two of his CIA "companions" were already waiting for him.

"Jimmy?"

He glanced over his shoulder but didn't turn to face her. "Yeah?"

"Whatever you're doing, be careful."

This woman definitely jabbed a weakness in him. She drew him in a way he couldn't recall any other woman managing so quickly. He had to keep things light until he figured out where—if anywhere—they could take this.

Jimmy reached in his pocket for his keys and winked. "I'll bring you back some baby wipes."

FIFTEEN

No one could totally wipe away his or her own existence. He should know. He was an expert at erasing his identity as much as humanly possible.

Sometimes Mike Nunez just needed a hint of where to look for the connection. Luckily for him, Anya Surac had provided more than a hint. By listing a few of Aunt Marta's bars, Anya might as well have given him Map-Quest directions to others.

A few clicks through top secret land on his laptop had filled in the blanks. Parked in his cover-story hotel room in downtown Adana, he typed through the log-out menu to exit the NSA site and layer a Carvalho menu in place in case anyone tried to break into his computer.

Only one tiny piece of himself remained: a screen saver depicting a garden meditation labyrinth. He'd chosen an image of one in Spain to tie into his current cover, if anyone turned on his computer. He resisted the urge to lose himself in the twists and turns of the unicursal path. The time for release would come when this mission ended, and he left this upscale luxury behind in favor of his own spartan apartment in D.C.

Nunez stuffed his wallet into his back pocket and strapped his Glock to his calf. Marta Surac was, in fact, Anya's aunt. The woman owned eleven bars under different names. Two of them she shared ownership with none other than a corporate conglomerate that traced back to Spiros Kutros.

Interesting that the man had never mentioned Anya was his partner's niece or about his other holdings. His and Marta's joint and individually owned clubs were scattered through Turkey, Greece, and a handful of small countries in Eastern Europe, all situated near a military base or consulate.

Follow the money. It always painted a green path straight to the bad guys—or gals.

Almost certainly Chuck Tanaka had been stashed in Pasha's Palace in Istanbul, but for some reason the woman was moving him frequently. First south, on the outskirts of Adana, and now the tracking device indicated a northeast locale, deeper into the countryside.

All of which his people would investigate with the help of Lieutenant Colonel Scanlon's flight.

Nunez needed to get his head on straight for another night at the Oasis, laying the groundwork for Jimmy as a target—with Anya there in the possible line of fire. She appeared to be innocent in her aunt's business dealings, but he couldn't ignore her association with one of Marta Surac's bars.

He flicked his wrist to check the time. If he didn't get his ass in gear, he would be late meeting Anya for their supper together. Nunez locked his room and rode the luxury lift down to the lobby. The velvet-lined doors parted to reveal Spiros Kutros standing by a towering grandfather clock, his bodyguard nearby.

Nunez shoved his hands in his pockets to restrain himself from grabbing the gun strapped to his calf, pressing it to Kutros's temple, and demanding that the bastard talk. Adrenaline gushed through his veins as the op's momentum gained speed like a snowball rolling downhill, growing as everything came together. He could all but hear the thunder in his ears.

"Carvhalo," Kutros called, crossing to pass him a piece of paper, a printout with the hotel logo along the top. "I have covered the bill for your stay here thus far, plus an additional week."

"*Gracias*, but you did not need to do that." Even though that was exactly the bait Nunez had hoped the man would take.

"I know." Kutros clapped him between the shoulder blades. "I sense in you a kindred spirit, and I understand how inconvenient pride can become."

Nunez let Kutros play out the game. Sources indicated that the man had been very busy over the past three days checking into Miguel Carvalho's finances, which included a carefully constructed collapsing portfolio and a penchant for skirting the law.

Kutros had every reason to believe Miguel Carvalho was a flat-broke crook. The CIA and NSA had spread information building his playboy cover story well. All of which should bring him to the final stage in reeling the man in and saying good-bye to this region of the world. And Anya?

His adrenaline rush evaporated faster than if his snowball hit hell.

Nunez folded the invoice in half, then quarters. "I will pay you back."

"Of course you will." Kutros gestured toward two claw-footed chairs tucked beside a gold fountain conveniently sloshing loud enough to dull conversation. "I have some business ventures that have proved profitable in the past. If you're interested."

"I'm interested in listening." He took a seat, back to the wall for a better view of the bustling lobby full of tourists and bellhops pushing loaded luggage carts. The revolving door gusted the cigar smoke from the hookah bar across the street.

Kutros stretched his legs in front of him. "My work isn't for the squeamish."

"I am only nauseated by the thought of bunking in three-star accommodations."

Kutros threw his head back with a bellow laugh that echoed up to the gilded dome ceiling. "Definitely a kindred spirit."

Nunez waited. The less a person said, the more others spoke. And revealed.

"Do you have plans for this evening?"

Shit. Anya. Their supper date. He should be halfway to her place by now, but he couldn't afford to let this opportunity pass. "What do you have in mind?"

Kutros pushed to his feet. "Let's go to a place where we can talk freely. I will have supper catered. If you are on board, you will be a richer man before the night is over."

That fast? Of course they would move that fast, because once Miguel entered that world, there was no leaving. If he turned down the offer, he might as well sign his death warrant. Those who knew even the smallest details of these kinds of plans could only comply.

Nunez stood and gestured toward the revolving door spilling out of the hotel and closer to this mission's end. "Lead the way. You've piqued my curiosity."

"I am pleased to hear that." Kutros smoothed the fine fabric of his suit jacket over muscles surprisingly pumped for a man of leisure, especially for one who kept a bodyguard lurking nearby at all times. "You've chosen well. I'm going to make you very wealthy before you see forty."

"I cannot think of anything that would make me happier."

Starting now, Miguel Carvalho could only surrender to

the inevitability of becoming the evil he worked to bring down. What a difference a few days and indiscriminate spending could make.

And Anya? He wouldn't have time to meet her and didn't have a number to call. On the positive side, if she was innocent, he intended to do his damnedest to keep her clear of the action. However, if she was in collusion with her aunt? Then he would almost certainly see the beautiful Anya at the shakedown.

Because if his instincts were right, tonight he would kidnap Jimmy Gage.

* * *

Captivity sucked.

Chloe huffed a lank curl off her forehead as she rolled off her bed and to her feet. Her iPod thunked onto the carpet. Not even Debussy's entire body of work could bring a woman peace when she was this cranky.

How much longer until security concerns eased, and they could carry on with the performances? Maybe she should just go home after all and sign on for another USO trip later.

Except Jimmy wouldn't be around for the next tour.

Cranking open the window, she inhaled the fresh air to ease the encroaching claustrophobia. Surely if she blasted the AC and opened a window, she could achieve the best of both worlds in a cooler but aired-out bedroom.

As it stood now, her small space with a double bed and desk grew more oppressive by the second. From the heat and kitchen smells weighting down the air, of course. Not because she'd spent the past four hours chewing her nails to the quick worrying about Jimmy, a situation she could do nothing about. So she focused on what she could fix: her smelly room.

A gentle breeze drifted inward and over her, carrying the soothing scent of spring blossoms. Oh yeah, pump that window wider. Chloe stuck her whole upper body through and into the small courtyard. Security lights played off the pink and deep purple flowers. She thought about plucking blooms to scent her room, but the rustle of night creatures in the bushes kept her hands firmly planted on the windowsill.

A movement outside, larger than from any rodent or animal, startled her back into her room. Then curiosity drew her forward again. The sill bit into her palms as she squinted to peer into the dark, and yes, someone was darting around trees. Her stomach knotted. She cranked the window closed again, her body already stretching toward the door so she could alert security.

The intruder sprinted across a bare patch of lawn, under a lamppost. Chloe relaxed.

Livia.

Everybody seemed to have somewhere to be tonight. Chloe tugged a peasant shirt on over her tank top and khakis, and shoved her feet into sandals, hopping on one foot, then the other on her way to the door. She cleared the exit without finding a guard in the hallway. She shivered at the possibility that they might all be on call for whatever dangerous mission Jimmy was off to tonight.

Hopefully they were just outside, checking on Livia. Chloe searched the courtyard. Livia sprinted toward the other side. Holy cow, she sure made speedy time in heels and a dress. Oversized Gucci shades nearly swallowed her face.

Shades? At night?

"Hey, Livia," Chloe called into the dark. "What are you doing?"

The diva pirouetted on her spiked pumps and promptly grabbed a tree for balance. She reached down to pry her high heel out of the sandy lawn. "Getting out of this place."

"You're going home?" Chloe strode closer, drawn to

the kind of person who could spring herself from captivity, elude the guards, and wander through the base alone at night.

"Just out." She smoothed a hand over sleek black hair pulled back in a bun, the going style for all the females in need of a serious shampoo. "I finally have a moment free of my colonel guard."

"He stays near you for a reason, as do the rest of the security personnel." She scanned the area for their guards, who were apparently all taking a break. In fact, the whole courtyard and small lot were deserted, other than a lone car rumbling a few feet away.

Livia fluttered her ringed fingers through the air. "Those people, I can lose easily enough. I have been doing it for years. Go back to your room and stop worrying about me."

The pop star charged past a row of palm trees to a parking lot behind their quarters. She made a beeline toward the black Mercedes chugging exhaust into the night, a driver silhouetted behind the wheel, the backseat empty. Chloe hotfooted after her, only just managing to catch up.

"Stop." She grabbed Livia's model-thin arm as she opened the back door. "What about the café bombing? Don't you care about your safety, or the people who could be hurt trying to protect you?"

Chloe lowered her voice and nodded toward the bearded man behind the wheel, puffing away on a thick cigar. He sure as hell wasn't wearing a military uniform. "Do you even know that you can trust this driver?"

"I believe this is like that saying about lightning never striking the same place twice. I have already survived a terrorist attack. I am now safe from that coming my way again."

"If that's the case, why don't we just send you into Al-Qaeda camps and let you negotiate a peace treaty, since you're so immune?"

Livia shrugged free of Chloe's grasp. "I may not speak perfect English, but I can detect sarcasm. No one asked for your help. Now be a nice little rule player and go back to your room."

"Apparently I don't have a lock on the sarcasm market. Please, listen. It's not about the rules. I'm being a good friend like you've been to me."

"I appreciate your concern." Livia's face softened. "I only want a real shower. I'm tired of shaving my legs in a sink with bottled water. I will be back and tucked into my bed before the colonel even notices I am gone."

Chloe plumbed her brain for some kind of rebuttal. Livia might be a diva, but she'd never been a dunce. Until tonight.

Headlights striped in the distance. Some help. Thank God.

"*Merda!*" Livia's curse split the air as a cop cruiser crested a hill. She gripped Chloe's wrist and jerked. Chloe tumbled into the car. Livia slammed the door closed behind her.

"Why did you—"

"Drive," Livia ordered the man in front before turning to Chloe. "The police were coming. You left me no choice but to bring you along."

"You've got to be joking."

Nobody laughed.

Chloe tapped the driver on the shoulder. "Sir? Please, sir? I would like to get out of the car."

The chauffeur glanced up to meet her eyes in the rearview mirror. "No English."

Tires squealed as they peeled rubber out of the parking lot, only to slow to the posted base speed limit. If only he would do something reckless so the security cops would pull them over, but no luck.

"Stop. *Durmak*?"

The driver didn't respond to the Turkish request, even though no how, no way could he have missed her intent.

Fine then, she would just get out next time he . . . slowed . . . for a corner. She reached for her door handle and yanked.

No luck again.

Her stomach clogged her throat. She pumped the latch repeatedly. Nothing happened.

Chloe sagged back in her seat, icy hot prickles of fear tingling over her. "You can't expect to kidnap me."

"Kidnap is too harsh a word." Livia clicked her seat belt. "I am simply being a good friend to someone else. Steven, my backup dancer, is stranded drunk at a bar downtown. He's certain Melanie is cheating on him, and he left the base to track her."

"But he's cheating on her."

"That's just a rumor he started in hopes of making her jealous. If anyone finds out he's gone, he could be fired. He has a sick mother to support."

The driver followed posted limits all the way through the front gate while Livia detailed at length the reasons she had to help Steven Fisher. Chloe pounded on the tinted window as they passed the gate guard, but base security were only stopping people coming into base, not those leaving.

She sagged back into the leather seat in defeat as they reached the main road, the driver's cigar smoke already swelling throughout the vehicle. What the hell had she gotten into? Could Livia really be saving some drunk, lovesick idiot?

Or was her friend less trustworthy than Chloe had assumed?

Sixteen

★

Tonight was make or break.

Tension and anticipation kinking his muscles, Jimmy watched the man calling himself Miguel Carvalho weave around Oasis patrons toward him. One of two things would happen once Nunez reached the table. He would offer to buy more drinks, which meant the kidnapping was a go, or he would offer to pick up their tab, a signal that something had gone wrong, so it was time to *bail out, bail out, bail out.*

Carvalho stopped by their table. "Good evening, gentlemen. May I buy you all a round of drinks as thanks for your service?"

A green light.

He'd hoped for prior warning and a briefing at the base before they made contact with the abductors, but he sure as shit wouldn't argue with finishing this sooner rather than later. He squeezed the living hell out of the lime twist in his latest gin and tonic and knocked back the drink.

"Why yes, you may." Jimmy hooked an arm over his new drinking buddy's shoulder: Agent Mike Nunez.

Miguel, damn it. Jimmy shook his head as if that might somehow clear his brain. He had to remember the guy went by Miguel Carvalho.

He half-listened as Carvalho introduced himself to the table full of his own CIA paramilitary. Jimmy pulled a packet of mints from his back pocket and thumbed free two from the slots marked with a nearly indiscernible black dot. He popped the pills into his mouth and let them dissolve, preparing himself with additional drugs designed to counteract truth serums administered later.

"Breath mint?" He offered the packet to everyone else at the table, his cue indicating he understood Miguel's "message." The remaining white tablets were, in fact, simply breath mints.

By the time their drinks arrived, a mild burn tingled along his skin as the drugs grew roots. His stomach kicked over like a bubbling cesspool drawing him under. He could hold onto his secrets if he could stay awake with the mix of drugs and alcohol pumping through his system.

Thoughts of his crew flying without him proved plenty sobering. What if something happened to them? Survivor's guilt already crippled him.

He had to think positively, damn it.

This could all be over by daybreak, thanks to the radar lock on the microchip's signal. He would know if Chuck had survived. That possibility offered hope, as did this sting operation. Even if he wouldn't have the chance to fly with his crew and rescue Chuck, at least he could take a swipe at infiltrating the crime ring from another angle before more service members were snatched. Before national security could be seriously compromised.

Miguel Carvalho took the mint packet from the last of the agents and turned to Jimmy. "The waitresses seem to be overwhelmed. Come with me, and we can place an order for another round at the bar."

Jimmy went along with the charade and waved to his CIA rent-a-buddies at the window table. "Be right back, dudes."

He followed Nunez across the bar, threading through the press of bodies, weaving on his feet just enough to broadcast intoxication. Nunez nodded slightly toward a graying dark-haired man puffing away on a cigar, the same man Jimmy had seen the agent drinking with earlier.

He smacked the back of an empty chair on his way past, which did nothing to vent the pressure cooker expanding inside him. Tension, he could understand, but he hadn't expected dread and didn't understand why. He wasn't afraid, and he had experience.

Except what a time to realize that any dark ops he'd done involved action, aggression even. This passive role, waiting to be taken, chafed.

What had he been thinking signing on to voluntarily be held captive? Had he really been arrogant enough to believe his time in Afghanistan wouldn't roar up and bite him on the ass?

Focus on finding and vindicating Chuck. Afghanistan belonged in his past. Jimmy lounged against a barstool mounted into the hardwood floor while Nunez placed his order at the bar.

"What's your best Greek wine?"

The male bartender squeaked a white rag along a damp glass. "We have a fine selection in our wine cellar. We have a steward on hand if you would like to step in back and sample a couple to make your decision."

Nunez swept a hand to include Jimmy. "Well, my American friend? Would you like to make the choice for your companions?"

Jimmy swayed on his feet and plastered a goofy-ass-drunk smile on his face. "Lead the way."

Ever aware of the Greek's eyes on their progress toward the back of the bar, Jimmy eyed the four steps leading down into a dimly lit corridor. Sconces with low-wattage bulbs illuminated his descent, the air cooling with a cryptlike aura. The setting couldn't be any more obvious.

Nunez's hand fell on his shoulder where it met his neck. "Sorry, my friend."

The agent pinched, his fingers clamping on a major artery. Dots swam in front of Jimmy's eyes. He battled the urge to fight back, elbow or kick, even resort to the rudimentary moves he'd shown Chloe.

Chloe. Unconsciousness narrowed into a pinpoint until his mind's eye could only see her.

Then nothing.

* * *

Expect nothing, and never be disappointed.

Anya knew that but had allowed herself to dream optimistically for a brief weak moment. She hitched her purse higher onto her shoulder on her way to work. In the dark. By herself.

Hunger twisted her stomach. She had waited like a lovelorn idiot for Miguel to show up. Which he never did. Which left her with no time to eat before work. She blinked back tears, hating the weakness. Anya scraped her wrist over her eyes. No man should have that much sway over her emotions.

But ah, hope was bittersweet.

In relocating here, she'd yearned to discover a fresh breed of males from the ones her aunt attracted. Instead, for the past seven months in and out of the bar, she'd endured having her ass slapped, her breasts groped, and her optimism crushed.

Her flickering positive thinking these past few days had been flamed to life by Miguel Carvalho too quickly, too easily. She'd seen all the warning signs of a duplicitous male—the spending, the heavy drinking. She had allowed herself to believe he only did so because he was on vacation and wished to be near her. She must face the truth. She had given too much credence to one kiss.

Anya paused at a corner across the road from the Oasis. She waited for a Mercedes to swoosh past, then started across.

Brakes squealed in the sultry night. She jolted, searching the dark lit only by sputtering shop signs and streetlamps with dirty globes. The black sedan now idled in a narrow side street beside the Oasis. No one exited the vehicle. A wooden door along the stone wall creaked open, and a dark-suited man stepped out of the tapestry shop behind the nightclub.

Someone waiting for a ride. Nothing unusual. How paranoid she had become. Just because a man let her down didn't mean she should see the world as bleak.

A honking horn snapped her attention back to her own path. A tiny Fiat inches away beeped twice more. She raised a hand in apology and finished crossing.

Perhaps she needed to find another job, even if it paid less. She could make a true fresh start with people who didn't lie on a regular basis.

"Help!"

A woman's scream split the night. Anya's hand snaked into her purse, and she gripped her switchblade. Without hesitation, she looked first at the Mercedes.

The dark-suited man leaned half-in, half-out of one back door on the Mercedes, while the burly bearded driver rushed to the other. The slick fellow backed out quickly, his arm looped around the waist of a tiny young woman with black hair. On the other side of the car, the driver leapt away from the vehicle to dodge a pair of dainty feet pedaling straight for his crotch. Two women?

Anya eased into the shadows, out of sight. She knew

better than to interfere. They would only take her, too. She searched for help but found local pedestrians scurried in every direction except the one that would lead to a rescue.

Where was the Oasis's doorman, Omar? Not at his post.

Would he have even bothered to assist? The haughty employee always seemed more concerned with what went on inside the Oasis, rather than outside. She looked back at the unfolding nightmare, not sure what she could or should do but unable to abandon these poor women.

"Release me, you *bastardo*," the small woman shouted with an Italian accent.

God, she felt like a child again, watching from under the bar as her father barked at a waitress. She hadn't known the root of the fight then, only that evil and fear tainted the air. Years later she had learned her father pimped out his waitresses, even his waiters.

The jagged stone wall bit into her back much the way splinters had snagged her skin long ago. The past and present merged in her mind as she watched the two women fight back against unbelievable odds while their captors dragged them toward a door labeled as a drop-off point for a tapestry store. Snippets of the conversation mingled with the sound of honking horns and rumbling trucks.

"No." The skinny woman twisted and jerked in her captor's hold. "No, no, no, you do not understand. I have a friend in trouble. He needs my help."

The other woman shouted in outrage, her wild, curly hair bouncing free from a loose bun. "Don't you realize Steven freaking set you up?"

"*Dio*, no! Steven would never do that."

The larger man backhanded the Italian woman. "Shut up. Both of you."

"Livia?" the woman with a mass of hair said.

"What, Chloe?"

"Run." Her hand snapped behind her to grip the inside of the man's thigh.

Skinny Livia kicked off her strapless heels and bolted toward the alley. The other woman—Chloe—pinched her captor. Hard. Her fingers all but disappeared into his fleshy leg.

He doubled over, screamed in agony, releasing Chloe. She sprinted after her friend.

Anya's grip on her knife eased. It seemed this Livia and Chloe could protect themselves even without weapons.

Chloe raced down the side street. Her hair streamed behind her as she tried to catch up with Livia disappearing around a corner. The dark-suited man leapt over his incapacitated friend and made tracks after the women racing away, taking them farther from Anya.

His arm darted out and he snagged a fistful of blond curls and yanked. "You made a mistake angering us."

Her scream gurgled with outrage and tears. She fell backward. Her hip slammed into the cobblestones, her legs pumping as she struggled for balance that would release the pressure on her hair. An empathetic burn echoed along Anya's scalp.

Chloe shrieked, thrashing in an attempt to free herself. "Help! Help!"

Anya sure could use some of her aunt's street smarts right about now. Marta feared nobody.

"You will find no help here." He tugged Chloe again, looping a length of her hair around his wrist mercilessly as he hauled her up. "Baris?" he called. "Get the hell off the ground and take her while I catch the other one."

Anya's heart pulsed up to her ears. Those poor women could be black market sex slaves by morning if no one interceded. Why hadn't anybody other than her tried to help? Not that she had stepped forward with any great aggression.

Scratching her still-aching scalp, she realized she could not hide in the shadows any longer. Moving away from her family's legacy of crime meant nothing if she passively let malevolence thrive around her.

"No!" Anya started forward, whipping out her knife, flicking the blade free.

Before she could take more than a trio of steps, the bearded man limped forward and threw the woman toward a door, ignoring Anya. They disappeared inside the tapestry store.

Her eyes stung. She had acted too late.

"Oh, God, oh God, oh God," she prayed to a deity she'd rarely had the chance to meet while growing up in the moral void that made up her family heritage. Something she had to rectify now.

She raced into the Oasis and straight to a telephone. She punched in the numbers of the people she'd been trained from birth were the enemy.

Anya's hands trembled as she called the police.

* * *

Ohmigod. After surviving two kidney transplants, an exploding boat, and a terrorist attack, she'd reached the end trying to save someone else.

Chloe forced herself to go limp in the brutally tight grip of her captor, Baris, a bearded bastard who now had a serious grudge against her for pinching his thigh. If he wanted her at the bottom of the cellar stairs, he could carry her every damn step of the way. Not that she was sure she could have walked anyway on her shaky legs.

Please, please, please she hoped Livia managed to escape the other man racing after her and could call for help. The dank stench of mold growing up the walls gagged her. As much as she wanted to lay blame at Livia's pedicured feet, the reasons for staying on base had been clear. She should have dragged Livia away from that car back at Incirlik.

Was this another terrorist incident? If so, there went Livia's lightning theory.

Baris limped to a stop outside a thick metal door. He booted a knock twice fast, three times slow, his steel-toed shit kickers at odds with his sleek suit, hinting at the darker underbelly he obviously possessed. The door creaked open like something out of a B-grade horror flick.

Real-life monsters scared her more than Freddy Krueger.

A smoothly handsome Latino filled the portal. "What is going on here?"

"A special gift for the boss." The driver-turned-villain shouldered past.

She stole a peek back at the guy sporting what looked a lot like a Savile Row suit. He seemed familiar, but she couldn't place where she'd seen him before. He spoke with a Spanish accent, but that didn't do anything to stir her memory.

Desperately she searched for some sign of hope as the guy with arms as thick as her legs carried her deeper into the bowels of this underground maze. Sconces lit the way. They passed racks of wine at an odd angle. The wall of bottles had been pivoted open like a secret door connecting this basement to another chamber. Could it be a possible path to escape?

Voices drifted down the lengthy corridor, becoming clearer as she neared to find a man looming over another man tied to a chair, his back to her. Even from behind, those shoulders looked heartbreakingly familiar.

"What do you know about tracking devices implanted under the skin?" asked a man with a Greek accent.

The man in the chair laughed. "Sounds pretty Star Treky to me."

Her skin prickled, her insides colder than the rapidly dropping temperature in this cave grave. Those shoulders, that voice . . .

Her captor advanced toward the open door and eased her to her feet, while keeping a death grip on her arms.

The Greek even smiled. "A smart-ass. We've seen many of your kind, and your mouth costs you far more than it costs us. I will ask you again."

Diamond pinky ring glinting, the man fisted a handful of hair and yanked back his captive's head.

She bit off a cry. Even with the bruises staining his face, Chloe recognized Jimmy.

SEVENTEEN

★

Of all the gin joints . . .

Bogey's words bounced around in Jimmy's battered head as he took in Chloe standing in the doorway. For a second he'd hoped the "breath mint" drugs were making him hallucinate. Or perhaps it was a reaction to the truth serum they'd injected him with minutes after he'd come to in this cellar jail. He blinked again, and still Chloe stood in the dank room.

How had she landed here? Something must have gone wrong. Way the hell wrong.

Jimmy risked a look at Nunez for an answer. The agent backed deeper into the shadows by the small video camera on a tripod, his eyes narrowed. Nunez seemed to be as clueless as he was about this latest kick in the _cajones_ development.

Even with his limited view of Chloe, he could see the fear she tried to hold in check. He could have kept his head together while they beat him into the ground, but he couldn't stomach the sight of that bastard's hands on her, and far worse would be in store for them if Nunez didn't get them out of this cluster fuck soon.

The hold on Jimmy's hair eased, and he restrained the urge to crank around in his chair for a better look at Chloe.

The pugilist with garlic breath and a Greek accent temporarily abandoned his pummeling to address the bearded goon in the doorway. "Damn it, Baris, you said you would bring the famous one."

"I tried, but this one came along, too." Hairy Barry shoved Chloe deeper into the room. "We lost the Italian babe, and this one fought like hell. Careful. She's an unpredictable bitch."

And Barry was a dead man once Jimmy got free.

The Greek—Spiros, Nunez had called him one night in the bar as they'd walked past—eased around the chair. "You expect me to believe two women overpowered you and my bodyguard? Are you weak or just an idiot?"

Barry's chest heaved, but his tight lips showed some restraint. He limped into the room. "Livia Cicero slipped away while we were restraining this woman. The rock star must have a lot of practice in escaping fans, but your bodyguard is tracking her down."

They'd set up an international celebrity to be snatched? What did that have to do with kidnapping military personnel and trying to beat him into spilling his guts for the camera? Jimmy struggled to put the pieces together in his messed-up mind. Maybe he should have offered Chloe a crash course in ditching the paparazzi rather than his half-assed self-defense course.

Spiros assessed Chloe with a leer. "This one is useless to us." He waved an unlit cigar through the air, his knuckles raw and red. "Have your way with her quickly, then kill her."

Chloe's brave face faltered before resolution set her chin. Her bravado vise-locked pressure against his temples.

"Wait," Nunez stepped out of the shadows. "She may

have an unexpected value. I do believe our guest here likes her."

The screws tightened.

* * *

"You screwed up." Marta gripped the disposable cell phone, pacing around the kitchen of the small safe house. She'd given Baris a mission and help on the ground. She had not given him permission to run rogue. "I won't even ask what you and Kutros were thinking kidnapping such high-profile targets. We're supposed to stay under the radar."

If she understood human nature—and she liked to think she did—Baris had made use of their USO security leak to impress her, and Kutros used Baris in an attempt to generate extra money on the side. She should have assessed their weaknesses better. Kutros would do anything for money, and Baris would do anything for power to feed his feeble ego. It was her fault as the boss for not foreseeing this, a mistake she intended to address.

Baris cleared his throat on the other end of the line. "We're already moving both the man and woman in case anyone comes looking for them."

Poor consolation when they'd already botched and possibly ruined her lucrative business. "Find Cicero before she makes her way back to base." Marta paced, her brain racing with ways to salvage something from this leaking dam of stupidity. "Kill them all and dump their bodies where no one can find them. I do not want to risk anyone finding evidence on their bodies. Burn them if you have to, but do not fail me again."

"Of course," Baris agreed from the other end of the airwaves, a slight huskiness to his tone the only sign he realized his balls were in a vise.

"The singer will *not* make it back to the air base."

"I understand."

"So you say."

Marta thumbed off her cell phone. Her fingers fisted around the cool metal. Incompetent ass. Baris had thought to impress her with his brilliant plan. He'd lured the singer off base with a cry for help from one of the backstage hands, their inside connection, who would be compromised if the Cicero woman made her way back to base and relayed her story.

Why had she trusted Baris with such a sensitive mission before testing him over time as was her standard procedure? Marta flung the phone across the room, chest heaving. She knew why. Her business acumen had been blinded by a surprising lust, which made her every bit as disgusting as Uncle Radko. She resisted the urge to shove away the memory of killing her uncle. Instead, she embraced it and the memory of warm blood between her fingers.

At least Erol would lead the military astray up north, and perhaps Baris might even manage to salvage some valuable information from their new military guest. She eyed the cellar door and thought of her captive. He still lived.

Perhaps she would do well to resurrect some of her old interrogation skills.

* * *

Hands and feet tied with disposable cuffs, Jimmy blinked to adjust his eyes to the cavernous darkness inside the van. Steel flooring offered no relief to his aching body.

He thought he heard someone breathing to his left. "Chloe?"

No response.

The van doors slammed, and the engine rumbled to life. The dashboard lights illuminated two men up front in profile, Spiros behind the wheel and Nunez in the passenger seat. The rice-sized earpiece linked to the one in Nunez's ear stayed silent. Either the two men weren't talking, or the thing had malfunctioned.

Something back in that cellar jail had set the agent and the goons packing fast. Just when Jimmy had thought they were making a breakthrough—if they were asking about a special tracking device, they could well have Chuck—then Chloe showed up, and Baris's phone had rung. Minutes later, Jimmy and Chloe were tossed in the back of a van. It seemed their captors had some other mission to complete before they beat the crap out of them.

At least the relocation provided more time for Nunez to turn this operation back around. Something he'd better do soon, or Jimmy would be taking matters into his own hands.

His vision cleared to a murky gray, just enough for him to discern Chloe lying on her side an arm's stretch away—if he had use of his arms. The steady rise and fall of her chest reassured him, even while countless potential land mines exploded in his head.

What if Kutros pumped Chloe full of the same drug he'd injected into Jimmy right before the interrogation started? With her transplant and regular prescriptions, her body chemistry could catapult out of whack. How long could she last without her medication? Nunez would need to know soon, even if it meant alerting their captors as well.

Jimmy rolled to his back, searching the too-empty van for something to free his hands. Then he could pummel Barry into finding Chuck while Nunez scratched his ass. Thoughts of those bastards aiming their fists at Chloe's vulnerable kidney area dumped acid in his gut.

The driver ground the gears, popped the clutch, and the van lurched forward. Jimmy used the momentum to propel him across the floor toward Chloe. His roll landed him nose to nose with her, and ah hell, but they'd bound her hands and feet, too.

"Chloe?" he kept his voice low, but loud enough to hear over the whoosh of cars zipping past. "Chloe? Are you with me?"

Her lashes fluttered open, confusion darkening her eyes. Her nose scrunched as the smell of reeking oil and rotting food swelled through the close space. "Jimmy?"

He inched closer until his leg pressed against her with as much reassurance as he could offer with his hands bound. "Are you all right?"

The van rattled along the road, jostled in a pothole and slammed them both against the unforgiving floor. Chloe's head thunked against metal. She moaned. He bit back a curse.

When would Nunez make his move? Jimmy needed to keep Chloe as calm as possible until that moment. If the listening devices in their ears were working, then at least Nunez would get a status check on Chloe.

He nudged her feet with his and asked again, "Are you okay? Did any of those punches injure your kidneys? Do you need your transplant meds?" That should provide Nunez with the heads-up he needed—as long as their listening devices still worked.

"Aside from being scared to freaking death?" She shrugged, almost managing to stifle a wince. "Yeah, I'm good."

No amount of truth serums or ham fists could have made him talk. Would he be able to hold as strong if they put the screws to Chloe? What choice did he have if spilling his guts would only ensure their deaths? "How did you and Livia end up outside the base?"

Chloe huffed a curl off her forehead, revealing a bruise just starting to purple up. "I shouldn't have left under any circumstances. You can say I told you so anytime now."

"Pointless." He searched her face as best he could with the dim lighting streaking through as they passed streetlamps. "Why *did* you come chasing after me?"

"The ego roars." Her laugh turned sniffly. "Sorry. Bad joke. I wasn't looking for you. I was trying to keep Livia from leaving the base, and she all but kidnapped me."

Now, that was odd, but hadn't Nunez been concerned enough about Livia to have the commander guard her?

The Greek *had* mentioned the Circero woman while he was twisting a fistful of Jimmy's hair out by the roots. He'd been busy gluing his jaws together so he didn't let a groan slip free in front of Chloe and freak her out. Well, any more than an average woman would be freaked after being kidnapped and then seeing someone pulverized.

But back to the Cicero comment—good God, his mind wandered thanks to all this crap in his system. "Why was Livia trying to leave the base?"

"Something about helping a pal with girlfriend troubles and a sick mother to support. I'm so mad right now, I could kick Livia's tail."

Spunk in the middle of a nightmare. Her take-no-prisoners grit that had so irritated him before struck him as a handy trait right now.

"Jimmy, if you have an escape plan, now would be the time to spill it."

"Sorry, maestra." He couldn't risk telling her about Miguel Carvalho, not when she could be next on the rack.

"What are *you* doing here? What's going on?"

He jerked his head toward the driver, then pinned her with a hard look he hoped she would realize meant he couldn't discuss his presence here. She searched his face through two grinding gearshifts before she gave a small nod of understanding.

"Talk to me, please?" She inched closer, her full lips close enough to kiss. "The dark isn't as heavy when I can hear your voice. Tell me more about your family."

He stole a look at the two men up front. The driver stared straight forward into the dark night. Nunez dropped his arm, palm flattened in an unmistakable "hold your position" signal. Since Nunez had use of his hands and weapons, he called the shots.

Jimmy returned to keeping Chloe calm so she didn't draw undue attention to herself. "I have two brothers."

A crack of thunder sounded just as raindrops tinked along the van roof. A plus or minus for them? Slippery bodies would be tougher to hold on to. Maybe he and Chloe could make their break for it when the van stopped.

She chewed her bottom lip, the plumpness freshly split and swollen in one corner. "And your sister, the one who had leukemia?"

The windshield wipers slapped away rain while he gathered his resolve to wade into a part of his past he rarely revisited, even in his thoughts.

"Jenny was two years older than me. For a while, we thought she would beat the odds. God, she was so fearless, a real fighter."

"Like her brother."

But he hadn't been strong enough. "I was a bone marrow match, and we went the transplant route." He worked his jaws to create saliva in a mouth gone dry from more than lack of water. "She stayed in remission for a full year and a half. Long enough to go to her junior prom."

He didn't want his emotional garbage out there for Nunez to overhear, but keeping Chloe preoccupied was his top priority.

"We were set to try another transplant. The week before the procedure, there was this scouting camp. I wanted to go, really wanted it, especially since I knew I would feel like crap after the surgery."

"Any normal boy would want that trip."

"We didn't have a lot of money for vacations anymore, so sleeping in a tent in the woods with my buddies sounded like nirvana." He looked away from her sympathetic face to the rain streaking down the van window. "I fell into a stream, kind of a waterfall actually."

"What?"

Her question pulled his gaze back to her. "It was the middle of the winter, and I took this dare to walk across stepping-stones in a stream. I got caught up in the current and went over the waterfall. It wasn't all that big."

"Yeah, right." She crinkled her nose. "The thing was probably freaking ginormous."

He shrugged, stifling a wince at the pull to his battered bones. "The pool at the base was deep enough I didn't break any bones."

"You were very lucky."

"Boys think they're indestructible." Except he'd been wrong. "I caught a cold that turned into pneumonia."

Chloe gasped. "The week before your sister's procedure."

"Exactly. I couldn't donate while sick." Her warm green eyes had a way of soothing him, urging him to keep talking, even when the words rasped like crushed glass coming up his throat. "We had to wait a full month before my marrow was safe. We went ahead with the second transplant, but she didn't last long." He clenched and unclenched his fists to restore circulation in his tingling bound hands. "I hate heights to this day. Take me to a rooftop and I'll probably puke like a wimp."

He'd only meant to distract her from fear, and somehow he'd fallen into some kind of confessional. "My folks swore they understood that it wasn't my fault, but things were never the same in our house after Jenny died." His parents had stopped coming to his and his brothers' sports functions, too afraid of running into friends of their daughter. "Holidays sucked most, missing Jenny and watching our mother try to hide her tears."

"Family tragedies have a way of tearing people apart at the very time they should be sticking together." Chloe's voice went husky in the darkening van, the streetlamps farther apart as they seemed to plunge deeper into the countryside.

"How do you understand this so well when my own brothers can barely look me in the eye?"

The rain hammered harder outside, leeching the sparse light, casting shadows over her face. "Before my mom died, she and Dad fought all the time, and I was certain it was because of my health issues. I don't have to explain to you how the bills pile up with a chronically ill child, then add my music lessons on top of everything else. I guess I'm trying to say that I'm certain your sister didn't blame you. Most likely she blamed herself for the problems she thought she brought to the rest of the family."

He hadn't seen the sickness through his sister's eyes that way. Mostly, though, he hated that Chloe had gone through a childhood so packed with heartaches that she could see his hurts so fucking clearly. "When did you lose your mother?"

"In a car crash when I was twelve. She fell asleep at the wheel on her way back from visiting me in the hospital."

He wanted his arms free to scoop her up and comfort this woman who'd already experienced enough pain for three lifetimes. How could her mother put her kid through that?

Her brow puckered a second before her eyes widened. "You jumped out of the back of an airplane into an ocean full of sharks, even though you're scared of heights, to save me."

"I said I was afraid. I never said that would stop me. I had a first-rate example in bravery watching what my sister went through."

Her eyes fell to his mouth, stroking with her gaze as effectively as if she'd kissed him in reality. "That's why you say fear is for the weak. You're honoring your sister."

He eye-stroked her right back. "You got it, maestra."

She understood him too well. A scary prospect. So why had he, a man who prided himself on facing his fears, been running from her?

The van lurched forward faster, jarring him against Chloe. He only hoped they lived long enough for him to explore the rest of that thought.

EIGHTEEN

"Want to take it easy there, Kutros?" Nunez braced his hand against the cracked vinyl dashboard on the cheapo foreign model, determined to control something in a mission going downhill more rapidly than the van. With Chloe Nelson's surprise appearance, he would have to cut his losses once they reached the farm and pray that enough info could be gleaned there. He couldn't afford the luxury of spending time there in hopes of gathering more intel.

"Damn it all, someone is following us." Kutros careened the utility vehicle around a corner on the unlit country road about ten miles north of Adana.

A tail?

Had his operatives come out of their unobtrusive stance? Nunez checked the rearview mirror, and even with the piss-poor visibility of a stormy night, he could see enough. They were being followed, but not by his people.

Two Turkish police cars barreled behind, accelerating at breakneck speed through the sheeting rain. Then sirens blared, lights strobing through the haze. The authorities weren't supposed to make their move until the van reached Kutros's destination.

And the authorities weren't supposed to be Turks.

Forcing his heart rate to stay even, his pulse steady, Nunez organized all the players in his mind, moving them about mentally like chess pieces. Cops with sirens blaring would screech everything to a halt and could very well shut down the investigation, cutting off all hope of getting Chuck Tanaka back. Sure, the safeguards he'd put into place became problematic with the Nelson woman along, but at least the people listening in understood the potentially explosive dynamics.

Unlike local cops looking to issue a speeding ticket.

Kutros ground the gears, downshifting up a rolling hill. "Would you like to weigh in with a suggestion?"

End this now in a standoff with the Turkish police who knew nothing about the situation? Or ditch the cops so his agents could continue following the GPS tracker he'd slipped under the seat?

He didn't even have to wonder. "Floor it."

Kutros nailed the accelerator and fishtailed along the muddy road before gaining traction. Twin geysers spewed from the back tires, flinging up a wall of water the Turkish police would be hard-pressed to see through.

The Greek spun the steering wheel in his hand. "Roll down the window and shoot."

Uh, not a good idea. "Can't see them. I'm not wasting my ammo on a blind shoot. And I am definitely not sticking my head out there for them to plug a bullet into my skull."

Kutros mumbled something under his breath, no doubt insulting Nunez's masculinity.

Jimmy's whisper piped through Nunez's earpiece. "I'm getting antsy. Something's gotta give soon. Not gonna stand by if they touch Chloe."

"Hold," Nunez mumbled, windshield wipers slapping double time. He'd heard Jimmy's warning about her kidney transplant and would do his best to keep her safe. Although so far, the Nelson woman appeared quite capable of taking care of herself.

Kutros's unibrow pinched tighter together. "What was that you said?"

"I'm going to hold on to the woman when we get out of the van."

"Nunez," Jimmy muttered, "why not let the cops help?"

He didn't want to risk whispering another word to Gage, not with Kutros already on edge, so Nunez settled for, "How much longer until we get to that farm? You are going to have to trust me sometime, partner."

"You'll hear soon enough. I cannot risk going there until our police 'friends' are taken care of." Kutros rolled down his window and whipped out a semiautomatic handgun.

Nunez lunged across and chopped Kutros's wrist, sending the gun rattling in the floorboards. "Drive, damn it, and I'll take care of the rest."

"You are beginning to irritate me, Senor Carvalho." His thick, dark brows lowered until his evil eyes almost disappeared. "Perhaps you brought the authorities."

"I don't know what you are talking about." He scooped the weapon off the floor. "Look in the mirror. You lost the police."

"I intend to make sure they stay lost." Kutros continued silently for another two kilometers before pulling the van off the road alongside a field of fig trees. He left the engine on idle. "Unbuckle your seat belt.

Something was off. Nunez had the distinct impression he'd better grab his sunscreen, because this operation most definitely was about to take a rapid southerly turn.

He kept the gun loose in his grip, preparing to press it to Kutros's temple if necessary. So many lives in the balance depended on which choice he made. "Where's the farm?"

"We are stopping here until a few things are settled." Kutros pulled another gun from beneath the dash.

Definitely south. He'd waited too long.

He hated second-guessing and couldn't waste the time on any thoughts but getting the two people in back out alive. Nunez slid his hand under the seat, pressing the alert button on the GPS that would call his people in ASAP. They would covertly swarm the van in minutes.

"All right then." He needed to keep Kutros talking. "Bring me up to date on what we need to discuss before you trust me with the farm's location." Even if he was too late to save Chuck Tanaka, Nunez would damn well bring a body back with him Stateside.

"Oh, we will not be talking." He leveled the long barrel dead aimed at Nunez's chest. "It is time for you to prove you are with us."

Us. More people in the chain. Marta Surac, most likely. He stuffed aside thoughts of Anya and her possible—hell, probable—involvement. He would deal with her when and if necessary.

"Be reasonable, Kutros." He patted the air in the universal *calm down* signal. "If anything, you owe me an apology for mucking things up with our extra passenger. I have proven myself by giving you the airman."

"In my business, we have many levels of tests. The more you pass, the more you will be compensated."

He didn't need to hear the price for failure.

His semiautomatic steady, Kutros nodded to the weapon in Nunez's hand. "Kill them both. Now."

* * *

Chloe searched around her frantically as the man with a Spanish accent—Miguel—opened the back doors of the van, an ugly black gun in his hand. The torrential rain had already saturated him, plastering his clothes and hair into an even darker shade of doom.

She set her chin and her resolve for the fight ahead. She hadn't gotten this far in life to waste the precious gift that unnamed kidney donor had blessed her with. If this Miguel thought he could simply pull the trigger and make her disappear, he had another think coming. Not that she had a clue how she would stop him, but she would make damn sure the guy felt the brunt of her inner Captain Kirk before he fired that big ass scary weapon.

Her throat closed, and she swallowed gulps of cold fear and damp air.

"Jimmy?" she hissed. "What should we—"

"Stay calm, quiet, and don't piss off the Greek guy."

She wanted to ask more, like what had Jimmy been whispering about earlier to some guy named Nunez? Did he have a bug wired somewhere? Because if he had reinforcements tucked away, now would be a really good time for them to jump out of the trees in their weedy looking ghillie suits or whatever it was those military sorts did when they were trying to be covert.

Her inner Captain Kirk might be willing, but her lessons with Jimmy hadn't progressed to fighting with her hands bound. She seriously doubted she would inflict much damage on these guys before the bullets flew.

Miguel called over his shoulder. "Kutros, free their feet so they can get out of the van. I don't want to risk any bullets ricocheting around inside that metal cave."

The Greek man—Kutros—pitched the keys to the other man. "Do it yourself."

Miguel leaned inside, something flickering in his eyes that she could have sworn was reassurance, then gone. He mumbled to Jimmy, but she couldn't hear over the pounding percussion in her ears and drumming rain.

"Out," Miguel ordered.

Chloe scrambled across the van floor toward the gaping back doors. Between the storm and the clouds covering the moon, the night waited like a hungry void.

Jimmy moved quietly next to her as she stumbled out of the vehicle onto the small patch of ground near a line of trees. Rain poured over her in pounding pellets, her clothes soaked in seconds. What a way to get the shower she'd been longing for.

The humidity smelled of thickly pungent cigar smoke even as she gave Kutros a wide berth. Why couldn't those police have caught them earlier? They were probably too far away now to hear any shots.

At least she and Jimmy had their feet free. She wasn't sure how much good that would do them against two armed men with full use of their hands, but she'd seen Jimmy in action before. At least they had a chance. She couldn't even let herself think he would die because he was hamstrung protecting her.

Miguel strode over to Jimmy, gun held loosely in one hand. Thunder clapped overhead, followed by the snap of lightning.

Panic ramped up inside her. She'd prepared herself to die more times than she could count. She hadn't wanted to go, yet she'd been resigned to the seeming inevitable.

But she couldn't wrap her mind around even the possibility of something happening to Jimmy. Damn it, she refused to resign herself to that. She would do *something*, no matter how small, bite, kick, spit in someone's eye, throw herself at them like a berserker.

She launched forward just as Miguel slid one hand behind Jimmy's back. To brace him from falling over at the impact of a bullet to the brain? *No, no, no.* She swallowed bile, too far away to make it in time.

The intense eyed Miguel took his time bringing the gun up, his finger on the trigger. His mouth moved with low pitched words apparently meant only for Jimmy.

An apology?
Gloating?
The gun popped. Jimmy fell.

* * *

His hands now free from the moment when Nunez had leaned in to warn him, Jimmy slapped the muddy ground to break the momentum of his fall. Kutros clutched his shoulder, blood pumping between his fingers as he stumbled back against a fig tree.

The shot Nunez had squeezed off a scant inch in front of Jimmy's face had hit true into Kutros.

And probably popped Jimmy's eardrum, but he didn't have the time or inclination to complain. They were alive. Most importantly, he'd kept Chloe alive, even if she'd almost managed to throw herself in the bullet's path. That nightmare moment was guaranteed to wake him up in a cold sweat more than once in the future.

Nunez shouted. In pain? Jimmy rolled to a crouch, rain beating his back, as he scanned for the agent. Nunez stumbled around the small clearing, shoes slipping in the muck.

With Chloe on his back.

Her legs were wrapped around Nunez's hips, her teeth clamped into his shoulder to hold herself in place even without her hands. God, she was amazing. And taking a serious chunk out of Nunez.

Jimmy vaulted to his feet and clasped Chloe around the waist. "It's okay. You can let go. He's with us."

She sagged against Jimmy. He lowered her to her feet while Nunez backpedaled. The agent ground his teeth through curses, gripping his shoulder on his way over to Kutros.

Chloe stared from him to Nunez, her hair a wild, wet tangle stuck to her face. "What in God's name is going on?"

Jimmy waved a hand in the air to Nunez for the cuff keys, his body still tensed from the fight. He wanted to haul Chloe up close and shake her all at once.

He settled for sliding a hand along the nape of her neck, his thumb grazing the reassuring throb of her pulse. "We'll talk later."

"Like hell," her chest pumped with gulping gasps, as he uncuffed her hands, "we'll talk now."

Sirens wailed in the background, cutting her short and saving his ass for now, although Chloe's eyes assured him the reprieve was only temporary. Her ire fired him up all the more at a time when his emotions were already on a fast rise from simmer to boil.

A pair of police cars streaked their headlights over the clearing in a blinding flash that had Jimmy shielding his eyes with his arm to his forehead. Both vehicles screeched to a halt by the roadside, spewing water over Kutros, now cuffed and moaning in a puddle.

Nunez swiped his face off, approaching Jimmy and Chloe fast. "We don't have much time. Play it cool. Keep the answers minimal until we can get to the stationhouse and my credentials can be verified. With a little luck and some diplomatic pressure, we should be back on base within two hours."

Despite Nunez's reassurance, this showed all the signs of turning into a tangle of governmental channels that could land them in Turkish cells for an indeterminable amount of time when they needed to find that farmhouse before Kutros's people disbanded. However, taking down four local police officers didn't sound like a wise option, either.

Damn. Make that five. One of the cop cars had an extra passenger.

The back door swung open on the first squad car. Nunez had his attention focused on the well-dressed man sporting a fedora and a high-end suit, climbing out of the cruiser with an umbrella. Jimmy searched his mind to place the familiar face . . .

The doorman from the Oasis, Omar. Turkish police a step behind, he strode closer, his fine leather shoes squishing in the mud. "I understand from Mr. Carvalho's girlfriend that you are in need of assistance."

NINETEEN

A simple call to the police shouldn't have warranted this kind of attention. After phoning in her report about seeing what looked like a kidnapping attempt, Anya had been picked up, forced into a police car. And, most confusing of all, she'd been transported to the local NATO air base.

Waiting alone in a small interrogation room, Anya eyed her coffee suspiciously. It had come from the authorities, after all. Growing up, she'd seen authorities take money from her father and later from her aunt. She had even tried reporting her aunt to the police before leaving, only to have Aunt Marta threaten her the second she got home. Of course the police were on her payroll.

Their track record made her wonder why she'd reached out to them this time, but who else could she have called? Her conscience wouldn't allow the incident to go unreported, even if the end result had her trembling in fear. She slid her hands under the table to hide her nervousness.

Anya studied what looked to her like a two-way mirror
and wondered who waited on the other side. She'd heard
of women disappearing into the justice system here. Of
course, those stories had been from her family and their
friends, so she hoped perhaps they were distorted out of
their disdain for the law. She rubbed her throat, already
aching for outside air.

The doorknob twisted. She stilled, tamping down nau-
sea. The thick metal door swung wide for a man in loose-
fitting dress pants and a button-down shirt rolled up at the
sleeves. His tousled black hair attested to multiple finger
combs of frustration.

How nice to know she wasn't the only one having a
stressful day.

Her eyes skipped to the man standing behind him. She
studied Omar, the door guard back at the Oasis and apparently an undercover detective for the Turkish police.
Having him respond to her call to the authorities had been
a surprise, but she should have guessed. The police were
always tied up in her aunt's dealings. They must have
been watching her. Sharing the family name had distinct
disadvantages.

She hated to think the Oasis might be as corrupt as her
aunt's holdings. Was there any safe place for her? Anya
sagged back in her chair and waited for the man with
Omar to quit lurking in the doorway, staring at her like
they were caught in some childhood blinking contest.
Fine. She would blink first.

Then she blinked again, but this time in shock.

Anya straightened in her chair slowly. "Miguel?"

Gone was the aristocratic tilt to his head, the slow
grace with which he moved. The man before her now did
not appear a privileged heir enjoying life to its fullest but
an intense, driven man with a light in his dark eyes she'd
never witnessed. Most telling, he unmistakably belonged
here in an official manner.

Had he been following her, too? Getting close to her

for the sake of trying to reach her aunt? Did he suspect *her* of something sordid?

Her stomach roiled upward, and she lurched for the trash can beside her to empty what little churned around in her gut. She had missed a meal, after all, thanks to her no-show dinner companion, a dining companion who might well have been lining up a warrant for her on some bogus basis rooted in the accident of her birth into a crooked family.

A handkerchief appeared in her line of sight, proffered by a hand now devoid of expensive jewelry.

"Thank you," she dabbed at her lips, straightening. "I do not appreciate being stood up for supper."

She met his dark eyes again, hoping perhaps she'd somehow misread the situation. But no. His freedom of movement in this place left her with no doubts. He was some kind of police official or military personnel, and she'd been used.

Miguel showed no emotion. "I'm sorry about the past week."

He didn't even have an accent? Of course not. Everything had been a lie, even his kisses.

She moved the coffee aside, leaning forward on her arms and to hell with Omar, she did not care what anyone thought. "For lying to me or for using me?"

That stopped him cold for two heartbeats before he recovered. Miguel—oh God, she did not even know if that was his real name—pulled a chair out and sat across from her.

"I can send someone to find food if you're hungry. Would you like a doughnut to go with your coffee?"

"No thank you." She couldn't sit here and simply eat a pastry with him in some sad mockery of their dinner plans. "I just want to get this over with as soon as possible."

He withdrew a small tape recorder and pressed a button. "Tell me more about your aunt."

Irony burned away any tears welling inside, and she

laughed, painful gasps that grated her throat on the way up and out. She should have known.

Everything always came back to Marta.

* * *

Moving to the next holding room at the base security police station, Nunez worked like hell to put Anya's look of betrayal out of his mind for the moment. She'd maintained her innocence throughout, but her distrust of the police couldn't be missed.

Yet she'd called for help.

As had Livia Cicero after her sprint for freedom.

He was lucky the whole flipping Turkish police force hadn't come charging after them in a hailstorm of gunfire.

At least he'd convinced Turkish authorities this fell under the military's jurisdiction, even allowing him to bring Anya back with Livia for questioning. If anything, the local cops seemed glad to turn the mess over to someone else. Anything involving Livia Cicero equaled paparazzi. They all agreed this would be best kept out of the press if possible.

They'd sent Omar, their undercover dude at the Oasis—and wasn't the door fascist's role a real kick in the ass?—to be their official representative. Beyond that, this was Nunez's show. Thank God. Keeping this quiet was in the best interest of finding Chuck. They'd scanned a five-mile radius beyond where Kutros had pulled over and found no suspicious farmhouses, and Scanlon's crew hadn't found anything at the site farther north.

Work definitely required all his concentration right now. He needed to focus on questioning Livia Cicero and hopefully pry some answers from Spiros Kutros. If the bastard survived surgery.

Later, he would think about what Anya's seeming innocence meant for him.

For now, he needed to find out why Livia Cicero had

left the base and if she had any ties to Marta Surac. Jimmy Gage had requested to sit in on this interview. Since he'd been there when the goons brought Chloe to the cellar, he could well have impressions or memories that would help validate—or negate—Livia's story.

The singer perched on the edge of the steel chair, cupping her coffee in both hands as if she couldn't get warm enough. Nuances. Look for the subtle clues. Her makeup was smeared, unusual in and of itself for the always cool diva, but even more so, given her simple jeans and tank top. Not a sequin in sight.

She glanced up at the three men entering the room. The mug rattled against the scarred wood table as Gage and Omar set up shop in the corner by the two-way mirror. Ah, she held the cup to hide her shaking hands. A scared suspect he could work with.

Nunez grabbed a chair, flipped it around, and slammed it to the ground near her. Livia flinched.

He straddled the chair backward, leaning toward her, crowding her. "Why did you leave the base when you were told explicitly to stay put?"

Her chin quivered as she tried for a face tip of bravado. "I have already spoken to the Turkish police and the base security police. Why am I being questioned again?"

He stared at her without speaking, waiting.

"All right. Fine." Her normally sultry voice turned curt. "I will repeat it all if you will just tell me what happened to Chloe Nelson."

No one had told her? An oversight? Or downright cruel. "She's alive and in our custody."

"Thank God." She blinked back tears as she crossed herself. "I left the base because I received a call from a friend performing with the USO."

"A friend?"

"The American backup dancer, Steven Fisher, had a fight with his girlfriend, Melanie." She swiped her fingers just below her red-rimmed eyes, sniffling but keeping up the steady stream of words. "He thought she was cheating on him, and he left base to track her. His taxi ride never showed up at the Oasis, and he needed my help to get back."

The story would be easy enough to check out. In fact, his people taking notes on the other side of the two-way mirror were probably already dispatching someone to bring in the backup dancer for questioning. "Why didn't you just call the security police to retrieve him?"

"He was drunk and crying. He was afraid of getting fired. He has a sick mother to support."

The Kevin Federline look-alike had a mother? "You do realize your story sounds thin."

"I have so many threats made against me. Perhaps I have grown a bit blasé when it comes to security." She shrugged, her eyes flicking to Omar and Gage nervously. "Wrong of me, I realize now, but at the time, I never thought I would be in danger, and I believed I could help. He sounded desperate and pathetic, and yes, maybe I was looking for an excuse to leave this place. I'm just grateful no one was injured."

Gage straightened from his post by the two-way mirror. "Do you really think your actions had no repercussions? Can you imagine what Chloe must have been thinking? How terrified she must have been?"

Her wide eyes flicked from one man to the other. "I truly am sorry. Tell me what you need me to do to make this right."

Nunez leaned forward, blocking Livia from Gage's line of sight before the pilot blew a gasket. "Ms. Cicero," he pulled an eight-by-ten from his file, a picture of Marta Surac taken at a bank in Germany. He'd been able to locate a clearer image after Anya listed some of her aunt's bars, and Nunez started following the money trail. "Do you recognize this woman?"

Livia edged the photo closer with one finger, nail polish chewed off the tip. "No." She shook her head, nudging the picture back. "I'm afraid not."

"Have you ever heard the name Marta Surac?"

Again, she shook her head. "Does not ring a bell."

Nothing in her body language indicated she was lying. She truly appeared to be a woman terrified after a near kidnapping. Either way, he sensed he'd gotten everything out of her that he could. "That's all for now. You should return to your quarters and stay there. You'll be pleased to hear the water is working again."

Quiet ticked away seconds louder than the clock on the wall. She didn't so much as fidget with any sign of guilt. "Thank you for bringing Chloe back safely."

"I will escort you to your room. For your own protection." Hopefully, Kutros would be out of surgery by then and ready to talk.

A smile ticked the corners of her mouth, chewed clean of lipstick. "I am not going to make a run for it."

She shoved back her chair and rose with a prima donna grace, waiting for him to open the door for her. All of which would have pissed him off, but her hands still trembled.

Outside the interrogation room, Lieutenant Colonel Scanlon stood by a water fountain, lounging against the wall. Interesting. The man's expression revealed nothing. His presence, however, spoke volumes. Maybe he was waiting to speak with Jimmy Gage . . .

But no. The commander's attention stayed firmly fixed on Livia Cicero.

Scanlon searched her up and down with inscrutable eyes. "You're all right?"

She nodded tightly. "I am sorry if I got you into any trouble by leaving the base."

"I'll survive. I'm glad you did, too."

He shoved away from the wall and strode down the hall, rounding a corner and disappearing from sight.

Her haughty exterior slid into place again, but with a thin veneer. "I am ready to return to my room for my shower."

* * *

Jimmy scrubbed his wet hair with a towel one last time before tossing it aside. The water wasn't hot, but it was definitely wet. The pipes had been repaired, and so many people on base were lining up to wash off, the water heater couldn't keep up.

All the same, the cold shower did nothing to lower his steaming blood pressure. The shakedown with Nunez had turned into a cluster fuck because the waitress had called local police. That paled, though, in comparison to the news here at the base.

His crew had returned, but without Chuck.

They'd run a cursory imaging scan of the building blaring the tracking device's beacon, only to find no sign of their friend. But there had been plenty of ground fire. They'd hauled ass back to base empty-handed. Not that he'd expected anything positive to come of the flight once the kidnappers had asked about a tracking device. In fact, it seemed the crew may have even been set up.

The chances of Chuck being alive were next to nil.

Jimmy flung the wadded up towel under the sink. Even though he knew his presence on the plane wouldn't have made any difference, he couldn't dodge the sense of failure. From the start, this mission had carried a sense of doom he'd tried to attribute to too many reminders of his own POW experience.

At least Chloe survived. That much he could hold on to in a death spiral day. The need to check on her again kicked over him. He zipped his jeans, shrugged into a polo shirt, and toed on his deck shoes.

Jimmy jogged down the hall, knocked on her door—waited—no answer. She might be asleep. He knocked again anyway.

The next door down opened, and the stage manager stepped half-out in a black satin bathrobe. "She's in the practice hall."

"Thanks, dude."

"No problem. It's my job to know where everyone is," Greg answered with an oblivious smile.

Greg sure had dropped the ball on that tonight.

Two flights of stairs down, Jimmy passed the commons area on his way to the rooms allocated for individual practice. Not a tough task finding her now, since he only had to follow the music.

He didn't know a lot about the subject, but even a tone-deaf seven-year-old could have recognized the speed and mastery of Chloe's playing. The emotions swelling from the notes, however, he wasn't ready to think about.

He nodded to the guard outside the practice room door.

"Is Chloe Nelson in there?" Jimmy asked just to be sure.

"Yes, sir."

"I'll stick around for a while if you need to take a break."

"That would be nice, sir. Thanks. I can hit the cafeteria, then hang in the commons area at the end of the hall. Call when you need me."

"Take your time, Sergeant."

Jimmy opened the door quietly and stole a moment just to watch her at the grand piano. Bent over the keyboard, she swayed with the runs of her fingers up and down the Steinway's keyboard. Intent on her song, she didn't even notice his arrival.

Her damp hair spiraled down her back in locks heavy with water. An image of the first time he'd met her flashed to mind. So much intensity had been packed into the few days they'd known each other. He understood that sensation well from other edgy missions. The senses increased, soaking up life at an accelerated pace.

She swayed in synch with her fingers dancing along the keyboard. Like a few days ago when she'd joined the villagers, she merged with the music. Her body rocked in a fluid accent to the sounds. Hell yes, this woman stirred things inside him he would rather not face, her unflinching grit challenging him to dig deep.

But turning away was no longer an option.

* * *

Chloe poured herself into the emotionally passionate swell of notes and hoped the pain and fear of the evening would empty out as well.

Caressing the final echoes from the Brahms ballade, she found her frustration level only increased. She segued to pounding the keyboard with Rachmaninoff. Her fingers burned with intensity. The strength of the piece flexed her muscles and infused her with a sense of power she desperately needed after the helplessness of her kidnapping, the anger over not being told help was so close.

She pounded harder, her feet on the pedals and the sway of her body squeezing every ounce of emotion from the piece. She couldn't ignore the glaring reality that Jimmy did more than just fly airplanes. He put his life on the line, and she'd made things worse for him by landing in the car with Livia. She could have made things worse for others, because surely whatever he and the undercover man had in the works had been compromised by her presence.

She nailed the last chords, waiting for the final notes to fade before placing her hands in her lap and slumping with the release of energy. Slow, deliberate applause snapped her upright again. Jimmy lounged in the doorway, and she didn't even recall hearing the door open.

Her emotions still too close to the surface from her music, she couldn't miss the raw magnetism radiating from him as tangibly as any tone plucked from the keyboard. Her fingers itched to test the soft texture of his well-washed polo shirt over defined muscles, explore the rasp of crisp denim hugging his lean hips. After a night like this, she'd witnessed firsthand how that strength and vitality weren't just for show.

"I didn't see you there." She picked at the wrinkles on her pants, boring khaki at a time when she wanted to be bold. "I must have been pretty zoned out."

"I don't know much about classical music, but even I can tell that's amazing. It's the sort of playing that sucks in whoever's listening until you're really in the moment. Kinda like how flying works for me, if you get what I mean."

"I totally understand what you are saying, and thank you." His praise meant more to her than it should. She wanted to be mad at him for keeping her in the dark about help being in reach, but she couldn't deny her own culpability.

And bottom line, everything else seemed small in comparison to how close they'd come to dying.

"Do you want me to step back outside so you can keep playing?"

She shook her head, battling with the need to hold his warm, alive body—or kick him in the shin for letting her think the faux Spanish guy really intended to shoot him. "I want you to stay."

"I sent your guard for a break, because I need to talk to you, too." He stepped into the room and closed the door behind him. "You really held your own tonight and more. No one would have thought less of you for just stepping out of the way when the guns came out, but instead you stayed brave. You even kicked some serious ass in a way that put Street-Smart Barbie in the shade."

She snorted. "I almost chewed up a secret agent on our side."

"You had no way of knowing, and before you say

anything more, I couldn't risk letting you know about Nunez—uh, the guy calling himself Miguel. We couldn't take the chance you might telegraph that information with your body language. We did it for your protection. I won't apologize for that." Jimmy folded his arms over his chest, arms bulging tight against the short sleeves on his polo shirt.

Well, hell. She couldn't tout her need for independence now without sounding petty. "I'm sorry for putting you in greater danger, and I'm sorry I messed up whatever you were working on."

"Apology accepted."

She couldn't stop from asking him the question burning a hole in her brain. "Can you share *anything* about what happened?"

"We're looking for a missing military friend." His clipped answer iced the air.

Guilt piled on top of the already huge pile of shame filling her gut. "He must be an important friend for so many people to risk their lives."

"Every one of our brothers- and sisters-in-arms is important. But yes, this friend carries secrets that could endanger a lot of lives."

"Thank you for letting me know that much. Can you tell me what you really do?"

"I'm a test pilot," he said simply.

She could see in his eyes there was more but sensed she couldn't push. Chloe feather-brushed her fingers over the keyboard, the glassy smooth ivory a familiar comfort in a world suddenly turned on its axis. If only she could bring colors to her life the way she milked rainbows from the keyboard. She'd hoped with this tour . . . "What about the tour?"

"I believe it's in everyone's best interest for the troupe to leave." Jimmy braced his elbows on the edge of the piano, leaning closer.

"What if I want to stay anyway?" To see him. She couldn't imagine leaving things like this between them. Everything felt unfinished, like a symphony missing the final movement.

He skimmed his callused fingers over the top of her hand, comforting, arousing. "Unless something radically changes in the next twenty-four hours, I don't believe you're going to have a choice."

She resisted the urge to bang out her frustration on the piano again and instead forced herself to focus on the real source of her agitation. "Will we see each other again? I've never even thought to ask where you live. I imagine you can tell me that much."

"I'm stationed at Nellis Air Force Base outside of Las Vegas."

Not what she'd hoped to hear. And why couldn't he show some disappointment on that too-appealing face of his? "That's quite a commute from Atlanta."

"I'm occasionally TDY in your area."

Some of her anger melted away so fast at even the possibility of seeing him again it almost scared her into bolting out the door. "TDY?"

"Temporary duty, like a business trip."

Keeping in touch, re-creating this surprise bond they'd formed, wouldn't be easy back in the U.S. The fear and adrenaline from earlier started up a depressing requiem in her head, reminding her of the reasons she needed to live in the moment. She was tired of being safe. Too often others had made decisions for her, were *still* making decisions for her. But this one decision she was taking control of right here, right now.

Chloe stood, closed the last few inches between them, and flattened her palms against his chest, the cotton every bit as soft as she'd imagined, the skin beneath even hotter. Just feeling him this close again reminded her of the horrifying time in the back of the van when he'd comforted her and confided secrets about his past just to keep her calm. He'd made himself vulnerable for her, and that spoke of strength she totally couldn't resist. "Jimmy?"

"Yeah, maestra?" His gaze fell to her mouth as he formed the word, inciting hunger.

"Lock the door."

Jimmy slid the bolt shut. "I hope you're not planning to leave anytime soon."

TWENTY

The clicking lock and Jimmy's bold promise of a lengthy stay echoed in Chloe's ears, committing her to the moment.

Jimmy made a slow but purposeful turn back toward her. His heavy-lidded eyes cruising her body broadcast loud and clear how much he wanted her, too. He pulled her flush against him, the clean scent of his soap and something essentially *him* sending her senses on overload.

And she hadn't even kissed him. Yet.

He lowered his head to hers as she arched up on her toes. No restraints. No more holding back. Later she would worry about his overprotective urges when it came to her transplant. Later she would wade through his issues with his sister's death.

For now, she deserved to explore the attraction that had snapped between them from the moment his head broke through the waves that day in the Mediterranean.

Jimmy slid his hand up into her hair and palmed the back of her head. He slanted his mouth over hers, no hesitation, fully demanding, and she demanded right back. She wriggled against him, aching to get closer, skin to skin. He scrunched her white cotton blouse up and over her head, pitching it to the side. His fingers fell to the front clasp of her bra, and with a single flick from him and a shrug from her, a cool breeze from the air conditioner gusted over her bare breasts. Her nipples tightened from anticipation more than the cold.

Then his warm mouth fell to her shoulder, lower, lower, until she went wobbly, and he slid his thigh between hers to help her balance, bringing the delicious bonus of muscled heat nudging between her legs. She threw her head back, her spine bowing her closer to his intent tongue.

She wanted, ached to feel him. She tore at his polo shirt, his mouth leaving her for the second it took her to tug the finger-bunched cotton over his head. Warm flesh against flesh sent a humming along her nerve endings. Chloe sighed against his neck, sipping away a bead of water dripping from his freshly washed hair. Her fingers teased frenetic runs over him, greedy to learn everything she could about him in case they didn't get another chance.

He toed off his shoes as she kicked away her sandals, and somehow she managed to peel off his pants while he helped her shimmy out of her own, the rasp of fabric against her skin teasing her with the promise of better touches yet to come.

Jimmy clamped her against him, both of them finally fully naked. His hands stayed blessedly clear of her scar, something they would have to deal with, but not now. Her hands shook as she explored him, unable to remember the last time a man had touched her this way, as if she was the only woman in the world.

She urged him to the floor with her, side by side. She savored every sensation: the rasp of the industrial carpet, the *shoosh* of the air conditioner overhead, the feel of his strong hands over her body. Her own warmth ratcheted up the scent of her lavender perfume to mingle with his scent. Much longer, and she would lose control, forget about practical concerns like . . .

"Jimmy," she took the hot length of him in her trembling hand and stroked, continuing, wresting a groan from him, "we need a time-out for birth control."

His lips and teeth teasing her earlobe stilled. He tipped his face to look at her, his eyes slowly focusing back in on her. Then his eyes slammed closed as her meaning must have finally penetrated his brain.

"Ah hell," he rolled off her, his forearm over his face.

"What's wrong?" She teased her fingers along his chest, circling one flat nipple, then the other.

His arm fell away, his breathing hitching with a rasp that flattered her. Clearly he didn't want to stop any more than she did. "Nothing. Condoms are always wise these days. We just have to relocate to my quarters. I didn't intend for things to go this far here."

"I have some." She took in his surprised expression. "What? I'm not allowed to carry condoms?"

His eyes darkened in a way that said he would be all over her again. Soon. Her body shivered in anticipation, her skin humming with need of his touch.

"Of course you are. I simply didn't expect that you would."

"Not to put a damper on things, but they're not a testament to any girls-gone-wild leanings. I keep them on hand because it's wise. Pregnancy would be a big and risky deal for me." She grabbed her purse from beside the piano bench and whipped out a tiny pink zipper pouch. "You owe me for being prepared."

He filched the pink bag from between her fingers as he lowered his body over hers again, making his intent known. "Yes, ma'am."

She teasingly reached to snatch it back. He held it farther from her grasp while taking her mouth with his. They

rolled along the carpet, again and again, until he stopped
with her beside him.

Under the piano.

She plucked a condom from his hand. His eyes turned
from brown to a molten black as he stared back at her.
She tore into the packet and rolled the protection inch by
tantalizing inch over him, watching his eyes slide to half-
mast.

He gripped her hips, shifting the balance of control his
way again. He positioned her against him, the carpet a
tantalizing abrasion against skin suddenly supersensitive.
Carpet, for crying out loud. This man had her twisted in
knots.

The thick nudge against her core sent delicious shivers
over her that beat any shower. His hold eased on her hips
as he left the next move up to her. Without hesitation, she
hooked her knee on his hip, urging their bodies closer
until he filled her, stretching, adjusting, settling in place.

His smile echoed hers. Ah, she'd definitely chosen the
right path to forgetfulness.

She rocked against him, and he met her stroke for
stroke, his eyes intent on her the whole time. He caressed
her shoulders, arms, along her side, dodging her scar in
favor of reclaiming her breasts. She writhed against him,
her back arching. He cupped her head and brought her
closer to him, safe under the confines of the piano. Would
she ever be able to play again without thinking of this? Of
him?

Pleasure swelled inside her to a near-painful cres-
cendo, fuller, until her skin felt too tight for her body. He
slowed, delaying her release, until she nipped his shoulder, demanding, rolling her hips against his harder, harder
still, until . . .

Release shuddered through her. Again and again. She
squeezed her eyes closed to draw in all the colors spark-
ing behind her eyes. She glided along the after-echoes
while his raspy shout of completion rumbled in her ears.

She sagged against him, and he gathered her closer. The forgetfulness she'd wanted, the escape, was fading. Reality seeped back through her mind in whispery bursts much like the air conditioner puffing away overhead. Her fingers played along his back, forcing her to process what she'd shied away from when she'd touched him during sex.

She felt the knotted skin, reason insisting on a dawning horror she desperately wanted to deny, but couldn't. The pads of her fingers registered dime-sized scars. Jimmy had been burned by cigarettes or cigars. More than once.

What the hell had happened to him? Here she'd been concerned about how he would deal with her transplant, little knowing he still held deep secrets of his own.

She wanted to cry, except he wouldn't want that any more than she would want sympathetic tears for herself. She ached to ask him, though, but she understood how scars had a way of going deeper into a person's soul. Sometimes it helped hearing others share their own vulnerabilities. But still, his secrets were his to spill when he was ready.

Would she even be in his life long enough to find out?

* * *

Jimmy tugged on his pants, the rustle of Chloe sliding into her panties and bra echoing in the small rehearsal room. He didn't consider himself Captain Sensitive, but even he could feel the weight of her unasked questions hanging in the air.

He should have thought about the fallout from her finding the scars on his back. He'd dealt with the issue over the past three years when he'd slept with other women. Of course he'd lied to *them* and attributed the marks to an aircraft fire, a camping trip gone awry, anything he could think of except the truth.

With Chloe, he couldn't bring himself to tell the casual lie.

Where were his shoes? He needed air, space, an escape from too much past shit in his head.

Chloe tugged her cotton shirt over her head, a sexy siren in just her underwear and top offering a distraction he wanted back. How many condoms did she have in the pretty pink pouch? And how often could they have sex before he should mention, *Hey, I'm disease-free and shooting blanks, so how about we ditch the rubbers?*

She retrieved her khakis from the corner and returned with one of his shoes as well. "I didn't have many friends growing up. Practices gobbled free time, and my health problems kept me out of school a lot. But I had this one particular music teacher, an artistic eccentric, who became a mentor-friend."

Where the hell had that come from? He wasn't sure where she was going with this, but having her fill the silence was easier than digging around inside himself for something to contribute. Like, *Hey, I had this mentor once, but I couldn't save him any more than I could save my sister.*

Jimmy took the shoe from her and unearthed the other from beneath the piano bench.

"Mrs. Crenshaw taught piano and music history at the local college. I started taking lessons from her shortly after my mother died." She tugged on her khakis with a wriggle that sent his pulse pumping when he should have been an hour away from ready for another round. "Nobody can replace a parent, but Mrs. Crenshaw helped fill a void."

"That sounds nice." Wow, way to go, pal, with holding up your end of the conversation.

"She performed at Carnegie Hall in her youth."

"With the piano?"

"Actually, she sang." Chloe dropped to sit on the piano bench, her bare toes curling against the carpet. "Eventually, smoking took a toll on her voice. Man, she loved to smoke, but she was a frugal lady. She always told me how much she resented the rising prices of cigarettes, so she started rolling her own."

The woman rolled her own *cigarettes*? Doobies more like it.

Could Chloe's sheltered life have left her that naïve? Jimmy sat beside her on the bench, his feet crossed at the ankles next to hers, almost brushing. He couldn't decide if touching her would offer more distraction or flay him raw.

"I would stay after lessons sometimes and help her roll them while we watched *I Love Lucy* reruns." She snagged a hair band from beside the keyboard and gathered her tangled hair into a haywire ponytail. "Then she would make the most amazing cheeseburgers."

If you had to get the munchies . . . "She sounds like a real character."

"Oh, she was a character all right." Chloe clasped his hand and sketched a lone finger along his palm. "Around the time I was fourteen I showed up early for my lesson and found her prepping her stash of *tobacco*. Except it wasn't tobacco. She had a marijuana garden in her back-yard."

"You must have been surprised." He settled into the soothing sound of her voice. They'd come a long way from sniping each other's head off a few short days ago.

She leaned back against the keyboard with a light tinkle of the higher notes. "To this day, cheeseburgers give me a buzz."

"For someone who vows to have led a sequestered life, you sure have packed in some strange situations."

"I tend to stumble into unique experiences." She dismissed her life-or-death brushes with a half shrug. "After I walked in on her that time and figured out what was really going on with the 'cigarettes,' I never went back. I convinced my dad to find me a new teacher without mentioning her weed garden."

"That was probably for the best. There's no telling

what might have happened to you if you'd lived with that kind of easy access to drugs as a teenager."

"If only life were that simple when it comes to right and wrong decisions." Her other hand fell over their clasped ones and she started tracing again with a cool touch. "Turns out that was only half the story. Six months after I found Mrs. Crenshaw's plants, I learned from one of her other students that she smoked the marijuana for her glaucoma."

Ah hell. "Why didn't she tell you?"

"I don't know." Her thumb massaged back and forth over his wrist. "I never asked, and now she's in a nursing home totally out it. I still feel guilty. I think maybe I was taking out an unreasonable anger at my mother for dying on the one woman who was still around trying to give me a semblance of maternal love."

He couldn't get away with a bullshit auto-response for this one. "You were just a kid. You deserve to cut yourself some slack."

"Thanks for trying to let me off the hook, but . . ."

"But forgiving yourself is tougher."

"You're perceptive for a card-carrying member of the testosterone club."

She squeezed his fingers, and damn, what a time to realize she hadn't been sketching absent patterns over his hand. She'd been tracing the thin ridge of scar tissue along his wrist from when it had been stomped back in Afghanistan. And the marks on his back? Astute Chloe wouldn't have missed those either, a fact echoed by the glint of tears in her green eyes. He may have managed a bit of Captain Sensitive after all, but talking about his POW time, tonight, with the reality of having failed Chuck pouring salt on unhealed parts of his soul . . . Forgiving himself wasn't on the agenda tonight.

His BlackBerry buzzed, the sound louder than normal from vibrating against the piano.

Jimmy shot up from his seat beside her and snagged

the messaging device like a much-needed lifeline in shark-infested waters. "Sorry. I have to check this."

Chloe's eyes damn near bored new holes in his back. Was he using work to avoid a confrontation? Hell, yeah. He might be Hotwire when it came to bar fights and strapping his ass into a risky new piece of equipment for the DOD, but when it came to the touchy-feely emotional stuff? His Hotwire ways short-circuited.

Jimmy cupped the BlackBerry in a death grip and scrolled through Nunez's message, blinked to be certain he'd read it correctly.

Gage, your undercover work paid off. We were able to break Kutros. We know where they're keeping Chuck Tanaka.

* * *

Why couldn't a woman locate a decent knife when she needed one?

Marta yanked open another kitchenette drawer and shoved the spoons and spatulas from side to side. An idiot must have outfitted this efficiency apartment attached to the barn-turned-holding-cell. How many ladles did a person need? When she found out which one of her employees set this place up, she would toss him or her into the same deep pit where she planned to bury airman Chuck.

Today was day seven, the end of the extra week she'd allowed for prying information from him. Apparently she'd taken a few hours too long, given what happened with Kutros. She should have aborted this mess earlier.

Hopefully Kutros would bleed out in surgery before he could unload everything he knew in exchange for a deal. That inept idiot had been sucked in by an undercover agent, a tidbit she'd learned thanks to the bug she'd planted on Kutros, a bug now in some hospital laundry bin. To make matters worse, that traitorous bitch Anya had been lusting after the very same agent.

Marta hip-slammed the drawer closed and slumped back against the counter, nothing but four dull dinner knives to show for her search. Hardly worth the effort. Not that she needed a blade.

She rubbed her thighs together against the cool efficiency of the tiny pistol strapped high on the inside of her leg. However, shooting offered a certain detachment, and she preferred contact with her victim. Tonight she needed the rush of power brought by an up close and personal kill.

She also needed to clean up here fast and go to ground. Except hiding cost money. Her organization was stretched thin financially with her expansion into Turkey. Given how the agent had planted a military member in her club, authorities were onto her scheme of kidnapping service people. She definitely needed to do something about that "fake hostage" and the woman he cared about, the one who'd been taken as well.

No one escaped from her, damn it. She built her reputation on that. People feared and respected her as a result.

She would simply have to tap into an alternate means of generating the funds she needed to lay low and regroup. She could sell other brands of information.

Marta snatched her keys from the table to unlock the door to the holding cell. The cool metal of Uncle Radko's cigar clippers comforted her, reminding her of her own strength even early on. She would survive this. She always survived.

Marta turned the snipper over and over in her hand, then stared at the thick wooden door, inspiration smoking through her until she rubbed her legs together to ease an unexpected ache. Removing Chuck's fingerprints would be a wise move, not that she expected anyone to find him. But just in case.

She could leave the actual shooting and disposal of the body to Erol. Or perhaps Erol could just break Chuck's thick, strong neck. Regardless, she needed to turn her attention to the business of freeing up cash quickly.

What a shame she no longer had time for a bidding war on the tracking device and USO leak. Damn Kutros, Anya and those blasted "escapees" for all they'd cost her. She would have to take the bird in the hand offer already on the table from a local terrorist cell, the group responsible for the recent suicide bomber attacks.

Selling them her information on the USO's weak link in security would generate enough capital to relocate and lay low. Given Kutros's screwup with the kidnapping attempt, she really should dump her information about the USO immediately, before the police had time to delve deeper. She would also need to rein in Anya. Marta had indulged the girl's rebellion long enough.

But first. Marta unlocked the door and swung it wide, the kitchen light slanting over Chuck curled unconscious in a corner.

Time to say good-bye to a worthy opponent.

TWENTY-ONE

★ ───

An hour after takeoff, Jimmy stared at the airspeed indication as if he could somehow squeeze more velocity from the already maxed-out CV-22. They'd gone from alert to airborne in twenty-one minutes, every second critical, since their intel could go cold in a snap. None of them knew if Chuck was dead, only that he'd been alive last night, according to Kutros, who'd been all too happy to trade information for a deal.

The tilt-rotor aircraft bounced around at 300 AGL— above ground level. Nasty squalls on the edge of a weather system prohibited the lower approach Jimmy would have preferred. Hadn't the clouds emptied themselves out enough last night? Every thirty seconds or so the aircraft lost twenty or thirty feet of altitude in an unpredictable roller-coaster ride as mind-scrambling as sex with Chloe.

An encounter he definitely needed to put out of his mind if he expected to stay focused.

A collective swell of determination filled the metal

confines. The crew, the half-dozen CIA paramilitary, Nunez—they wouldn't go home without Chuck this time.

Vapor flew beside Jimmy in the other pilot's seat. "The weather is total crap."

Lieutenant Colonel Scanlon manned the surveillance equipment wired in back. "At least we have the sky to ourselves."

With a little luck, the weather would help mask their approach and reduce the risk of taking ground fire. If the CV-22 didn't smack the earth first.

Jimmy pushed a button on his multifunctional display and keyed up his mic, "Smooth, how are the spooks doing back there? All this bouncing around must be wreaking havoc with their last meal. They probably think we're screwing with them on purpose."

"They seem unfazed," the flight engineer answered. "Beauty. We need some steely eyed motherfuckers tonight."

The aircraft hummed, engines at max revolution, beyond what the tech orders noted as safe, but then as testers, they made their bread and butter from pushing standards off the chart. If ever a flight warranted it, this one fit the bill.

"Ten minutes to go, Smooth," Jimmy updated, training-honed instincts overriding emotions. If only he could stay this detached around a certain pianist with a mermaid body and a will to survive that damn near humbled him. "Give them a heads up."

"Wilco." Will comply.

From the copilot's seat, Jimmy peered out into the darkness. "I haven't seen a ground light in a half hour."

Good thing this baby had terrain-following radar. If they'd been stuck eyeballing the flight, they would have been roadkill by now.

Vapor stared at the radar display that automatically guided their aircraft through the weather and over craggy terrain. "Tower coming up, slight climb."

Jimmy scanned to the right more out of a good aviator habit pattern than because he thought he might see something through the sheeting rain. "Clear right, for what that's worth. Come right to heading zero-five-zero now."

"Zero-five-zero, copy." Vapor tipped the stick. "Coming right."

Jimmy cycled through the navigation screens, tapping into more of that calm gained from training hard. "Five minutes, boys and girls. Get up and ready in the back."

"Wilco," Smooth responded.

Vapor looked over at Jimmy and gestured toward the front window. "Eyeballs out for a visual on the landing zone."

Adrenaline buzzing, Jimmy punched up a screen. "Right five degrees for wind correction. LZ is four miles ahead, begin transition."

The aircraft angled right in a smooth sweep, all things considered. Jimmy strained his eyes for a glimpse of the treetops and outcropping of rocks that marked the drop-off point for the operatives in the cargo hold. Wait for it . . . Wait for it . . . Bingo.

Jimmy glanced fast at the control panel, sweat sealing his helmet to his head. "Two miles out, Vapor."

"Copy, slowing."

The engines transitioned from a blades forward airplane to the blades upward helicopter mode, slowing, engines *whump, whump, whumping* louder now that they were overhead as they landed. The back ramp groaned open, wind gusting in through the ass end of the craft.

Narrowing his focus to the moment, not what waited a distracting few yards ahead, Jimmy monitored the MFD again. "Fifteen seconds. Slow to fifteen knots."

Vapor moved the engines to the final helicopter setting and continued decreasing speed. So far, so good. No sign of bad guy bubbas in the woods waiting to plug a hole in the engines.

"LZ in sight." Jimmy pointed left of the windscreen,

the landing zone landscape murky from rain and the cloud-eclipsed moon.

Vapor followed the finger to a clearing in the trees. "Tally-ho, bringing it in for a landing. Little help, please, Smooth."

"Clear back here on the load ramp. About thirty feet to go."

Vapor brought the aircraft to a hover and began to settle it down. "How're we doing, Hotwire?"

"Twenty feet. Good rate of descent. Keep her steady," Jimmy monitored. Smacking terra firma sucked on a good day. Crippling the craft tonight was beyond considering. "Ten feet, five feet, come to a hover."

Vapor stopped just above the ground. "Thumbs-up, Smooth. Roll them out."

Jimmy had pulled his fair share of time in the cargo hold, learning about all crew positions as part of his test training. He could envision every step of the movement behind him: CIA agents and Nunez pounding down the ramp, jumping to the ground, and disappearing into the mist. Smooth backing inside and raising the ramp.

"All clear, sir. *Go go go!*" the flight engineer shouted.

Vapor put the aircraft into a climb and began transitioning the engines to aircraft mode. "Colonel? I'm not seeing anything on the infrared camera. Is your equipment picking up any warm bodies hidden in a bunker looking to pop us out of the sky?"

"Hold," Lieutenant Colonel Scanlon answered low. "So far I'm not seeing anything other than small night critters. Scanning over for a view inside the barn."

Exhaling hard, Vapor flexed his fingers inside his flight glove, switched his hold on the stick, and worked the other hand. Jimmy cycled through screens on his MFD until the communication page glowed. He tapped through the keys. "Red team comm check."

Agent Nunez's voice came over in a whisper. "Red team loud and clear. In place about two mikes out."

Jimmy double-clicked his own talk button to acknowledge the call.

The colonel tapped his mic, "Red team, display shows two warm bodies in the barn, belowground."

"Roger that."

A surge of triumph swelled in Jimmy's gut, which he quickly hammered back down. This looked right, felt right, but no jinxing the mission with premature hopes.

Three minutes passed in a roar of engines and rain, and totally quiet airwaves, before Agent Nunez's voice broke the quiet. "Breaching."

One shot, then a second popped through his headset, followed by a grunt from Nunez. Tension buzzed through the plane. Jimmy's hand hovered just over the controls for the nose gun, ready for any surprises.

"One guard down," Nunez updated softly. "Looking for the second warm soul."

Chuck? Or another bad guy, because God, they had every reason to believe Chuck could already be dead inside that building. Jimmy's gut twisted harder than some newbie pilot on his first rescue. All their work and planning would play out in a matter of minutes as Nunez and his men now slipped around inside the barn.

Vapor powered full speed toward the wooden building, putting them in place to assist and for immediate pickup if things went to shit. The silence stretched.

Finally, Nunez's voice piped though, "Red team secure. Package secure, ready for extract."

"Package condition?"

"Cannot determine."

What the hell did that mean? Either Chuck was the second warm body, or there was another guard out there lurking. "Copy all, two mikes out. Can you give us a beacon?"

"You bet, beacon on now. Make it quick."

A flashing light blinked dead ahead.

"Got the beacon on visual. Coming in fast," Jimmy

called to Nunez before shifting back to Vapor. "Take a little jog to the left."

Vapor maneuvered the aircraft left and lined up on the glimmer through the darkness, his arm straining as he held the stick firm against the battering winds. "In transition."

The aircraft began to slow into a glide path toward the faint light. Jimmy scanned the area with the infrared camera and found the team crouched beside the farmhouse. "Area clear of bogeys. The team's right next to the building. Heads up, Smooth. On the ground in just a sec."

"Copy, sir, manning the gun for cover."

The test-modified CV-22 they flew had a nose gun for the copilot and one mounted on the back ramp for the flight engineer to use in defensive fire. Jimmy eyed the gun controls in front of him, his hands itching.

Vapor settled the aircraft into the pasture beside the wooden building, the back ramp open and gusting in the scent of muddy rain. The team of agents peeled away from the side of the barn and plowed through the muck toward the aircraft. One of the agents carried a man in a fireman's hold over his shoulder.

The team sprinted out of Jimmy's line of sight, and he turned toward the rear. The agents jogged by Smooth and into the aft cabin, collapsing onto the red seats.

Smooth's voice echoed through the headset as he counted each agent boarding. "And that makes seven, plus package. All onboard. Ready to clear out of here, Vapor."

"I don't need to be told twice." Vapor guided the aircraft straight up into haze and began transition to forward flight, the CV-22 twice as fast as the helicopters it replaced.

No one asked the burning question about Chuck. Jimmy stole another quick look behind him into the steel belly of the aircraft.

Two dripping-wet agents were securing Chuck to a stretcher. He looked like shit, barely recognizable. Thank

God he was strapped in his seat, or he would have fallen to his knees, puking his guts out anyway. No wonder they couldn't discern if Chuck was unconscious or dead. Where would they even start feeling for a pulse in a guy swollen all over?

He did know one thing for certain. Whoever had held Chuck was a monster.

* * *

Chuck fought against consciousness, trying like hell to will himself back into the place where he didn't have to worry about what he might slip and say. Damn that witch Marta for poking at his arm again with a needle. He had to fortify his defenses against her drugs.

He thrashed. Or intended to. A twitch was about all he could muster.

"Hold still, Captain Tanaka," a distinctly male voice instructed. "I'm a certified medic, and I'm here to take care of you until we transport you to a hospital."

Captain Tanaka? They knew his name now? But wait, that was an American accent. He grappled through the layers of fog, slowly assimilating the smells and sounds around him.

The musty scent of hydraulic fluid and wet gear.

A low *whump, whump, whump* of aircraft rotors.

All the knowledge he'd repressed for the past two weeks offloaded back into his brain. He even knew what kind of rotors. He recognized the distinctive sound of the new CV-22 Osprey, an aircraft he'd helped field-test. His eyes burned with air tears, his body too dehydrated to pony up even a drop of moisture despite the need to weep like a newborn.

They hadn't left him behind.

Tension seeped from his muscles until he damn near melted into the stretcher, while he let the smells and sounds of home wash over him. The medic finished inserting the needle but didn't pull it back out. An IV?

Coolness seeped into his veins almost as fast as gratitude and mind-numbing relief.

"Nunez, what happened back there?" The voice was distorted by drugs, but the edge of impatience was all too recognizable.

Jimmy Gage. Of course Jimmy was here, just as he would have done anything to be on the rescue flight if the roles were reversed. Chuck might be known as the most bullheaded in the squadron, but Jimmy was known as the toughest.

Chuck tried to move his head toward his friend, but they'd put him in some kind of collar lock. He settled back and listened while the medic continued checking him over with efficient but careful hands.

"We made it just in time. We caught a guard standing over him with a gun pointed at his head."

"I heard two shots through the headset—" Gage hesitated with a low hiss. "Holy crap, Nunez, how's your arm?"

"This little scratch? It was worth deflecting the guard's attention, since it gave one of my guys the opportunity to pop the bastard." The man called Nunez moved closer, his broadcaster-like accentless voice growing louder. "I just wish we could have taken that guard alive for questioning."

"Things shook down pretty fast. You didn't see anybody else except that one guard?"

"The place was deserted. Eerily so."

Chuck tried to push Marta's name past his cracked lips, but he could only manage an inarticulate groan over his swollen vocal chords. Fuck. He couldn't even write a note with his hands such a swollen mess—if he even had the energy to lift his arms. He wanted her to pay. He needed to make sure she didn't do this to anyone else.

And he burned to let his friends know he hadn't betrayed them.

"Captain Tanaka," the medic said, the IV pole clanking

from the bumpy flight. "I'm administering fluids, and I'm also going to give you something for the pain."

He didn't want more drugs. He didn't want to . . . lose control. Miss a minute of living, if his injuries were too severe.

Another groan slipped free, louder this time.

"Dude . . ." Jimmy Gage's voice penetrated the pain.

Chuck pried his eyes open enough for a narrow view. He couldn't speak, but he tried to translate his feelings with a look and prayed his friend understood. *I didn't talk.*

But Jimmy was staring at the shot being added to the IV before glancing back up at Chuck's face. "You had to know we would find you." Jimmy looked up and down the stretcher, his eyes telegraphing loud and clear his pity for the pulverized mess in front of him. "I'm just damn sorry it took so long."

Chuck tried again to relay his thoughts through his expression. *It's okay, man. You're here now.*

"You did the right thing, hanging on. Don't give up now."

I didn't talk, he tried again to say, but just the effort of being awake sapped him. He closed his eyes and surrendered to the painkiller dousing his system. Or was it a death euphoria? Either way, after the hellish two weeks of holding strong, he didn't have any fight left inside him.

He didn't expect to live, but at least he wouldn't die staring up at Marta's evil face.

TWENTY-TWO

Nunez may have been winding his way around rows of military cop cars like all was well in his world, but he couldn't get rid of the tic in the corner of his eye, a tic that had started the second a security police sergeant informed him that Anya Surac refused to leave the air base.

This should have been a time for victory dancing. He'd retrieved Chuck Tanaka alive. Spiros Kutros was spilling information faster than the man used to puff dragon trails of smoke from Cuban cigars.

Sure, the backup dancer, Steven Fisher, had lawyered up, stating only that no way in hell was he ending up in a foreign jail. He wanted to go to the embassy, then home. Frustrating, but at least they had him in custody.

Could they accept Fisher's story at face value, that he'd just called a pal for a ride and emotional support? Or had he set Livia up to be kidnapped? Hopefully, Kutros would answer those questions as well with time.

Nunez bit back a curse. He needed to be downtown at the hospital overseeing Kutros's interrogation. Instead, he

was back in Incirlik's security police station to spend
more face time with a woman who—innocent or not—he
should leave the hell alone. How could he stay objective
about her aunt with Anya up in his grill?

Sweat stung his eyes. He swiped his arm over his brow.
Was it already daytime again? Tough to keep track when
you didn't sleep.

Nuncz tugged the front door open and strode inside the
station lobby. A poof from the tepid air conditioner met
him along with the low drone of a television. A trio of
uniformed cops from different NATO countries strode
out, discussing where to eat, clearing his line of sight to
the far corner. Anya sat in a corner chair beside her assigned military escort.

Nunez held up the ID clipped to his shirt. "Good afternoon, Sergeant. Agent Nunez. I've got this."

"Yes, sir. Uh, good luck."

She'd been that stubborn? Great.

Anya looked as weary as he felt. His anger ratcheted
down a notch. She still wore her red silky dress from
work, minus the apron, but with plenty of wrinkles along
her willowy curves. Blond locks straggled from her tired
ponytail.

He stuffed his hands in his pockets to keep from dropping to sit beside her, maybe stretch his arm along the
back of her seat to pull her against his side. He couldn't
escape the fact that she attracted him. Her toughness. Her
apparent struggle to free herself from Marta. "You can
leave anytime. We don't have evidence to hold you."

He didn't mention how much he hoped it would stay
that way.

"I want to help." She clutched the front edge of her
chair in a white-knuckled grip, her dusky eyes darting
from him to the oblivious traffic of people going about
their workday. "The police here said I could stay until I
check with you. Maybe I will think of something else that
will help you find my aunt."

Was she faking the nerves, angling for a deal by playing the sympathy card? "That would be good."

"Do you believe I am staying here for another reason?"

"Are you?"

Her chest rose and fell with erratic breaths, and she began to rock almost imperceptibly. "I am staying here because she scares me like death."

His brain translated her meaning well enough. He'd seen how Chuck Tanaka fared after two weeks with Marta Surac. Anya was right in believing that woman was enough to scare anyone to death.

He dropped to a crouch in front of her, eye level. "Has she ever hurt you?"

"Not physically, but I've seen what she does to others." She paused, visibly gathering her nerves until her dark-shadowed eyes met his again. "I want to stay here until you find her, and I'm willing to earn my keep. Ask me questions, anything you want to know about her." She swept an expansive gesture, opening herself up to his interrogation.

Okay, she was winning him over. Maybe he should wrangle some deal for her with people who could stay objective. "I can talk to the Turkish police about—"

"No." Her breathing hitched again in that near panic attack pattern he'd seen while questioning past suspects. "Aunt Marta pays the police. When we lived in Hungary, I tried to report her, and they simply told her what I had done."

Hungary. Nowhere had he found anything to send him searching there. He started to ask her what city, when she gasped.

Anya reached, her trembling fingers hesitating just short of his arm. "You're hurt."

He glanced at the bandage peeking beneath the edge of his rolled-up shirtsleeve. There hadn't been time for him to think when the gunman had turned the weapon on him. Thank God for training and reflexes, or the bullet would have hit his heart. "It's just a flesh wound."

"Did my aunt do that?"

"No." He stood again.

"But one of her people did." She held up a hand. "You don't need to answer that. I can see the answer in your eyes. Yes, Mr. Secret Agent, you do show things in your expression on occasion."

Now, that surprised the crap out of him after an eleven-year career when he should have been past surprising. "Nobody else thinks so."

"I guess that makes me different." Some of her old starch crackled back to life.

"You've been different from the start."

A tentative smile eased tension lines around her eyes. "I take that to mean I am no longer on your suspicious persons list."

He couldn't go that far, but he kept most everybody on his suspect list until a case closed. He nodded toward the door. "Let's get some fresh air."

For once, he startled *her* quiet. Hell, he startled himself quiet at the request he hadn't planned. But Anya Surac had gotten under his skin, and he would be lying to himself if he thought otherwise. He held the front glass door wide, waiting for her to exit into the parking lot. She strode alongside him, her heels clicking on the way to his car. Again, he opened the passenger door for her.

"Where are we going?" she asked as he settled behind the wheel of the nondescript blue sedan.

"Somewhere we can talk." Where he could learn more about her and figure out who she was underneath all the layers he'd seen in the past week.

A few winding turns deeper into the base later, he pulled up outside the recreation center baseball field. As he stepped from the car, familiar sounds of home rode the wind. Two teams of airmen played an intramural game: shouted calls, good natured heckling, the crack of a ball against the bat, families cheering from the metal bleachers. Over the years he'd embraced classic American moments to help bring him out of the grip of his undercover persona.

He took Anya's elbow and pointed to an empty corner on the first row. "Over here."

She followed alongside, picking her way through the patchy grass to their seat, regally ignoring the curious glances from women in jeans checking out her red dress and heels.

The bleachers felt hot even through his suit pants. "Is this okay with you?"

"Of course," she answered without hesitation but with plenty of confusion. She adjusted the drape of silk over her knees.

"Good." He shifted his attention front.

A big dude stepped up to bat with an accent Nunez pegged as Czech. Not exactly a country known for its Little League teams. The guy swung and rocketed the ball into foul territory, all torque, no aim, but having a blast.

The sun baked away two days of rain and tension. Elbows on his knees, he watched the game, ever aware of Anya beside him, yet still not sure what he felt for her. Ditching his Miguel Carvalho guise should have ended his attraction to her.

It hadn't.

She tugged the band from her hair and shook it free down her back. "Do you play the baseball?"

He could listen to that accent all day, a realization that reminded him he wasn't tamping down the attraction by not looking at her. Even her voice tempted him.

"No, I just like to watch." He took the opportunity to think about the question and not the woman. He'd wanted to play baseball once upon a time. His parents had signed him up for a team twice as a kid, but they had to move halfway through the season.

No more avoiding. He needed to get back to business. "You've been helpful in rounding up people who work for your aunt when you could have just as easily gotten away with playing dumb."

"My aunt's workers? You still haven't found *her*?"

"We posted an alert bulletin out for her and her body-guard." He could safely tell her that much, obvious information anyway.

"What about Baris and Erol?"

"Excuse me?" The bearded man who'd participated in Chloe's kidnapping had been named Baris.

"She has two bodyguards, Baris and Erol. I am sorry, but I do not know their last names."

"Will you work with a sketch artist?"

"Of course." She spun the hair tie around her fingers. "You still did not say whether or not you have crossed me off the suspect list."

"I am as sure of you as I can be of anyone."

"Trust is a difficult thing. I imagine trusting would be all the more difficult because you spend much time doing your beneath covers work."

He choked on a cough, and an image of just how hot sharing a bed with Anya could be. "Pardon? Beneath covers?"

"Your pretend persona. Miguel."

He unbuttoned his suddenly too-tight collar and pulled free his tie. "Uh, that's called undercover work."

"Ah, right. I will remember that." She stared at the ball field as a lady on the blue team whacked a home run and emptied the bases. Once the roar of the crowd dwindled, she said, "No wonder you do not have a quirk."

"Excuse me?"

"Quirk. A character trait. I believe I have the right word this time." The exotic melody of her accent thick-ened the air between them.

"What is your quirk?"

"I do not have one either. Mostly, I tried not to bring attention to myself. It is safer that way."

"Sounds like we have more in common than I

thought." He slid his arm along the bleacher behind her, allowing his thumb to graze her arm in comfort.

"My aunt is sentimental."

"You're going to have to explain that one, because I'm having a hard time understanding how anyone who tortures other people could be sentimental."

Anya blinked fast, her mouth sealing thin.

Shit. "I didn't mean to hurt your feelings."

"You're only speaking the truth about her actions." She fought back the tears.

"Explain to me what you meant about her being sentimental." He would be a fool not to tap into her insights. And yeah, he wanted to get to know Anya as much as he needed to understand Marta.

"You have a show in your country about the Mafia. I believe it is called *The Sopranos*."

"Right, but the series is over now." He tucked his feet under the stand to make room for a mother passing by with a double stroller.

"Still, you know what show I am referring to. It centers around one Mafioso in particular, the leader."

"Tony Soprano is probably one of the most recognized TV characters ever."

"I believe that is because he had a human side with a quirk as well as his evil side. Even bad people are not . . . uh . . ." She wiggled her fingers beside her head as if searching for a word. "Flat?"

"Correct. Flat. One-dimensional."

"Yes, my aunt has many dimensions. One of them, she collects things that remind her of the past. That is why I say she is sentimental."

"Vulnerabilities. The downfall of anyone, good or evil. You would have made a damn fine agent, Anya." He would be wise to stay alert around her.

She twisted the hair tie around and around her fingers tighter until the tip of her index finger turned blue. "I am not as innocent as I would like to be."

Ah shit. Here it came. Her confession would blindside him after he'd convinced himself she really had tried to escape her aunt. He could see how it would unfold and hated what he would have to do, but he was completely helpless to stop the end result. "I'm listening."

"I ran packages for my parents as a child without knowing. After they died, I continued, but understood my actions. I transported drugs for my aunt, and I smiled at men to get them to tell me things." Her tumbling confession began to stutter. "S-s-sometimes I did more."

He numbed himself, almost. For some reason his normal defenses weren't working at optimum levels. Her revelation explained the sadness and regret, and yeah, even shame he saw in her, her sense that she could never be just an ordinary girl on a date to a ball game.

"I am not proud of what I did, and I will not make excuses." She studied the shortstop as he fielded a routine ground ball. "I knew what I did was wrong. Plenty of people are scared and still choose to do what is right. I did not stop until she asked me to kill someone. That is a line I could not cross. That is the day I went to the police."

"The time you discovered the cops were on the take."

"On the take?" Then her face cleared. "Right. That is also when I began saving to leave, to become clean. How silly of me to think I could escape her reach."

Relief funneled through him. How damn strange that hearing her confession made him trust her more. Maybe because he was beginning to really grasp what she already knew about quirks and layers to people.

"What sort of things has your aunt kept?"

Anya blinked fast, confusion skirting across her eyes. "She has a ring from her mother, and she carries a cigar clipper with her always. She told me once it belonged to her uncle, Radko."

Radko. He made a mental note to look up more on the guy.

"She told me one day that ring would be mine. I do not

want anything from her, but still, it seems strange knowing that I will never have that ruby." Her dark eyes softened with sentimentality. "Just as it makes me sad I will
not kiss you again."

Her surprise admission cleaned his clock like a ball
upside a batter's helmet—for all of one shouted call from
the ump. Nunez tucked a knuckle under her chin and
tipped her face to his. He skimmed his mouth over hers
once, again, lingering.

"Get a room, dude," called a teenage batboy staring up
at them from the first base line.

Anya's smile stroked his kiss for a final second before
they eased apart. "I know your last name is Nunez. What
is your first name?"

"Mike."

Her smile widened, reminding him of the feel of her
mouth on his. "Thank you, Mike, for taking me to my
very first baseball game."

And there she went, blindsiding him again with how
she forgave him so easily for lying to her. Of course there
hadn't been a choice. He'd only been doing his job, but in
the past, some hadn't been as magnanimous.

God help him, wise or not, he really believed her. Now
he just had to figure out what the hell to do with her.

* * *

To hell with waiting around to be told what to do next.
Chloe intended to take charge starting right now.

She kept her eyes locked on the door to the briefing
room. She'd actually wrangled one of the guards into telling her where to find Jimmy. Apparently he was doing
some kind debrief with his crew. Perhaps because of
whatever had happened last night after they'd made love
under the piano?

When he'd read that message on his BlackBerry, his
face had hardened with an unmistakable mix of fury,
determination, and a brief hint of pain. She knew he

couldn't tell her everything about his job, but she wouldn't let him avoid her.

She still wasn't sure where they stood with each other or even where she wanted things to be between them. She couldn't risk a relationship with someone who couldn't accept her unconditionally. However, she also couldn't deny the fact that Jimmy drew her in a way no one else ever had.

The briefing room door snicked a quick warning, and she straightened. Jimmy's crew poured out, all somber: the older boss with horn-rimmed glasses, the shaved bald jokester, the flirt who'd helped pull her from the water.

And finally, Jimmy. His desert-tan flight suit bore more than a few wrinkles attesting to how long he'd worn it.

He walked straight toward her. "Wanna get a cup of coffee?"

Jimmy looked like he needed a bed far more than caffeine, the shadows under his eyes attesting to how much of himself he gave to this job.

"I don't want to keep you awake. I just wanted to see for myself that you're okay."

"I'll walk you back to your room then." He hitched his flight bag and helmet into his grip more securely and started down the hall.

More framed posters mingled with official photos of airplanes and past commanders. Seeing those scenic shots of Turkey reminded her of Jimmy's "tour guide" stint in the rec room when they'd talked about the Maiden's Castle and his Turkish grandmother.

That mellowed-out, chatty man was nowhere in sight. Even the crabby Jimmy she'd first met, the one who made her feel mad and alive all at once, was MIA.

"Jimmy? Are you all right?"

"Sure."

He lied. She knew it. Did a week in his life and a night of getting naked under a piano give her the right to press? She wasn't sure, but she did know that she seemed to be the only one around to try. She scrunched her toes inside her tennis shoes, the purple socks she'd begged off Livia urging Chloe to be bold. "What happened after you got that e-mail?"

"We flew out last night to get the missing friend I told you about. He's not in good shape." Jimmy pushed open the door, the sun blindingly bright.

"Is he going to be all right?" She shaded her eyes with her hand as she looked up at him.

"There are a lot of levels to 'all right.' " His words came out flat, devoid of emotion. "Will he live? Maybe. Will he carry this inside him? Forever."

Cars swooshed by, and a crowd cheered in the distance in seeming defiance of the dark mood pulsating from Jimmy. She could feel the ache radiating off him as tangibly as when he'd read that BlackBerry message. Except, damn it, every time she saw him, his pain pricked her a little deeper.

The whole way to the lodging facility, down the long hall to her room, she stayed quiet, waiting.

He followed her into her room without asking. He closed the door and sagged back on the wood panel. She gave him his space and sat on the edge of her bed. How strange that she'd never realized how inaction on her part could also be proactive, because she knew without question that he needed her quiet support right now far more than words or fix-it deeds. How many times before had she mistaken his silence for rudeness?

Jimmy studied his crossed feet with excess concentration, not that his combat boots offered him much to see except for long laces and a dog tag to match the one around his neck. The one on the boot was there to identify him if he was ever burned beyond recognition in a plane.

Now wasn't that a cheery thought? But after seeing Chuck, grief for his friend tangled up with the hell he'd been through himself, all of it boiling up inside him until he couldn't contain it anymore without exploding. Right or wrong, Chloe was the only person he could bring himself to talk to.

But he needed to stare at his boots, damn it. Looking at her would only weaken him when he needed everything inside him to open this vein and pour out the destructive lava from his past. She deserved to know.

"I was a POW in Afghanistan for four months. The hospitality sucked."

She gasped, then quickly stifled her shock. And thank God, she didn't speak. It was hard enough just talking.

There was so much more he could say, should say about Socrates, his bones out there somewhere. Or about the guy one cell over who'd lost his head just before Army Rangers showed up to rescue them. "That's when I got the scars. I can't even begin to explain the twisted shit some so-called humans do to other human beings."

"The kind of things that were done to your friend?" She paused, still not touching, but he could feel her eyes on him.

An image of Chuck's battered face filled his head. He had a fair idea what had happened, but apparently there were recordings out there as well. In Kutros's confession, he had explained that they ran a video camera through all torture sessions with their military captives, recording everything a prisoner said. Then they attempted to blackmail that person into going home and stealing additional secrets. If anyone went to the authorities, the video of that person spilling national security secrets would be released on the Internet. The only real choice for those kidnapped? Talk or die. "Yeah, Chloe, they put him through hell."

"The way you were put through hell," she stated rather than questioned.

Perceptive woman.

He nodded, memories clogging his throat. Everything was crashing in on him at once, like a hurricane picking up all the garbage in his past from Jenny's death to Socrates' murder. Chuck and Chloe and their pain swirled right into the mix.

Existing took all his concentration. If she touched him, he might fly apart, but he couldn't figure out how to leave the room. This week had left him so fucking raw he was hardly functioning.

"Jimmy?" she said softly, rising, crossing to stand next to him and help hold up the wall.

"Huh?" he grunted for want of a better word.

"It's okay that it's not okay. It's not a matter of weak or strong. Some things will never be right, no matter how much we rationalize them."

In an unexpected way, her words made total sense to him. This wasn't a matter of weak or strong. Some things would never be right no matter how much he rationalized. A sigh shuddered through him, the exhale carrying out slivers of the pain. Not the whole package, but still a few less pieces to scrape around inside him.

He glanced down at her. "I can't cry about this, Dr. Freud, so don't bother bringing out the tissues."

"That's not my expectation or my call to make." Her eyes broadcast enough pain for the both of them.

"It's not because I think tears are for the weak." He tried for a laugh and actually managed half a chuckle.

She placed her hand between them on the wall, not touching but out there and ready if *he* wanted to touch her.

"Thank you." He linked fingers with her. Damn but he liked this woman.

A little more of the rawness eased.

"You're more than welcome."

He angled to kiss her, just a thanks kiss— Ah, man, who was he kidding? He didn't have the strength to say no to the one thing that felt good and right in his world today.

Being with Chloe.

She eased away to whisper against his mouth, "Jimmy, we used up my stash of condoms."

"Actually," God, he didn't want to dig any deeper, but with the increasing sense that Chloe could be an important part of his life, she deserved to know. "I can't have kids. Another by-product of those four months I guess I should mention and deal with."

Maybe someday he would tell her the details on that one, if she stuck around that long, but he'd had his fill of sharing this garbage for one day.

She squeezed their clasped hands. "I am so sorry for the pain and for what you've lost."

"You understand." A bit more of the hurt slid away, allowing room for other sensations to bombard him. Like the feel of Chloe's soft skin. The barely there flowery scent of her that was so sweet and clean and feminine it made him want to get closer to inhale her.

"I do." Her voice sounded like music to the beast, and he knew he wasn't leaving this room without thanking her in slow detail for the gift she'd given him.

What a stunner to realize with this woman, he didn't have to pour his guts out. She got it, got him, without some owner's manual. She was his personal freaking test pilot. Chloe offered him peace on one helluva bad day, and call it weakness on his part or strength of conviction, he knew exactly where he had to be right now. "Chloe?"

"What, Jimmy?"

"Lock the door."

TWENTY-THREE

Committed to the moment, determined to stop wondering why this woman had gotten to him so fast, Jimmy hooked his hands behind Chloe's thighs and scooped her up against the door. Just that quickly, they were hip to hip, chest to breast, mouth to mouth. He breathed in her minty breath, brushed his lips across hers, soaked in the feel of her pressed against him. She hooked her legs around his waist and dove back into a deeper kiss.

Yes.

The powerful wave of protectiveness he felt told him that sex with Chloe wasn't just something he wanted. This was something he needed.

She tugged his flight suit zipper down the length of his torso, chasing away any remnants of the crap thoughts in his head. She was his for the taking, offering herself up to him to burn away every ghost of the past that messed with his mind. Her hand slipped inside, into his boxers, seeking, touching . . .

His head fell back, his groan filling the room. He stumbled and almost dropped her. Way to go, Romeo.

He steadied his hold on her, needing to keep that contact with her. He wanted his hands all over her. "I flew. I need a shower."

Toying with his dog tags, she arched her hips closer, shimmied against him until he thought he'd go crazy if he didn't get inside her now. "That sounds like an invitation."

He tugged her toward the shower with the last shreds of his discipline. "Do you want it engraved?"

"I want you."

Ditching his combat boots went a helluva lot faster with both of them working on the task. She tore at his clothes as intently as he dispatched hers until a haphazard pile of khaki, uniform, and lace filled the floor. A flash of purple distracted him. Chloe's socks fluttered to rest on his flight suit.

Purple?

"I'm trying to add color to my wardrobe," she answered his unasked question, reading his thoughts again.

He urged her under the spray before following her inside. Yanking the industrial shower curtain closed behind them, he sealed them in a stall of steam. Just the two of them for however long he could last, and he intended for that to be a long time. Or as long as was humanly possible, given she looked so damn good naked. She lathered soap in her hands, and he willed himself to slow down and enjoy the moment as she infused the humidity with a flowery scent he recognized as hers.

"Lavender." She smiled. "It relaxes the spirit."

"I'm feeling anything but relaxed, maestra."

"Give it time." She flattened her palms to his chest, testing his willpower with sweet, seductive strokes.

Her hands worked over him, tempting and teasing but never lingering in one place. Not lingering on his back. Nothing about her smearing the suds over him tele-

graphed any healing ritual that would have left him all the
more raw. In fact, her acceptance of him as he was relaxed
him far more than any tearful display of "washing away"
his pain.

But then maybe she'd spent even longer trying to pretend everything was normal in life than he had. For that,
he kissed her. With slow deliberation, he took her face in
his hands and tasted her, tugging gently on her tongue
until her busy hands stopped their cleaning all together.
She moaned softly against him, her wet body melding to
his.

Shower beating his back, he took the bar from her.
Soaping his own hands, using his palms as a washrag in
kind, he left no part of her slick body untouched, lingering
on the sweet fullness of her breasts for so long he thought
he might have to press her to the wall and finish it now.

Instead, he dropped to his knees in front of her, urging
her legs apart with his shoulders while the soap fell to the
floor. Her fingers landed on his arms, lightly scoring his
skin.

"Think about that lavender," he puffed over her swollen flesh, "and relax."

He took her, laved her with the most intimate kiss, and
her fragrance soothed and stirred him far more than any
scented soap. Her legs sagged, and he supported her, drew
on her, soaked in her whimpers while coaxing even louder
cries from her.

"Jimmy." Her fingers dug into his shoulders, nails bit-
ing tender moons into his skin as she squirmed restlessly
against him. "Enough. More."

He smiled against her, teased with a final flick of his
tongue that sent her shuddering in his arms, shouting her
"Yes, yes, yes" completion in that beautiful voice of hers
that stroked over his senses.

Not that he needed any coaxing. He'd held back for as
long as possible, but he needed to be deep inside her.
Now.

He stood quickly, urgently, looping her legs around his waist again. Pressing her to the tile wall this time instead of the door, he drove deep, full, her after-spasms clamping around him in a hot grip that sent his already revved body over the edge. He pounded and pulsed and took her gasps into his mouth, or maybe she took his, until he slumped against her.

Her legs slid down until she stood again, steam fogging around them, sweat mixing with the shower pellets. His head fell to rest against the wall. The taste of her still on him, the scent of them around him, he couldn't hide from the truth. Keeping her safe wasn't just about the job anymore.

Somewhere between her conducting an iPod song and seeing her in nothing but purple socks, this had become personal.

* * *

Parked on his bed, Nunez clicked through secure websites on his laptop. He'd procured a room for Anya for at least one more day until he could figure out what authorities could offer her in the way of protection.

He should have gone to sleep hours ago. He'd even tried to unwind with the palm-sized meditation labyrinth he carried with him, tracing the path with his finger rather than walking it on a life-size course.

The pewter disk now lay on his wadded bedspread, where he'd pitched it after realizing no amount of meditation, prayer, or ritual would slow his brain enough for rest. He'd given up and gone online to the NSA site for research on Anya's genealogy now that he had additional hints for where to look. The cyber network certainly saved manpower hours, often cutting fieldwork in half.

Searching in Hungary, he located the name he'd been looking for. *Radko Surac*. Luckily, the uncle didn't have a different last name. A tiny archived news article reported he'd died at forty-two from a stab wound with—

Nunez sat up straighter. With a corkscrew? Holy crap. The assailant was listed as a vagrant found beside his body in a dark alley. Nobody thought to question why that nameless drifter just happened to have a corkscrew in his bag of homeless man goodies?

Clicking the back button, he returned to the sparse family tree he'd lucked into. Marta's mother and father. Marta's one older brother and the man's wife.

Wait. Something wasn't right.

He searched again, and the family tree read the same as before. Anya was adopted. She'd never mentioned that, and given how much she wanted to break free of her criminal family, he thought she would be glad to disclaim their blood connection. Perhaps she would even want to search for her biological parents. He would bet big money that she didn't know about the adoption.

A possibility he didn't even want to consider scratched at the back of his brain like a beast demanding to be released. Pieces of evidence shuttled around in his brain: how much Marta and Anya looked alike, their sixteen-year age difference. Anya had talked about her sentimental aunt wearing her mother's ruby ring, a piece of jewelry Marta promised to Anya. The pieces came together as the beast latched hold with sharp teeth.

Marta Surac wasn't Anya's aunt. Marta could only be Anya's mother.

* * *

Where the hell was Anya?

Marta hid in a tiny, smelly room over a rundown bar. She could have been sixteen, scared, and pregnant again, living under her parents' thumb, enduring the disdain of her brother and his wife. As if they all hadn't been grateful for the information she bought on her back.

She was in control then, taking from the men rather than being taken from, as Uncle Radko had tried. Only when the brat had latched on inside her had she lost some of her power, a mistake that would never happen again, since she'd had her tubes tied.

The shower sounded a simple door away. She'd made it clear to Baris he couldn't have her until he washed. She hated the grime that seemed to come with being poor most of all.

Kicking her shoes to the ratty rag rug, she swung her feet onto the lumpy mattress. Perhaps she needed this reminder of her past to get her through the next twenty-four hours. Erol was dead, killed while trying to shoot Chuck. Kutros was talking. She would never give up looking for Anya, but Marta also accepted she couldn't have back her old life. She must move forward.

To do that, she would focus on what she had left. She still had Baris, even if he was a poor replica of a man. She could use her power over him to ensure he did exactly what she wanted. She had a connection to a powerful terrorist cell frantic to hit an American icon. She had information about the USO troupe.

And she had the courage to do her own dirty work in planting the bomb. That bomb would blow her enemies out of the way, especially the two undercover men who'd tried to infiltrate her world and that Chloe woman who'd somehow managed to escape when stronger men couldn't.

* * *

Covers tangled around her damp legs, Chloe rested her head on Jimmy's chest and flipped his dog tags between her fingers.

In the quiet moment, she finally let the reality—the horror—of what he'd shared sink in. Jimmy had been a POW. Even thinking about what he'd been through . . . She blinked back tears she knew he wouldn't want to see and sealed herself to his side instead. She listened to his steady heartbeat, each thud a reminder that he had survived.

How long could they lounge around after their power nap before work called him again? She eyed the Black-Berry on the bedside table with a low-lying sense of dread.

How ridiculous to resent a piece of technology, especially when he held such an important job, but that same job had also nearly killed him. She listened to the steady reassurance of his heart against her ear, his sparse but loaded words from earlier echoing just as loudly in her mind. His intense lovemaking was still fresh on her sensitive skin.

And oh man, the rest of her felt just as sensitive and more. What she'd shared with him had opened up a well-spring of feelings deeper than she ever would have expected in a week's time.

Jimmy tugged a lock of her hair, winding the wavy strand around his finger. "The friend I told you about, he's from my test squadron. He was kidnapped two weeks ago during a TDY to Turkey."

No wonder he'd been on edge thinking about his friend going through the same hell. She would have been more than just irritable in his shoes. "Thank God you were able to save him in time. Why didn't I hear about his kidnapping on the news?"

"There really wasn't anyone to tell, since Chuck doesn't have family, and the air force kept a lid on the details. We didn't want to risk his identity getting out."

"He's someone important?"

"I can't go into a lot of detail, but we do dark ops testing."

Her fingers slowed toying with his dog tags as she began to comprehend the kinds of "secrets" he and his friends held. "I know the military does secret testing, and they have dark ops units, but dark ops testing?"

"Suffice it to say, if you can imagine the technology, we can make it, and more. It was dangerous on a number of levels for him to be taken."

The night she'd been nabbed and hauled to the cellar rolled over her, making her wonder. She bolted upright. "You were trying to get kidnapped, too, that night in the wine cellar? These are people who kidnap often?"

He'd risked captivity even after all he'd been through in Afghanistan? The people he worked with hadn't thought twice about asking that of him?

How could he be so fearless on the one hand and seem so afraid of accepting her health concerns? This guy seriously confused her.

He cupped her shoulder and tugged her back down into the crook of his arm. "You put things together quickly. The investigation is still ongoing, but you're going to hear some things on the news soon."

"A news leak?"

"A carefully worded statement to the press. Basically, the people I'm working with have made a break in finding a group responsible for the disappearance of a number of military personnel overseas. This group breaks them and then sells the information to the highest bidder. They don't appear to have any political or ideological loyalties."

She kept her breathing steady while her heart clicked away like a pegged-out metronome. For years she'd watched stories on the news featuring people living through these sorts of dangers, but no breaking broadcast could relay the gripping fear when something like this affected someone you loved.

Loved?

Jimmy?

Ohmigod, just when she'd thought her heart couldn't pump any faster. She clenched her fists until her nails cut a steadying pain into her palms. She admired him but didn't want to love him, not with so much unsettled between them. She hadn't even thought past putting their feet on the floor.

His fingers grazed up and down her bare arm. "We're still gathering information, and I can only share with you what's in the press statement. Basically, they've been staging deaths to look like an accident or a mugging gone bad. Eventually, though, we noticed a trend."

"This kidnapping ring kills people and ruins lives for money?" Maybe she was more ferocious than she thought after all, because right now she wanted to go back and shoot Kutros herself. And what about the driver and body-guard who'd gotten away? She embraced the anger that helped distract her from emotions she wasn't ready to dissect.

"Apparently so."

"That's totally amoral."

"You're right. That's why I want you to go home."

Whoa. Stop the music. How had this gone from talking about him to pitching her out on her ear? "Just this morn-ing we got the okay to continue on with performances."

"I know." He inched them both up higher on the head-board and pinned her with his exotically dark eyes she suspected he inherited from his Turkish grandmother. "That doesn't mean this is a totally safe region."

"There are troops in Iraq and Afghanistan expecting us." The defense sounded weak even to her own ears, but she didn't know what else to say, didn't know how to hide the kind of hurt this banishment incited. Once again, she was being relegated to the "practice room," while others lived lives.

"The show will still go on without you."

Why wasn't he barking orders at the others to go home? His dismissal of her role stung more than it should have, but damn it, her feelings were still raw from figuring out she loved him, something she wasn't ready to share, especially not now. "I know I'm just a backup singer, but you have to remember I'm also an orchestral conductor. I believe in the importance of everyone in the production. Beyond that, I *need* to do this, and you know full well why."

"It's not worth dying for."

"But it's worth living for." She tugged the covers over her breasts, already feeling more than naked enough around this man.

He cricked his neck to the side before turning back to her. "There's a medically tricked-out C-17 that's leaving in a few hours with Chuck. I want you to be on that plane back to the U.S."

She yanked the sheet around her and stood. "How convenient it's a medical plane for your weak and sickly girlfriend. Are you ever going to be able to look at me and not think of how your sister died?"

His mouth tightened. "I only meant there's a plane heading out, and you should be on it."

"No." She had to stand her ground with him now, or they wouldn't stand a chance at anything more. She secured the sheet into a tighter toga. "Unless they cancel the tour, I'm in for the long haul."

He swung his feet to the floor, bedspread around his waist. "Chloe, you could have died this week."

"So could you. This week and years ago and who knows how many times in between. I could have died more than once. Now I'm going to live."

He threw aside the covers with a curse and stalked toward the bathroom, no doubt to retrieve his flight suit and haul his taut butt out of her room. Why did she have to fight so hard for this? Why couldn't he understand after all she'd shared about herself why she needed to be here?

Her feet tangled in the sheet as she followed him. "You talked about TDYs to Atlanta, and I'm all for flying out to meet up with you, too. But if we're going to have more than just this week, you have to accept me as I am."

He pivoted in the bathroom to face her, already shrugging his flight suit over his shoulders. "Accepting a person works both ways, Chloe, and I can't stand by and watch you put yourself in harm's way again."

The set of his jaw allowed for no leeway. No arguing. Stubborn to the end.

What a time to realize managing a long-distance romance was the least of their worries. Despite the fact that she loved him, unless he could take her wholly and fully the way she was, illness and independence and all, she couldn't be with him.

TWENTY-FOUR

Her mood mirrored by the dim lighting, Chloe strode alongside Livia into the aircraft hangar for a final check before they left. Was it only a week ago she'd performed here for Incirlik's service members?

At least the USO tour was finally back on track, if not her life. Greg, dressed in his unrelieved stage manager black, held a clipboard, pointing and noting while backstage crew members rolled crated equipment, working with military personnel to load up gear into one of the two cargo planes outside. If all had gone as originally planned, she would have been finishing the tour with their final stop in Afghanistan.

She wouldn't have met Jimmy. She wouldn't have gotten her heart broken. Damn, she was in a funk.

After Jimmy had stormed away, Livia had tried to lift her spirits by offering more wardrobe "coloring up." The singer hadn't let her get off with just borrowing purple socks this time. Finally, Chloe had given in to end the discussion. She just wanted to pack up for the tour without another confrontation with Jimmy.

Would he phone her when she returned to the States? Would she even take his call? She honestly didn't know. If he could wreck her heart this fast, she feared what might happen in the long term. She'd fought too hard for her independence. She wanted to keep stepping into the light, bringing colors to her previously khaki world.

Chloe tugged at her borrowed shirt. The ruffles along the hem were a bit much for her, but the vibrant red wasn't half bad. Any other day, and it might have stood a fighting chance at cheering her up.

"Come on, *mia cara*, smile. Jimmy Gage is only a man. There are plenty more I would love to introduce you to, and of course there are plenty of very hot ones right here." Livia swept her arm to encompass the bustling hangar. "Just look around."

Seeing all those men in uniform only made her think of Jimmy again. She should have sent Livia on her own when Greg gave the last call before they loaded up.

Chloe rubbed her arms. "I appreciate you being so supportive, but can we stop talking about Jimmy?"

"Of course, you need time." Livia patted Chloe's cheek, then stretched up on spiky heels to peer past her. "Oh, I see the costume mistress over there. I will be right back."

Chloe spun away, wondering if she should just leave, but she'd already packed her suitcases, and she really didn't want to face her room where she and Jimmy had made love a few short hours ago.

Maybe Greg would have something on that clipboard of his to keep her busy. She started toward him only to have another performer snag his attention first. Melanie sidled up close to peer at his clipboard, a pair of black dance heels dangling from her fingers. Chloe hung back, waiting.

Melanie sure took her time. The backup dancer tipped

her head and laughed, her hand falling on Greg's chest. Seemed she wasn't losing sleep mourning for her jailed boyfriend either.

Chloe studied the couple more closely. Could Steven have been telling the truth about Melanie cheating? What did this mean in regard to the kidnapping attempt on Livia? Could Greg and Melanie have somehow played a part in that ill-fated call for help? Her instincts told her yes, and logic told her to pass along her hunch to Agent Nunez ASAP.

Chloe backed away from the couple and wished she had a good old-fashioned cell phone instead of her iPod clipped to her waistband. She searched for someone official-looking, but which uniform to pick from?

She waved down the nearest airman carrying a walkie-talkie. "Excuse me? Hello, I need help. I have to speak with the police, pl—"

An arm snaked around her waist, cutting off her air and her words. She flinched, looking around to see why she'd been dragged out of the way.

Nothing fell from the sky. The airman with the walkie-talkie hadn't even heard her. The steely arm yanked her even farther behind a towering stack of boxes right by an exit door.

Nobody in the cavernous hangar seemed to have noticed, either. Chloe opened her mouth to scream.

A beefy hand stuffed a rag in her mouth.

All-out panicked, Chloe stomped, kicked, drawing on anything she could think of from Jimmy's self-defense class, but God, he was right. It was hard to remember the moves when you were scared to death.

Rough hands spun her around, and she came face-to-face with the bearded man who'd taken her before. No, no, and hell no. Not again. Somehow the fog of fear cleared enough for her to see a woman with a gun who stood beside him in their little hidey corner.

How had they gotten on base, much less into the airplane hangar? They both even wore official ID badges of backstage hands. The answer bloomed in her mind like a toxic cloud.

The woman smiled with a twisted humor that never reached her empty eyes. "I saw you watching my new friend Greg, and I'm afraid I cannot let you alert the police. I've worked hard to create this security breach in the USO."

Trying like hell to spit out the greasy rag, Chloe struggled against the brutal arms holding her. Dimly the woman's words registered. Greg was a part of this just as she'd suspected.

The blond woman lifted her gun. "Baris, should we snap her neck or take her along?"

"A hostage is always an asset if things become sticky."

"A hostage she will be, then. You are learning fast and earning your take from the payoff."

"You've been a good teacher, Marta."

Oh great, they'd decided to speak English just for her. She really would have preferred they switch to their native tongue and spare her some of the gory details. The fact that they didn't bother hiding their names told her they had no intentions of letting her walk away alive.

His grip pinched harder until her arm went numb. "Killing her will be a special pleasure after she damn near crippled me outside the Oasis."

"Your turn will come, and we will not let her escape a second time. But we need to leave before Greg realizes we're taking our money and ending things ahead of schedule." Marta inched her gun down but not away. "My dear, it seems you will have to leave with us, but don't worry. Everyone will be too busy to miss you."

Marta lifted the lid on one of the crates and pulled out a briefcase. The payoff she'd mentioned? Chloe didn't have time to complete the thought before the black case cleared to reveal a tangle of pipes and wires and, ohmigod, the woman held some kind of remote device in her hand.

Fear gagged Chloe far more effectively than any rag. Why hadn't she agreed to leave like Jimmy asked? Now no one would miss her, because they would think she'd been blown to bits when this crazy woman exploded a bomb in a jam-packed military hangar.

* * *

Nunez stood on the tarmac, wind and airplane engines gusting dust around in a swirl that sent his suit tails flapping. Looming alongside the test crew's CV-22, two C-17 cargo planes sat parked twenty yards away. One C-17 was loaded up to transport the USO tour to Iraq then Afghanistan. The other was a medically equipped C-17 to transport Chuck Tanaka to the United States now that he'd been stabilized.

Defying the odds, Chuck was still hanging in there. If he managed to survive, he would have a long road of surgeries and rehab ahead of him. The guy sure had the steely will that kind of recovery would require.

Chuck had passed along valuable observations that helped in flipping Kutros. The bastard was alredy working to strike a deal in exchange for recorded discs that would lead them to blackmailed soldiers. He'd also offered up burial sites of service members who'd been kidnapped, murdered, and dumped. Families would have closure. Thank God.

Sunglasses in place against the fierce sun, Nunez scanned the flight line, watching maintenance personnel preflighting the aircraft, an aircrew doing their own walk-around, medical technicians and a flight surgeon sprinting toward the approaching ambulance.

He'd beefed up security for Chuck's flight, even bringing in a pair of Air Mobility Command's Ravens, specially trained security forces tasked to protect the cargo haulers from terrorists. Nothing was going to stop Chuck Tanaka from leaving here alive.

Along with Anya.

Getting her as far away from Marta—especially if the woman was truly her mother, and he knew in his gut she was—had to be a top priority. First he had to persuade Anya to agree to his plan.

Nunez stuffed his hands in his pockets, his right closing over the small pewter labyrinth as if it could lend some calm to a high-stakes moment. He still had work here to do tracking down Marta Surac, but he'd made arrangements for Anya to be on that plane. Everything she would need to start a new life was inside the C-17.

A small, open-top Humvee appeared in the distance, late afternoon sun a fat orange ball on the horizon. The vehicle raced closer until he saw Anya in the passenger seat, her blond ponytail sailing behind her. The Humvee squealed to a stop, and the guards unloaded, but he was a step ahead of them in reaching her side to help her down. Her soft hand fit into his, stirred him, distracted him.

The gusty breeze tore at her hair and plastered her jeans and blouse to the willowy body he'd hoped to explore. He kept their fingers linked, his other hand still in his pocket as they strode away from the Humvee toward the waiting plane. Her fingers in his were solid, real, reminding him of life yet to be lived, of relationships to be discovered. Because of the two of them, Chuck Tanaka had a chance at those. Because of him, maybe Anya had a chance at a real life, away from danger. He had a lot to be grateful for today and just as many regrets.

Anya stopped him before he could lead her onto the C-17, sweeping her flyaway ponytail from her face to reveal her confusion. "What am I doing here?"

Showtime. He wished for a few more hours, days even, to ease her into the solution. Hell, more time with her, period. However, telling her in advance would only risk the very plan he'd put into motion if she slipped and mentioned anything to anyone. "You may have noticed I hold some pull on an international scale. You told me you want protection from your aunt. Did you mean it?"

"Of course I meant it." Her eyes confirmed her words.

"We're on the same page then." He hitched a thumb over his shoulder. "You can be on that airplane and out of here in minutes."

The confusion on her face shifted to outright shock. "What? Where? I don't understand."

"Once you're onboard, you'll be offered three choices for a new identity in the U.S. or one in Great Britain. We have identities prebuilt for just these sorts of occasions." He forced free the words that would send her away, knowing damn well there wasn't any other way to keep her out of danger. "In America, we call it witness protection. You've helped us gather evidence against your aunt, now we owe you safety from her backlash. It's your decision."

Her gaze skipped to the plane and nervously back. "If you catch my aunt, I could resume my old life?"

"Do you really think she will let you go that easily?" He sure as hell didn't, and using some of Kutros's information, he could make sure she understood as well. "She knew you wanted to leave. She made sure you heard about the job opening at the Oasis, and she had one of her partners watching you the whole time. She knows you were with me and that I played a role in breaking up her organization. You have to accept she would use any connections she has left to come after you, even from behind bars."

With each point he stepped closer, crowding, making her afraid if he had to, because this threat was very real and deeply lethal. "Fair or not, Anya, she's going to believe you betrayed her. Does she strike you as the sort of woman to just let that go?"

He held his breath, praying hard he wouldn't have to tell her his suspicion about her true parentage to tip the scales. "You have ninety seconds left to decide."

She picked at the collar of her shirt as if the loose blouse had somehow grown too tight around her neck. "Okay."

He wouldn't let himself regret his tactics, even if he hated the fear he saw on this strong woman's face.

"Okay what?" He needed to hear her say it, choose it.

She dropped her hands to her sides, fists tight, arms rigid. She could have been a soldier bracing for a mission. "I think you are right about the witness protection."

"I wish I wasn't." Angling closer to her, shielding her from the prying eyes of the ground crew milling about, he slid his fingers down her right arm, stroking her fist until it unfurled. "I understand how difficult it can be to become someone new." He pulled the palm-sized labyrinth from his pocket and placed it in her hand.

She stared down at the pewter disk. "A tiny maze? It is very beautiful."

"Not a maze. A labyrinth."

"Aren't they the same thing?"

Maybe he was being a selfish bastard by not making a clean break, but he wanted her to think of him. "They may appear the same, but their goal is entirely different. A maze has dead ends and false turns meant to confuse."

He placed one of his fingers over hers and began tracing the path from the entrance. "A meditation labyrinth has no dead ends and only one, unicursal path leading to the center. The same path leads back out again. When walking a full size labyrinth, you can release control, relax your mind and trust the path will lead you out. It frees the mind for mediation or prayer."

She kept her finger with his, following the miniature twists and curves until he forgot about the hot runway and waiting plane. He only knew this need to share something with her, a desire to give her some piece of himself before they parted ways forever.

"This pattern is modeled after a tile labyrinth in the floor of the Chartres Cathedral outside of Paris, France, installed around the thirteenth century. It's said that pilgrims who were unable to make the trek to the Holy Land because of the Crusades would walk the labyrinth on their knees in a symbolic *Chemin de Jerusalem* or Road of Jerusalem."

She looked up at him, her finger still staying in synch with his. "How did you learn so much about labyrinths?"

"When I was fourteen I had a tough time with our latest move . . ." He didn't go into his own experience with the witness protection program. Who knew if she would even believe him or merely see it as an attempt to manipulate her? He'd already lied to her in the line of duty.

He would rather offer her this part of the real Mike Nunez before she stepped up in the waiting plane and out of his life. "Our new neighborhood was pretty much crap. So after school, I hung out where my mom worked at a physical rehab facility. They had a labyrinth garden used as a healing tool. I started walking it to pass time. After a while, I found that there, inside the labyrinth, I could finally be me, regardless of where we'd moved."

Even if it was only for the twenty or so minutes it took him to walk the journey. "As an adult, I still seek out labyrinths at churches, hospitals, sometimes cut into a field. I find them . . . helpful after I finish an undercover assignment."

Understanding lit her dusky eyes, chasing away some shadows. "You shed the fake persona and all the darkness that comes with people like my aunt. You reclaim yourself."

This woman definitely had a scary-ass way of seeing inside his head. "I thought you might find something for yourself inside a labyrinth journey."

"A way to shake off my past?"

"And keep track of yourself." He lifted his hand from hers, the path back out complete.

"I don't know what to say except thank you. I will treasure it." She tipped it to catch glints from the sun, her thumb running over scratches that attested to its well-used life. "This is yours, I am guessing. You will get yourself another just like it?"

"I'd already planned on it." He liked the notion of thinking of her using hers while he traced his. It beat the hell out of looking at the same star thousands of miles away from each other.

She cupped his face. "You are sentimental after all." Her fingers caressed lightly along his cheekbone, the smile leaving her eyes. "If I can't have any connection with my old life, I'm never going to see you again."

He should answer how she was right, and that was simply a sad fact of surviving. Instead, somewhere in his black-and-white world of right and wrong, dead or alive, he found a tiny strip of middle ground. "If you want, I can check up on you. I'm really good at my job. No one will ever know. Except you, of course, since you can see through my 'beneath the covers' persona."

"I would like that very much." She tucked the labyrinth into her purse and stretched up on her toes.

Onlookers be damned, he angled his mouth over hers for what wouldn't be their last kiss after all. She tasted sweet and familiar and every bit as good as he had wondered if she possibly could be.

"I will see you later, Mike." She didn't smile, but she waved, backing away as long as she could before turning to join her Raven escorts onto the medical C-17.

Stuffing his hands back into his empty pockets, he watched her board, the back hatch closing behind her and Chuck. The cargo plane taxied down the runway, engines roaring louder as it gained speed. He stared until the aircraft disappeared into the horizon, and for the first time in—well, he couldn't remember when—he had something to look forward to.

He pivoted back toward the hangar, away from the empty sky. The rumbling under his feet gave him less than a second's warning before an explosion vibrated the earth.

A black cloud of smoke plumed from the hangar.

TWENTY-FIVE

Jimmy sprinted toward the burning hangar half full of USO equipment . . . and people. *Chloe.*

His heart pounded double time the rhythm of his boots. He should have insisted she leave on the C-17 with Chuck. He should have pitched her over his shoulder and dumped her on that fucking plane. Sure, she would have screamed the whole way and then never spoken to him again, but she would have been safe.

Please, God, let her be safe now.

Fire trucks and ambulances screamed across the tarmac toward the hangar. *Ambulances.*

The column of black smoke scared him spitless. Maybe she'd been delayed packing. If he hadn't stormed out of her room earlier, he would have known where she was instead of having to play guessing games while his stomach fought to claw its way up his throat.

He shoved and shouldered and pushed through the crowd of onlookers. Someone cursed at him, but if the guy hadn't wanted to land on the ground, he should have damn well moved. The noise swelled to near-deafening levels. The crackle of the flames. Sirens. Bullhorn announcements and shouting.

And nowhere could he find any sign of Chloe.

Jimmy charged toward the open hangar only to be stopped by a firefighter and cop grabbing him by the arms.

"Back away, sir," the firefighter barked. "You're keeping us from doing our job."

He started to argue anyway but heard his name. He searched, listened.

"Gage, over here." Nunez flagged him down from twenty feet away.

Jimmy brushed free of the firefighter and cop—"Sorry about that"—and jogged over to the agent. "What the hell's going on? Where's Chloe?"

"Don't know, but I'm going to find out."

Two medics shoved a gurney free of the smoke, and holy crap, Livia Cicero was strapped down and groaning. Nunez cursed low and long. Livia stretched out an arm toward them as she tore aside her oxygen mask.

"Hotwire . . . Jimmy . . ." she rasped before coughing.

He and Nunez sprinted alongside, careful to stay out of the medics' way. God, was that a bone sticking out of her calf? With blood everywhere, it was tough to tell.

Livia hacked through another cough. "Chloe . . ."

Jimmy leaned closer. "Do you know where Chloe is?"

"Saw her, before explosion. Tried to help." She gripped his arm with surprising strength, insistence even. "Find police."

Alarms blaring inside him as well as outside, Jimmy kept his hand on the edge of the gurney, running. "Why do we need the police for Chloe?"

"Man with a beard who took us," she gasped, groaning at each rattle and jostle of the gurney. "And that woman, the one in the picture."

Nunez pulled up closer. "What picture?"

"Picture you showed me. Asked if I recog—" She wheezed, pulled the oxygen mask back in place for a long drag before trying again. "Recognized her."

The older medic held up a hand. "You'll both have to step back. We need to load her into the ambulance now."

Livia elbowed up, soot and blood streaking her face. "That woman took Chloe."

The picture in the interrogation room. Marta Surac. The evil woman who'd kidnapped and tortured Chuck, leaving him bloodied and broken, she had Chloe.

And God only knew if she was still alive.

* * *

Trapped sitting behind Baris and Marta in the Fiat with a pistol pointing at her through the seat, Chloe stared out the windshield at the approaching shoreline. The Mediterranean Sea lapped at the edges of the small fishing town. She estimated they'd left the base about forty-five minutes ago.

The second they'd cleared the front gate, Marta had detonated the bomb.

Chloe fought down the urge to hyperventilate. She couldn't think about what had happened back there. Fears for Livia and the others would cripple her at a time when she needed all her wits to salvage something from this hell.

She wriggled in her seat. Her iPod pouch clipped to her waistband was digging into her stomach like a son of a gun. At least they'd tied her hands in front of her this time. She slipped her fingers under the ruffled shirt and nudged the player aside.

Chloe leaned toward the front seat. "Authorities are going to find you. They already suspect you, and now there are going to be bulletins out for you all across the country. They'll be looking for me."

"They will think you died along with Greg in the explosion on base," Marta answered while Baris drove. "It will be days before they sort through all the rubble."

Very likely, but Chloe intended to press on. "If there is even one survivor from that explosion, he or she could tell the police what happened."

"Unlikely, but I know better than to trust luck." She hitched a slim elbow on the seat to look back at Chloe. "I am good at backup plans."

"The police will alert every airport, train station, and bus terminal." She had to keep the woman talking and distracted. "Everyone will be on alert. You set off a bomb with Greg's help and took all that money."

"Poor Greg. He thought he could manage me like he did his stage." She dismissed him with a wave of her hand, her ruby ring catching the final rays of fading sunlight. "As for alerts, they will not be everywhere as you think. Things do not work the same way here that they do in your country. Thanks to my newfound wealth, we can rent a speedboat from a 'sympathetic' fisherman. Once we make it to Cyprus, we'll board a private plane, take off, toss you into the water, then simply disappear."

Tossed into the middle of sea? Been there, done that, hate the sharks. And she wouldn't have Jimmy to save her this time. Oh God, she couldn't think about Jimmy right now and how damn sorry she was for wasting the chance to tell him how much she loved his stubborn, controlling, endearing self. "But what about—"

"Enough talking." Marta cut Chloe short as the Fiat pulled off the main road, jostling over the rutted dirt strip along the small seaside harbor. "Baris, park over there, then untie her hands. We don't want anyone to grow suspicious when we walk out on the dock. If she starts to talk, pinch her neck until she passes out."

Chloe swallowed down hysteria at the thought of them using a Vulcan neck pinch of all things, and tucked her iPod back in her waistband under the camouflaging folds of her ruffled shirt. Thanks to the new voice recorder feature, she'd spent the past forty-five minutes taping Marta's egotistical bragging about working with terrorists and snatching soldiers and about her Cyprus escape plan.

Chloe pressed her bound wrists against the tiny player/recorder, thanking God for about the thousandth time that she'd been able to use her fingers. She would only have one chance to get her SOS out there. A snap second to stumble against someone, pass over the iPod, and whisper the briefest of messages: *Help. Police.*

Since she wouldn't have time to ask if the person spoke English, she'd chosen those two words because they seemed the most universal. And if it somehow worked but help came too late? At least Marta's confession would be out there, hopefully in the right hands. Chloe knew she had her faults, but she was a fighter to the end.

She searched the sparsely populated dock. A burly teenager cleaned his catch. An old woman fished off the side. Men of varying ages repaired nets and sails.

Who could she trust?

TWENTY-SIX

★ _____

Jimmy had put his trust in a lot of things over the years when strapping his butt into the cockpit. Fliers were a superstitious lot, after all, with their rituals and good luck charms. But what a stretch, putting his faith in an iPod brought in by a little old lady with a fishing pole.

Luckily, he had the utmost faith in the integrity of Turkish grandmas.

Cruising his CV-22 out over the Mediterranean Sea, Jimmy prayed this grandma was as honest as he believed, prayed the Turkish authorities' take on the taping was accurate. Once they'd gotten the word of Chloe's recording, they'd been airborne in minutes. His crew couldn't waste time listening to the lengthy playback again, given Marta's head start. Jimmy plotted coordinates in flight for possible sea routes from the fishing village to Cyprus.

He had to shut down thoughts and rely on routine, training, instincts. Chloe had given them a window of opportunity. He wouldn't let her down.

Vapor maxed the throttles and peered through the windscreen, searching for the fleeing boat. "I'm not seeing shit out there, Hotwire. You're going to have to find them."

"I'm looking." He'd been searching and searching, and everything he found turned out to be a dead end. The radar sweep came around, giving Jimmy a view of the night water ahead.

Bright blips appeared in several spots on the display. Maybe this time. "I have six, no, seven contacts. One is heading back to shore, and so is that one. Two are too far north to be our contact. That gives us three to look at. Come right fifteen degrees, about four miles out."

Vapor angled the stick, guiding the aircraft. Jimmy slewed the infrared camera toward the contact and locked on the boat. He studied the screen and shifted his display back to radar.

Frustration cranked up the heat until sweat dripped in his eyes. "Damn. It's a barge. Come thirty degrees left, and I'll check another one."

He waited until they were lined up on the next target and switched back to the camera. He locked up and zoomed in for a closer look, grateful as hell for the technology that allowed him to see as much on a pitch-black night as anyone else saw in broad daylight.

A speedboat. Racing ahead in the dark with just the right heading to hit Cyprus. And please God, let it be carrying Chloe alive and well. He couldn't stop the insidious fear that they'd already dumped her body into vast depths of the Mediterranean, that he might never know what happened to her.

"This could be it. Dead ahead two miles." He stared into the screen and counted heads, zeroing in, tamping down hope. "I see three people in the boat. Do you want to come up from behind or offset to the side?"

Vapor looked into the darkness, appearing to weigh the options. "Let's blow right over them and see if we can give them a jolt while you get a closer look to confirm it's Chloe."

It had to be. He refused to accept any other ending. He refused to lose any more people he loved, and hell yes, he loved Chloe Nelson. He'd just been too stuck in the past to see what was right in front of him.

He kept his eyes locked on the screen, ready for that up-close view. The speedboat appeared ahead, chopping through the waves. The CV-22 swept over the boat about fifty feet up. He zeroed the camera in tight. Chloe's profile filled the screen, her hair trailing behind her. Just a flash of a look, but enough for him to be sure. "It's her. It's Chloe."

His gut turned to stone at the sight of her with a gun to her head.

Vapor broke into a hard left turn and climb. "Bring up the distress frequency and tell them to stop."

It was a long shot that Marta Surac would give up easily, but one worth taking. Anticipation hammered low and distracting in his gut. Jimmy dialed up the frequency and hailed the fleeing boat. "Attention speedboat six miles west of Antolik on a heading of two-seven-four. Heave to immediately. I say again, heave to immediately."

He watched, waiting for any reaction, but the boat powered ahead. Not unexpected, but still. "Fuck."

Vapor's cheeks puffed with a sigh. "All right then. Let's put a shot across the bow."

Jimmy homed in his focus tighter than ever, because if he thought about bullets flying around Chloe, he wouldn't be of any use to her. "Roger that. Arming the nose gun." A second later, he added, "Nose is hot."

He closed his fingers around the controls. The copilot's turret gun was the newer, less tested of the two weapons on board, but with a more precise optical sight.

And as much as Jimmy trusted his crew, this was Chloe. He had to be the one to take the shots. Nobody argued.

Vapor flashed him a thumbs-up. "Hotwire, single burst in front of the boat. Boss man, could you please take control of the infrared and keep an eye on the folks outside?"

"Roger that," Lieutenant Colonel Scanlon answered. "I have the camera."

Jimmy put the aim point in front of the boat. No second guessing. "Firing."

The aircraft hiccupped, and the sky lit up as the gun fired. Rounds ripped across the water just ahead of the speedboat, throwing spray over the bow. The boat blew through without altering course.

"Boys," Lieutenant Colonel Scanlon called, "this might require a bit more force. I'm seeing some action inside the craft. Uh, it looks like two women are fighting while the guy drives."

Jimmy stole a look at his camera and— "Holy shit."

Chloe gripped the older woman's hands overhead, fighting for a gun, kicking, kneeing, rolling out the moves he'd taught her and a few he'd never seen. Fear for her popped a cold sweat along his brow, even as he couldn't deny a gut-slugging admiration for how she held her own.

Not that he intended to leave her to fight this battle alone. Marta Surac had tortured and killed.

"Drop back, Vapor. I'm gonna put a burst down next to the boat, see if I can offer Chloe the edge of a little distraction."

"Roger that."

The CV-22 slid back, and Jimmy lined up the gun five feet to the left of the boat. "Firing."

Water spewed, eclipsing the boat from view. The speedboat cleared the spray in time for Jimmy to see Chloe score another wicked right cross. The weapon flew from Marta's hand into the sea. Just as Jimmy started to savor that major victory, the woman stumbled backward, grabbing a fistful of Chloe's hair.

Both women toppled overboard into the water. Chloe's

head slipped from view. The speedboat started circling like a shark ready for the kill.

Jimmy's hand twitched on the controls, ready to pop the bearded bastard who'd taken Chloe twice now. "Two in the water. Need to shoot the boat."

Vapor keyed up the interphone. "Boss man, what do you think?"

"Hell yeah, nail it."

He didn't need to be told twice. All his rage narrowed in as Jimmy locked onto the boat and speared a burst into the engine compartment.

The boat erupted in a pillar of fire.

Vapor turned the aircraft back toward the wake of the burning craft. Murky waves crested and rolled. Debris flamed like floating candles casting small circles of light.

Where was Chloe in all that churning water and wreckage? And what about the woman who'd hauled her into the sea? "Colonel, do you see Chloe or the Surac woman?"

"Roger, that. Think I've got them. Slow her down."

Dots prickled his vision. He blinked fast to clear it along with the relief threatening to rock him to his knees. "Both?"

"Two women, and we're damn near over them," Scanlon answered. "Looks like one is unconscious and the other is struggling to keep her afloat. I can't make out who's who, but I think we can safely assume the Surac woman would have let Chloe drown."

Only Chloe would have saved the person who tried to kill her. "Let's get a move on, Vapor. We don't want Marta Surac waking up and drowning Chloe."

"Roger that," Vapor responded. "I recommend we descend all the way down, rather than take time deploying the rescue hook. We can reach right in and haul them up the back ramp."

Jimmy was already unbuckling. "Colonel, come swap

seats with me so I can help Smooth pull them out. You guys are interested, but I am involved."

Scanlon double clicked his microphone in response. Jimmy hauled ass out of his seat on his way back, passing the colonel heading front.

On the run, Jimmy snapped on a walk-around safety belt. He pulled up alongside Smooth at the open back ramp just as waves started slapping up into the CV-22.

"Three feet to go," the flight engineer talked the pilots down to the water just above the women in some damn fine tight maneuvering. "Ease forward. Stop, that's it. Down one. Stop."

Water sloshing around his boots, Jimmy leaned over and grabbed Marta by the hair. He flung her back to Smooth. He might have to save the evil bitch, but he didn't have to waste precious time being gentle about it.

"Jimmy," Chloe shouted, bobbing in and out of reach.

"Come on, hang in there, damn it. I'm right here." He inched closer, closer again until to hell with it all, he dropped flat on his belly and commando crawled to the edge of the ramp. Waves crashed over him tugging, sucking. He grappled through the water, determination growling through him louder than even the roar of engines, wind, and sea roiling together.

His fingers brushed something solid. He stretched, felt, grabbed Chloe's arm. He tugged, muscles straining until the sea gave her up and her head broke free.

Gasping, she clutched his other hand, her wide eyes locked on his with complete trust

"Hey, Smooth," he shot back over his shoulder. "Some help, please."

Smooth gripped Jimmy's flight boots and pulled, the extra torque just enough to tip the scales. Jimmy heaved Chloe the rest of the way in. Backpedaling into the belly of the craft, he held on tight every step of the way, even after the back ramp sealed closed.

He dropped to his knees on the deck, taking her right

along with him. Out of the corner of his eye, he saw Smooth restraining the unconscious woman in a red webbed seat.

Which left Jimmy free to focus all of his attention on Chloe. "Are you okay?"

She scraped away her dripping-wet hair from her face. "You're really here."

"Because you're here."

All this time he'd been so wrapped up worrying about protecting Chloe, he'd missed how this strong, competent woman could take care of herself—with the help of an iPod recorder and a mean right hook.

Chloe sagged against him, teeth chattering, her arms and legs shaking. "God, I love you so much. I'm sorry for not telling you before, but I mean it."

Her words floored him, sucker punched him, and made his whole life at the same time. This woman never stopped surprising him.

"It's okay; you're okay. And damn straight I love you, too."

She stroked his face, her hand still trembling from cold or exhaustion or adrenaline letdown. Probably all of the above. "I guess red shirts are lucky after all."

★ AFGHANISTAN, SEVEN DAYS LATER

Chloe nailed the final high note of the last show in her USO tour. Seven blessedly uneventful days of entertaining the troops.

She'd had the perfect airman to set her sights on for this last performance, but she'd still swept her eyes and her smile to encompass the whole crowd. She and Jimmy would have time to talk backstage.

With Marta in jail, Greg dead, Steven cleared, and the small terrorist cell apprehended, the USO had inventoried how much backstage gear had made it into the C-17 before the bombing. With some equipment loaned from Incirlik's recreation center to fill in the gaps, they were able to go forward with the tour.

Minus Livia, who was recovering from surgery in Italy.

One of the backup singers—a past *American Idol* finalist—had taken on all of Livia's well-known songs to round out the playlist. The USO always delivered for the armed services. They'd dedicated the revamped tour to Livia Cicero and Chuck Tanaka, while newspapers already began to chronicle the downfall of Marta Surac and the roundup of criminals she'd brokered deals with.

Chloe waved her last farewell to the troops on her way offstage, her smile wide even if tears already streaked her makeup. She'd hoped to repay a debt over here. She hadn't even begun to realize how much she would gain.

She would even miss the sequins.

The lights went dark onstage and rose in the wings where Jimmy already waited for her. There hadn't been more than ten minutes for them to talk since landing a week ago, and she'd been too emotional after the rescue to do more than hold onto him and babble. Jimmy and his crew had spent the last seven days incommunicado on some new secret mission, while she'd finished her tour.

Finally, their time had come.

Sporting the same skimpy costume she'd worn the day she met him, Chloe flattened her hands to his chest and her mouth to his, totally unconcerned with the cameras snapping away at their Kodak moment reunion. His bold, hot hands slid low on her waist, stopping just shy of her bottom but hinting at the promise of what waited for them once they were alone.

Desire humming through her veins, Chloe ended their kiss. She kept her arms looped around his neck, her fingers toying with his hair. "You're here."

"Because you're here," he echoed their words from the second time he'd hauled her out of the water.

"That's really sweet of you to remember, but I mean

you're in Afghanistan." It was a place that held so many horrible memories for him. "We could have met tomorrow in Germany." Their stopover on the way home.

Jimmy held her gaze, and rather than just searching her, he let her see inside him. He didn't show vulnerability often—mostly never—but Chloe found this human side of him drew her just as much as his touch, his charm, and even his occasional grouchiness.

He knuckled a lock of her hair behind her ear. "A very wisc air force mentor of mine once told me that sometimes you have to go back to go forward."

"He sounds like a smart man."

"He was. His call sign was even Socrates. I'd like to tell you about him sometime." The intensity in his eyes slid away, an equally enticing gleam taking its place. "Did you just call me 'sweet' a second ago?" He reached into his flight suit pocket and pulled out his travel-size Sun Tzu's *The Art of War*. "Sweet is for the weak. Do you not realize I am a combat-honed warrior?"

He smacked the book against his palm for emphasis.

She plucked it from his fingers and fanned herself. "Am I about to get another martial arts lesson from Mars, god of war?"

He hooked a warm, muscled arm around her waist and ducked into a more private corner out of the human traffic flow. "I've learned you're more than capable of protecting yourself. You know, they say Amazons hailed from a place that's now part of modern-day Turkey."

"Amazon, huh? I think I like that nickname best of all. I take it that means you haven't come with a pair of bodyguards for my journey home?"

He didn't laugh. "I'm sorry for what I said back in your room at Incirlik."

"You already apologized shortly after you dragged me out of the water." But it felt good hearing it again. She needed for him to value her strength, a hard-won strength.

He pulled her in closer. "But I didn't explain why I

mean it. I wasn't just spouting off some bullshit because you scared the hell out of me."

Love for him tumbled through her all over again. Jimmy didn't admit vulnerability lightly—or eloquently. "You were scared?"

"Damn right I was. Then I saw you kick that bitch's butt. God, Chloe, you were as amazing that night as you are playing the piano."

"You were mighty darn amazing yourself with the guns and crawling into the water." His confidence in her strength stirred her more than any moving Brahms ballade or passionate Rachmaninoff offering. Jimmy was all the best melodies strumming over her emotions at once. "So you think I have a serious future as an Amazon warrior?"

"I'm not sure my heart could take your going pro with that, but if it's what you really want, I'm a hundred percent on board." His head fell to rest on hers. "I love you, Chloe. I love the way you calm me with your music and voice and lavender soap. I love the way you fire me up with your temper and conviction and smoking-hot body. I especially love the way you can absolutely take care of yourself. Damn it, I just love you."

She cupped the back of his head to anchor herself in this moment, since Jimmy had a way of sending her soaring. "That's a wonderful thing, because I happen to love you, too."

"So you told me seven days ago when you nearly had your way with me in the cargo hold in front of my crew."

"Oh, I did, didn't I? I just want you to hear why I mean it."

"That sounds good to me. How about you tell me at length over supper sometime back in Atlanta?"

"You're making a trip to Atlanta, are you?"

"I've got some leave time built up. Let's spend a couple of weeks hanging out, making love, watching that 'Tribble' *Star Trek* episode. Figure out how to make a cross-country relationship work."

"That would be time very well-spent. Given we're both such determined people, I'm sure we can come up with the perfect plan." She grinned up at him, staring her fill until she realized they'd stood there so long the backstage crowd had dwindled. She tapped the tab of the long zipper on his flight suit. "So you flew today."

He grinned back. "I sure didn't hitchhike."

She walked her fingers down his arm, tugging him along in an unmistakable invitation. "I think you need a shower."

"We, my Amazon maestra." He squeezed her hand, his boots picking up the pace toward her quarters waiting with a fresh bar of lavender soap. "From now on, we're one helluva team."

Turn the page for a preview of
the next Dark Ops Novel by Catherine Mann

HOTSHOT

Coming May 2009 from Berkley Sensation!

Major Vince "Vapor" Deluca didn't need to ask if there were Harleys in heaven. For him, hogs and planes both transported him from this world to brush the edge of paradise.

Not to mention both had saved his hell-bound ass on more than one occasion. And right now, he needed some of that heavenly salvation—on wings rather than wheels—in a serious way if he expected to pull off this potentially explosive mission.

Flying his AC-130 gunship at twenty-five thousand feet, Vince peered into a monitor at the increasingly restless crowd below in the rural Honduran town. With the help of his twelve crew members, he monitored the citizens pouring out of the hills to cast their votes in the special election, an election that could turn volatile in a heartbeat. The politics of this country were precarious and warlords were determined to stop the process. Local government officials had requested U.S. help with crowd control, using any means possible to keep the peace.

Vince cranked the yoke into a tight turn, flying over the voting place, a white wooden church. The sensors bristled along the side of the aircraft to scan the snaking crowd lining up. His sensors were so good the guys in back were able to study faces, gestures, and even guns worn like fashion accessories.

He knew too well how mob mentality could unleash an atomic *Lord of the Flies* destructive force.

His fists clenched around the yoke. "Okay, crew, eyeballs out. Let's score one for democracy."

"Vapor," the fire control officer, David "Ice" Berg, droned from the back, as cool and calm as his name implied, "take a look at this dude in the camera. I think he's the ringleader."

Vince checked the screen, and yeah, that guy had whacko written all over him. "He seems like a hard-core cheerleader yelling and flapping his arms around."

Copilot Jimmy Gage thumbed his interphone. "Those gymnastics of his are working." Jimmy's fists clenched and unclenched as if ready to break up the brawl mano a mano. He'd earned his call sign Hotwire honestly. Vince's best bud, they'd often been dubbed in bars the Hotwire and the Hotshot. "The crowd's getting riled up down there. Hey, Berg, do things look any better from your bird's-eye view?"

"Give me a *C* for chaos," Berg answered, dry as ever.

Vince worked his combat boots over the rudders while keeping his eyes locked on the screen scrolling an up-close look at the ground. "Roger that. All Cheerleader Barbie needs is a ponytail and a pair of pom-poms instead of that big-ass gun slung over his shoulder." A riot seemed increasingly inevitable, which was not surprising, since human intel had already uncovered countless attempts to terrorize voters into staying home. "Barbie definitely bears watching, especially with those ankle biters around."

He monitored the group of children playing on swings

nearby while adults waited to vote. Conventional crowd-control techniques could sometimes escalate the frenzy. This mission called for something different, something new. Something right up his alley as a member of the air force's elite dark ops testing unit. In emergency situations they were called upon to pull a trick or two from their developmental arsenal and pray it worked as advertised, since failure could spark an international incident, or, worse yet, harm a kid.

Today, he and his dark ops crew were flying the latest brainchild of the nonlethal weapons crowd. A flat micro-wave antenna protruded from the side of the lumbering aircraft. The ADS—Active Denial System—had the power to scorch people without leaving marks. Testing showed that as it heated up the insides, people scattered like ants from a hill after a swift kick.

Uncomfortable, but preferable to a lethal bullet.

Jimmy made a notation in his flight log. "Careful with your bank there, Vapor. Getting a little shallow." Once his pencil slowed, he glanced over at Vince. "Barbie might be providing a distraction for someone else to make a move."

Valid point. He increased the bank and smoothed the action with a touch of rudder. "Good thing there are thir-teen of us to scan the mob, because we're going to need all eyes out."

A string of acknowledgments echoed over Vince's headset just as Barbie grabbed the butt of his rifle and—slam—the past merged with the present.

A group of misfit teens festering with discontent. Four hands hauling him from his Kawasaki rat bike. Scream-ing. Gunshots.

A girl in the way.

Sweat stinging his eyes now as well as then, Vince reached up to adjust his air vents for like the nine hundredth time since takeoff. How could they make this airplane so high-tech and not get the damn air-conditioning to work?

"Time's run out for Barbie." The rattling plane vibrated

through his boots all the way up to his teeth. "Crank it, Berg."

"Concur," the fire control officer drawled from the back. "Let's light him up."

"I'm in parameters, aircraft stable, cleared to engage." Vince monitored as a crosshair tuned in on the infrared screen in front of him and centered on the troublemaker. He hoped this would work, prayed this guy was a low-level troublemaker and not one of the area's ruthless mercenaries. He didn't relish the thought of the situation escalating into a need for the more conventional guns aft of the nonlethal ADS.

That wouldn't go well for the "get out the vote" effort.

"Ready," Berg called.

"Cleared to fire," answered Vapor.

"Firing . . ."

No special sounds or even so much as a vibration went through the craft. The only way to measure success was to watch and wait and . . .

Bingo.

Barbie started hopping around like he'd been stung by a swarm of bees. His AK-47 dropped from his hand onto the dusty ground. The crowd stilled at the dude's strange behavior, all heads turning toward him as if looking for an explanation.

Jimmy twitched in his seat. "I halfway wanna laugh at the poor bastard, except I know how bad the ADS stings."

"Amen, brother." Before integrating the ADS onto the airplane, they'd tested it on themselves. It was disorienting and unpleasant, to say the least, but not damaging.

He was willing to take that searing discomfort and more to power through developing this particular brainchild, a personal quest for him. He could have been on the side of the evil cheerleader today if not for one person: a half-crazy old war vet who took on screwed-up teens that most good citizens avoided on the street. Don Bassett had never asked for anything in return.

Until this morning.

Vince relegated that BlackBerry e-mail he'd received minutes before takeoff to the back of his mind. "No time to get complacent, everybody. Keep looking. I can't imagine our activist with the automatic weapon is alone."

The system had the capability to sweep the whole group with a broader band, but he hoped that wouldn't be necessary, as it would likely shut down voting altogether.

Badass Barbie shook his head quickly, looked around, then leapt toward his AK-47 lying in the dust.

Berg centered the crosshairs again. "I think he needs another taste."

Vapor replied, "Roger. Cleared to fire."

"Firing . . ."

The rabble-rouser again launched into some kind of erratic pep rally routine.

"Stay on him." Vince eyed the monitor, heart drumming in time with the roaring engines. "Run him away from the crowd."

Berg kept the crosshairs planted on the troublemaker as he attempted to escape the heat. The wiry man sidled away. Faster. Faster again, until he gave up and broke into a sprint, disappearing around a corner of the building.

Hell, yeah.

Vince continued banking left over the village so the cameras could monitor the horde. As hoped, the crowd seemed to chat among themselves for a while, some looking up at the plane, discussing, then slowly re-forming a line to the church.

Cheers from the crew zipped through the headset for one full circle around the now-peaceful gathering. Things could still stir up in a heartbeat, but the pop from the ADS had definitely increased the odds for the good guys.

God, he loved it when a plan came together. "Crew, let's run an oxygen check and get back in the game."

His crew called in one by one in the same order as specified in the aircraft technical order, ending with Vince.

He monitored his oxygen panel. "Pilot check complete."

With luck, the rest of the election would go as smoothly, and they would be back in the good ole U.S. of A. tomorrow night.

Five peaceful hours later, Vince cranked the yoke, guiding the AC-130 into a roll, heading for the base, where he would debrief this mission and lay out plans for their return home.

And contact Don Bassett.

Vince finally let the message flood his mind. He couldn't simply ignore the note stored on his BlackBerry. The e-mail scrolled through his head faster than data on his control panel.

I need your help. My daughter's in danger.

That in and of itself wasn't a surprise. Bassett's only daughter had been flirting with death before she even got her braces off. Her parents kept bailing out Shay's ungrateful butt. What did surprise him, however, was Don asking for help. The dude was a giver, not a taker. Meaning that for whatever reason, he must be desperate.

Not that the reason even mattered. Whatever the old guy wanted, he could have. If not for Don Bassett's intervention seventeen years ago, Vince wouldn't need a motorcycle or airplane to transport him from his fucked-up world.

Because seventeen years ago, he'd led the riots.

Seventeen years ago, one of his fellow gang members had been gunned down by cops just doing their jobs.

Seventeen years ago, he could have been looking at twenty-five to life.

* CLEVELAND, OHIO, TWO DAYS LATER

"Suicide hotline. This is Shay." Shay Bassett wheeled her office chair closer to her desk. Tucking the phone under her chin, she shoved aside the steaming cup of java she craved more than air.

"I need help," a husky voice whispered.

Shay snagged a pencil and began jotting notes about the person in crisis on the other end of the line.

Male.
Teen?

"I'm here to listen. Could you give me a name to call you by?" Something, anything to thread a personal connection through the phone line.

"John, I'm John, and I hurt so much. If I don't get relief soon, I'll kill myself."

His words clamped a corpse-cold fist around her heart. She understood the pain of these callers, too much so, until sometimes she struggled for objectivity.

Shay zoned out everything but the voice and her notes.

Voice stronger, deeper.
Older teen.
Background noise, soft music.
Bedroom or dorm?

She scribbled furiously, her elbow anchoring the community center notepad so the window fan wouldn't ruffle the pages. "John, have you done anything to harm yourself?"

"Not yet."

"I'm really glad to hear that." Still, she didn't relax back into the creaky old chair in spite of killer exhaustion from pulling a ten-hour shift at the community center's small health clinic on top of volunteering to man the hotline this evening. "Can you tell me what's wrong?"

His breathing grew heavier, faster. "The line for one nine hundred do-me-now is busy, and if I don't get some phone sex soon, I'm gonna explode." Laughter echoed in the background, no doubt a bunch of wasted frat boys listening in on speakerphone. "How about you give me some more of those husky tones, baby, so I can—"

"Good-bye, John." She thumbed the Off button.

What an ass. Not to mention a waste of her precious time and resources. She pitched her pencil onto a stack of HIV awareness brochures.

The small community center in downtown Cleveland was already understaffed and underfunded, at the mercy of fickle government grants and the sporadic largesse of benefactors. Different from bigger free clinics, they targeted their services toward teens. Doctors volunteered when they could, but the place operated primarily on the backs of her skills as a nurse, along with social worker, Angeline, and youth activities director, Eli.

Bouncing a basketball on the cracked tile, Eli spun his chair to face her, his blond dreadlocks fanning along his back. "Another call for a free pizza?"

"A request for phone sex." She pulled three sugar packets from her desk drawer.

"Ewww." Angeline leaned her hip against her desk, working a juggling act with her purse, files, and cane.

Only in her fifties, Angeline already suffered from arthritis aggravated by the bitter winters blowing in off Lake Erie. Of course that was Cleveland for you, frigid in the winter and a furnace in the summer.

Forecast for today? Furnace season. The fan sucked muggy night air through the window.

"I apologize for my gender." Eli kept smacking the ball, the thumping steady as a ticking clock.

"Who said it was a guy?" Shay tapped a sugar packet, then ripped it open.

Angeline jabbed her parrot-head cane toward Shay. "You called the person John."

"Busted." She poured the last of the three sugars into the coffee, her supper since she'd missed eating with her dad. No surprise. They canceled more plans than they kept.

Angeline hitched her bag the size of the Grand Canyon onto her shoulder. "Always testing the boundaries, aren't ya, kiddo?"

Not so much anymore. "Calls like that just piss me off. What if someone in a serious crisis was trying to get through and had to be rerouted? That brief delay, any hint of a rejection, could be enough to push a person over the edge."

"You're preaching to the choir here." Angeline's cell phone sang with the bluesy tones of "Let's Get It On." "Shit. I forgot to call Carl back."

Eli tied back two dreads to secure the rest of the blond mass. "Apparently we're in the phone sex business after all."

"Don't be a smart-ass." Angeline stuffed another file into her bag that likely now weighed more than the wiry woman.

"Nice talk. Why don't I walk you to your car?" He slid the neon yellow purse from her shoulder and hooked it on his own.

"You can escort me out, but Carl'll kick your lily white ass if you hit on me."

"If I thought I stood a chance with you . . ."

Shaking her head, Angeline glanced back at Shay. "Make sure the guard walks you all the way to your car."

"Of course. I even have my trusty can of mace."

And a handgun.

She wasn't an idiot. The crime rate in this corner of Cleveland upped daily. Places like L.A. or New York were still considered the primary seats of gang crime. Money and protection followed that paradigm, which sent emergent gangs looking for new—unexpected—feeding grounds. Like Cleveland.

Hopefully, her testimony at the congressional hearing next week would help bring about increased awareness, help, and most of all *funds*.

"Tell Carl I said hello." With a final wave, Shay turned

her attention to the stack of medical charts of teenage girls who'd received HPV vaccines. At least she had all evening to catch up—a plus side to having no social life.

She sipped her now lukewarm coffee.

The phone jangled by her elbow, startling her.

She snagged the cordless receiver. "Suicide hotline. This is Shay."

"I'm scared."

Something in that young male voice made her sit up straighter, her fingers playing along the desk for her pencil.

Boy.
Local accent.
Definitely teen.
Frightened as hell.

Too many heartbreaking hours volunteering told her this kid didn't want phone sex or a pizza.

"I'm sorry you're afraid, but I'm glad you called." She waited for a heartbeat, not that long, given her jackhammer pulse rate, but enough for the boy to speak. When he didn't, she continued, "I want to help. Could you give me a name to call you by?"

"No name. I'm nobody."

His words echoed with a hollow finality.

"You called this line." She kept her voice even. "That's a good and brave thing you did."

"You're wrong. I'm not brave at all. I'm going to die, but I don't want it to hurt. That makes me a total pussy."

No pain?
No cutting or shooting.

"Have you taken anything?" Alcohol? Drugs? Poison? Last month a pregnant caller swallowed drain cleaner.

"Just my meds for the day."

On medication.
Illness?
Physical or psych?

"So you have a regular doctor?"

"I don't want to talk about that."

She knew when to back off in order to keep the person chatting. "What would you like to discuss?"

"Nothing," his voice grew more agitated, angry even, as it cracked an octave. "This is stupid. I shouldn't have called."

She rushed to speak before he could hang up, "Why are you scared?"

Voice changing.
14–15 years old?

"I told you already. I'm scared of the pain. It hurts if I live, and it's gonna hurt to die. I'm fucked no matter what."

She tried to keep professional distance during these calls, but sometimes somebody said something that just reached back more than a decade to the old Shay. The new Shay, however, shuttled old Shay to the time-out corner of her brain.

"You called this number, so somewhere inside, you must believe there's a third option."

The phone echoed back at her with nothing more than labored breathing and the faint whine of a police siren.

"Who or what makes you hurt?"

Still no answer.

"Hello?"

"Good-bye."

The line went dead.

"No! No, no, no, damn it." She thumbed the Off button once. Twice. Three freaking frustrated times before slamming the phone against the battered gunmetal gray desk.

She sucked in humid hot-as-hell air to haul back her professionalism. She had to finish her notes in case the boy called again. Please, God, she hoped he would call, and that he wasn't already as dead as the phone line.

Shay glanced at her watch. A four-minute conversation. Would that kid be alive to see the next hour?

She scrubbed her hand over her gritty eyes until the folder holding the rough draft of her upcoming congressional report came back into focus. It was a good thing after all that her dinner plans fell through. She was in no shape to exchange trivial chitchat with her father, who she barely knew and who knew even less about her. The report would make for better company anyway.

Each cup of coffee bolstered her to keep plugging away on fine-tuning her stats and wording. Maybe she really could find a ray of hope through political channels rather than picking away one shift at a time. She just had to hang on until next week for her congressional testimony at Case Western Reserve University.

The old Shay ditched the time-out corner to remind her that even one day was an eternity when every sixteen minutes someone succeeded in committing suicide. Thinking of how many people that could be by next week . . . The math made her nauseous.

Flipping to the next page, she spun her watch strap around and around over the faded scar on her wrist that still managed to throb with a phantom pain even after seventeen years.